CW00504482

MADAGALI

MADAGALI

WALE
OKEDIRAN

Abibiman
Publishing

New York & London

First published in Great Britain in 2022
by Abibiman Publishing
www.abibimanpublishing.com

Copyright © 2022 by Wale Okediran

All rights reserved.

Published in the United Kingdom by Abibiman Publishing, an
imprint of Abibiman Music & Publishing, London.

Abibiman Publishing is registered under
Hudics LLC in the United States and in the United Kingdom.

ISBN: 978-1-7397747-5-2

This is a work of fiction. Names, characters, places, and incidents
either are the product of the author's imagination or are used
fictitiously. Any resemblance to actual persons, living or dead,
events, or locales is entirely coincidental.

Cover design by Gabriel Ogunbade

To The Officers And Men
Of The Nigerian Armed Forces

For Their Gallantry and Dedication
In Spite Of All Odds.

CHAPTER ONE

The bullet that felled me on that foggy afternoon on the Madagali front was a .45 Caliber round. "You are lucky to be alive" the army surgeon, a tall springy fellow in a white bloody overall said as he finished strapping my right buttock where the bullet had lodged.

"The bullet missed a major blood vessel and your hipbone by inches. It also missed the sciatic nerve which would have crippled you for life or worse still, knock off your erection because it is the nerve that supplies your prick" he said, giggling as he signed my referral to the National Orthopaedic Hospital in Kano for further treatment.

I contrived to let out a soft giggle. I was in pains. War has taught me the harsh reality that is rampant among soldiers especially in the battle front. Whether they want to express extreme delight or extreme indignation, they resort to soldiers' talk, in a language devoid of emotion, replete with pungent phrases. Our families and our teachers would be scandalized if they heard the way we spoke, but out here it's simply the language everyone uses.

We had suffered heavy losses after Boko Haram terrorists ambushed us outside Madagali the previous night. Six dead and ten wounded. It was the second ambush in a week. We were all disconcerted. Boko Haram, whose name translates to 'Western education is forbidden' have killed thousands of people since their uprising in 2009. Two of our dead were women soldiers. We retreated and walked silently, crestfallen, one behind the other. The wounded were given First Aid and we carried the dead with us. The hitherto dusty weather had thickened as the strong wind of a coming rain lashed at our bodies. The whimpering and agonising cries of the wounded filled the air. It started to rain. We soon reached our trucks and got in. The engines revved, the trucks rattled and clattered along the pot-holed road.

The driver could not put on the headlamps because the lights would give us away, so we ran into holes and the trucks listed precariously from side to side. The rain got heavier. We ducked underneath the tarpaulins as the rain pelted them dripping off the sides in streams. The trucks splashed through the puddles on the road, we rocked along, tense, alert, our hearts in our mouths.

The night stretched out slowly and agonizingly to dawn as the wrenching moans of the wounded filled the thick, dark night. The drumming of the rain drops on the tarpaulin became monotonous. It later coralled into torrents that lashed our heads and the corpses stashed in the little space in front of the truck. It fell on the bodies of the wounded lying in our midst. It fell on their wounds. It fell on our hearts.

As we moved into the outskirts of Mubi, the evidence of previous Boko Haram attacks assaulted our gaze. Carcasses of shelled and burnt buildings, dotted the landscapes like pimples on an adolescent's face. Far out in the horizon was a shelled railway line with the rails ripped out and snarled upwards. On the far left was a Christian cemetery with coffins and corpses scattered as if suffering the indignity of a second death.

In a nearby thicket a few metres from the main road, a column of Boko Haram terrorists watched the approaching Nigerian Troops with deadpan attention. Before then, the terrorits or 'Munafukai' (the hypocrites) as the Federal Troops derisively refer to them, had sent some spies who usually disguised as beggars or destitutes to monitor the place they are to attack for days or weeks. Having received the reports of their spies about the strength and capability of the Nigerian troops, the terrorists had assigned duties to their men and in some instances, women. While some were assigned suicide missions, some others were to loot the remains of military barracks by carting away cache of weapons, ammunitions, tanks, vehicles, and other valuables of the troops. There were those assigned to record the onslaught on their cell phones and later post same on YouTube for propaganda. Other insurgents were assigned the duty of planting explosives on the attacked military bases to deplete reinforcement to the battlegrounds. The team also plant bombs on roads leading to their hideouts to evade military manhunt.

As our trucks continued to bounce along the pot-
holed road, I felt a pang of premonition. My heart
pounded against my rib cage. Cold sweat erupted in my
palms. The rain and the heartrending cries of the injured
further befuddled my mind. For the first time since
the beginning of the offensive in Madagali, I started
wondering if all our efforts at dislodging the dissidents
from the area would come to naught.

I was still in this reverie when it happened – the
ra-ta-ta sounds of a machine gun, from nowhere, broke
loose on us. We were under attack again. Bullet ricochets
filled the air. The driver applied the brakes as our truck
lurched to a stop. Before then, we had started jumping
off the truck to take cover. There came screeches here
and there. The earth shuddered, and men screamed as
shells smashed a few colleagues very close to us. We
threw ourselves to the ground.

With the first rumble of shellfire, an animal instinct
awakened in us as we all landed in a shallow, muddy
pond without waiting to know where the shooting
was coming from. The sounds of bullets and shrapnels
whizzed over our heads. If we had waited to think before
diving into the pond, we would have been cut to pieces
and there wouldn't have been any soldier left in our
column. As we landed in the puddle, my face became
a mash of muddy water. I felt a movement near me. It
was Private Dogo. Panic stricken, he made to crawl out
of the pond. I quickly dragged him back into the shallow
shelter just as another shell landed behind us. Someone

screamed — he must have been hit. A few minutes later another shell landed even closer. Dirt and mud splattered. Shrapnel buzzed. You could hear the thud as the noise of the blast receded. The air became hazy with smoke from the gun fires and fog. The thunder of the artillery fire made the earth tremulous; the fatal sound of gunfire reechoed through the surrounding valleys and hills. The next shell landed right in our midst. Screams of pain followed as shrapnels tore through fleshes. Our position had been identified. We needed to vacate the pond. All around us, the shells were sending up massive spurts of sand from the surrounding farmlands. I quickly looked around and saw a thicket nearby. I gestured to the others to make a dash for it. We bolted to the new have. But as I made to dive, I felt a sharp sting sear my buttock and I lost my balance and blacked out.

Five of us were to find ourselves at the National Orthopaedic Hospital, Kano. The hospital was filled with wounded men. A medical orderly came round and shoved a tetanus jab into each of us. We were separated. Those who needed surgery were put on trolleys for the theatre while those who just needed to recuperate were taken to the ward. My bed was next to another soldier's whose left leg had just been amputated below the knee. The bloody stump jutting out from underneath the bedsheet confirmed that the surgery must have been freshly done. He must have been around my age. He was surrounded by his family members whose looks were sullen, grim, subdued with the gravity that spoke a million words.

"Lance Corporal Bukar Salisu," the nurse called out to me. "You have visitors," she said as my Platoon leader, Captain Tunde Okaka and the Brigade Commander, Lt Col Bala Humus walked up to my bedside with a cellophane bag filled with beverages and fruits. We exchanged pleasantries while they dropped the bag on the cupboard beside my bed and stood over me as we talked. When Lt. Col. Bala Humus learnt about the size and type of bullet that had hit me, his face contorted into a loud, scandalized frown. "We are in deep shit," said the pint-sized Lieutenant Colonel, "these Boko boys mean business. From dane guns and pellets, our enemies have now graduated to SMGs and large calibre bullets. *Allah ya kiyaye!*" He exclaimed in Hausa.

"My main worry sir," Captain Okaka observed rather sadly "is the frequency of these ambushes. My hunch is that we have moles within our ranks."

"You have a point there Okaka", Lt. Col. Humus said. "Coming so soon after discovering some of our officers selling ammunition to the insurgents, we need to have a thorough overhaul of all our formations and services", Lt. Col. Humus added before they left my bedside a few minutes later.

After their exit, the nurse came again to inform me of another visitor – my course mate, Lance Corporal Tony Adede who had just been posted to the Janguza Barracks in Kano after a stint of action in Yobe State. Since I didn't know anybody in Kano, I had contacted him the moment I learnt of my referral to the Orthopaedic hospital. When

I informed Tony about Captain Okaka's suspicion about informants amongst us as the most likely cause of the incessant ambushes, he nodded in agreement.

"The captain is right. There are indeed moles in the army," he said. "About two weeks ago, a similar ambush in Borno State was reported. According to the report, more than 70 of our soldiers were killed by Boko Haram terrorists during an attack at Metele village in Guzamala local government area of Borno State. During the attack, terrorists had overrun the 157 Task Force Battalion in Metele and carted away large cache of arms, ammunition and military equipment after leaving the base strewn with soldiers' corpses. I learnt that the fight did not last for more than 45 minutes as our boys suffered a heavy casualty due to lack of adequate firepower. When our soldiers realised that the battle was not going their way, they retreated to the camp. But it was too late; the camp had been surrounded with barbed wire and the enemy fire was coming from the direction of the entrance. They had been surrounded and outnumbered. I learnt that when one of the drivers of the gun trucks decided to push through the barbed wire so that other vehicles could follow and escape, the truck got stuck. That was how many of our soldiers in other vehicles and those on foot were massacred. Those that managed to escape with injuries made it on foot through Kauwa to Monguno where they boarded commercial vehicles, some even sat in the booth of Golf cars to get to Maiduguri. The terrorists made away with about seven military gun trucks after outgunning our troops" Adede said.

Adede's account dampened my spirit. "So, in addition to sabotage, we also have to contend with poor equipment"?

"That's not all, my brother," Adede said. "Are you also aware that some of our commanders are pilfering our allowances?"

I stared at my friend with disbelief

"I don't know about your formation, but when I was in Yobe, for three months, our operations allowances were not paid. We had to rely on our meager salary for everything. From Battalion Commanders to Company and Sector Leaders, we were all in debt because our salaries were not enough to sustain us at the battlefront while feeding our families back at home. We joined the army to defend the civilians, is it not ironic that we had to go to the civilians in town to borrow money to fend for ourselves at the battlefront? The food we were fed were not fit for human consumption. Most times, there was not a single piece of meat or fish in them. The tastes were so bad that we had to add surplus salt to be able to swallow them. A plate of our food per soldier was about two hundred naira".

"Actually, our own meals were not that bad in the Borno/Adamawa sector" I said. "Our main problem was what we saw as a deliberate effort by our Commanders at prolonging the war."

"Prolonging the war?" the Lance Corporal asked. "Why would they do that? Don't they want to go home again?"

"For money, of course" I replied. "Many have enriched themselves by extorting motorists at check points. In fact, a state Governor had publicly complained about this nefarious activity. Another worrisome practice is that of some officers who hide under security maintenance to impose unnecessary curfews, ban fishing activities and weekly markets in some towns and villages and go on to take over commercial activities in these areas. It is disheartening to note that some of our soldiers are getting involved in commercial activities such as selling fish in Baga as well as foodstuff and drugs in Bama and Dikwa. We even have some cases of soldiers who sell relief marterial meant for refugees in Konduga while some of them even rear animals in Damataru, Katarko, Babbangida and Geidam. All these are in addition to onions, pepper and dried tomatoes which will later be transported to the southern part of the country at enormous profit"

"Seriously?" my friend asked, as he burst into laughter. "I can't believe all these."

"The most ridiculous and embarrassing was the case of some officers stationed in Kukareta who were caught using their personal vehicles to carry passengers to Damataru and Ngamdu village at exhorbitant fares," I said as Adede held his sides and burst into another round of laughter.

On the day of my discharge from the hospital, Lt. Col. Humus was back. "You have been given four weeks sick leave," he said as he handed me my pass.

"Thank you, sir," I saluted him.

"So, where will you spend your leave, my boy?" the burly soldier whom we all feared in the command asked.

"I will first see my sister in Kazaure sir before deciding on what else to do".

"In that case you will help me to take a bag of personal effects to my family in Achilafia. It is just before Kazaure. My brother will be there at the motor park to collect the bag from you so you can continue your journey to Kazaure."

As my superior officer, I could not ask him for the contents of the bag. Neither could I complain about carrying a bag full of 'personal effects' all that distance. He must have noticed the hesitation on my face as he said, "The parcel is nothing much, just a big 'Ghana Must Go Bag' laden with clothes and shoes for my family. Fortunately, you have your army ID and so you won't be bothered by any security check points on the way.

"All correct sir," I saluted in usual obeisance to superior command.

Because of the size and weight of the bag from Lt. Col. Humus, I solicited the help of my friend, Tony Adede to bring a car which would convey me from the hospital in Dala to the motor park at Naibawa.

Though I had been well treated at the Orthopaedic hospital, I still had frequent daily nightmares that the doctors could do nothing about. The booming sounds of guns and shells coupled with the screams and cries of the wounded and dying daily assailed my brain despite the drugs and injections from my medical handlers. The doctor stopped my medications and assured me that the nightmares would disappear "once you are back at home with your family."

I was ready for the trip to Kazaure. As instructed, I wore civilian clothes to avoid being marked out in case we run into the insurgents. For my protection, I neatly tucked my service pistol under my belt while my army ID was in my breast pocket.

Janbulo was still sleepy when Tony and I departed Kano early that morning. Moments later, as the water vendors commenced the day's commercial activities as they puffed and heaved heavy trucks of water containers. From the street corners, hazy serpentines of smoke could be seen floating in the early morning mist as *kose* sellers lighted their fires for the day's frying and selling business.

We were welcomed into Kabuga by a cacophony of noise from keke and taxi engines at motor parks. Already, the Almajiris, school children, civil servants and early morning travellers had activated the vehicular traffic in the area and Kano city was alive and well. We got to the motor park in Naibawa and Tony and I heaved the heavy bag to the Kazure bound bus. Luckily, my own travel bag which I strapped to my back was light.

"I wonder why the BC should saddle you with this heavy bag knowing fully well the state of your health." Tony blurted out of concern.

"I told him that I will cope."

"Only God knows what he packed in the bag that made it so heavy," he said.

"Stuff for his family, so he said." I replied as Tony took his leave.

As I showed the driver of the Sienna bus that was to take us to Kazaure the bag, he protested: "I don't think I can take you to Achilafia with this your heavy bag without paying some extra money. Those soldiers at the roadblocks will keep stopping us for a search and collecting money from me."

"But you have nothing to worry about. I am not carrying any contraband. I told you I only have clothes and shoes for my shop in the bag," I replied.

"That is not the issue. The soldiers check every bulky luggage they see. Apart from wasting our time, they will collect a lot of money from me. If not for the poor security report along the Kano to Kazaure road, we would have gone directly to Kazaure from Kano and cut off Dutse."

After haggling with the driver for a while, we finally agreed on what I should pay, and the journey commenced. We departed for Kazaure via Dutse with five other passengers in a Sienna vehicle just as the early morning sun was sneaking its way behind the cloudy canopy of the March morning. All was quiet in the vehicle as each passenger seemed occupied with his or her own thoughts. There was no traffic at that hour of the day, and we were soon in Wudil with the

University of Science and Technology hidden behind a green fence and foliage on the left side of the road. Next was a glittering array of pottery and silver merchandise resplendent in the early morning sunshine, displayed for sale by the roadside. At Shagogo Gayi, we chanced on farmers on both sides of the road, clearing and burning farmlands in preparation for the rainy season planting. Gaya, the headquarters of Gaya Local Government Area soon welcomed us after a series of mud walled villages on the left.

An hour after leaving Kano, the frequency of army checkpoints on the way increased.

"Kai, there are too many roadblocks on the way. It is a big problem for we commercial drivers," the driver moaned.

When I replied that the roadblocks were for our own good in view of the current challenge caused by the dreaded, Boko Haram sect, the driver grunted.

"Boko Haram? That is the excuse they are giving us to extort us"

"You mean the soldiers also extort money? I thought it was only the police that does that kind of thing?"

"Yes, the army too. When they first came, they were good, even very polite but they later became rude and started harassing us for money. And any small disagreement from you, they will arrest you as a suspect."

Although we still had to contend with the long traffic lines at military checkpoints, with my vantage position in front of the Sienna, our vehicle was always allowed to pass without inspection. As we sped along on our way, I was dumbstruck by a hovering early morning mist that made the nearby mountains magical and elegant. Mud walled villages, lush vegetation of dongoyaro trees and rivers with dry beds all flew past and soon we were in Ringim. It was market day in Kanya Baba when moments later, we passed the agrarian community with its loads of sugar cane and herds of goats and cows making their way to the market. Kanawa, Tasawa, Walawa, Dandi, Sabuwa and other mud-walled but lovely villages passed in quick succession.

We arrived in Yankwashin, as the early afternoon sun filtered through the nearby lush vegetation, bathing the bucolic environment with a magical lustre. Then we entered a large valley ringed all around by magical mountains. It was like a dizzy ride in a large bowl of earth. We continued like this for another half hour before we hit the outskirts of Achilafia. By then, the afternoon sun had set, and the wind was sighing amidst the stately dongoyaro trees that dotted the golden quilt of landscape. That was when my problems began. Before then, my army ID was enough to get the bus through the numerous military checkpoints without anybody checking it.

Just before Achilafia where I was supposed to hand over my Brigade Commander's bag, the Sienna was flagged down. All passengers were asked to disembark for a body and bag check. The checkpoint was manned by four young soldiers probably in their early twenties just like me. While two of the soldiers sat at a sandbag-fortified point manning a submachine gun, the other two checked the passing vehicles as they shone their florescent torches into the dark recesses of the booths of the vehicles.

As the one of the soldiers sighted my bulky lugage, he gestured to the driver to park. "From where?" he asked the driver in Hausa.

"From Kano, officer" the driver replied, trying to act jovial.

"Whose are these?" he asked as he shoned his torch at my luggages.

"Mine" I replied and quickly identified myself with my army ID.

"I'm sorry mate, we have orders to check everybody. The insurgents have been giving us too many problems these past few days. What's inside?" he said.

"Personal stuff for a friend's family in Achilafia," I replied, not wanting to involve my Brigade Commander.

"Can you please open the bag?" the soldier asked.

Quickly, I got out of the car and with the help of the driver brought out the large 'Ghana Must Go' bag. The soldier went through the bag with expertise of foresic doctor performing an important post-mortem. His eyes caught a package in a black nylon bag at the bottom of the bag.

"What is this?" The soldier asked.

"A package I was asked to drop for a friend." I replied.

"Please, open it," he instructed, pearing intensely at the package.

As I did, some black metallic objects, small cylinders and balls of electric wire came into view.

"What are these?" the soldier asked again.

"I don't know, I told you they were given to me by a friend in Kano to hand over to his family in Achilafia".

"How many of such packages are in the bag?"

"I don't know. I didn't check when he gave me the bag." I answered.

The soldier returned to the bag and fished out more of such packages which he had missed during his earlier search. The packages had the same contents.

By then, the second soldier had abandoned his work of searching other vehicles and joined his colleague to inspect my luggage. As they conversed in low tones the driver's face contorted into a sad expression. He turned to me.

"Haba Mallam, I thought you said you had only clothes and shoes in the bag? You have put me in wahala now."

"What wahala? They are just packages given to me to give to a friend". I maintained, unperturbed.

"But those packages are not clothes and shoes" he seemed to exclaim.

Before I could reply the soldier came over to me, "Old boy, you and the driver will follow us to our headquarters. These packages contain materials for making bombs and you two are under arrest".

"Subhanallah!" I exclaimed. "Bombs? Where? How? I was stupefied.

"Haba Mallam, you have killed me today," the driver wailed, his hands on his head. "And I didn't want to carry you. You told me you are not carrying any contraband... Now see this... what..."

"I was told that the bag contained only clothes and shoes," I stuck to my story, my truth.

"How about the bombs?" The driver thundered in panic.

"I don't know about that, the person who gave them to me will explain" I said calmly, trying to hide my confusion.

The traffic built up. The news of the bomb discovery passed from mouth to mouth among the motley crowd that had gathered.

"*Yanadebam*, he has a bomb," the crowd chanted as they passed the news from one to the other.

CHAPTER TWO

The decision that I should join the army was taken long before I was born. My father, late Captain Jallo Salisu, claimed to have been instructed by his own father, the late L/Cpl. Mahmud Salisu not to break the family tradition of military service by making sure that one of his sons joined the army. And since I was his only son out of a family of four children, I had no choice but to be the gatekeeper of what has become a family tradition. While my father saw action as a member of the ECOWAS Monitoring Group (ECOMOG) that served in Liberia, his father, my grandfather, L/Cpl. Mahmud Salisu was a veteran of the Nigerian Civil War. According to my father, my grandfather used to regale him with some of his heroism during the Nigerian Civil War of 1966/7 especially the famous 'Abagana Ambush' by Biafran soldiers. My grandfather had told him how on March 31, 1968, General Murtala Muhammed and his men were heading from Enugu to Onitsha with 96 military vehicles. Suddenly, down the road from downtown Abagana, their convoy came under heavy attack. It was later leant that the attack came from homemade "bucket bomb" or Ogbunigwe. The bomb exploded with such intensity that it tossed their vehicles like tin cans. Three-quarters of Muhammed's men died, and many others wounded. Gen. Muhammed and my grandfather were part of the few men who escaped unscathed.

In my father's case, he saw action in Liberia as a member of ECOMOG during the 14-year Liberian Civil War. It was in Liberia that he met and married a beautiful Monrovian girl, Sonia Johnson, my mother.

As a battlefield soldier, I did not know the wider socio-political dimensions of Nigeria's intervention in Liberia until after the conflict when I came across a news feature in the New Nigerian newspaper. The article claims that Nigeria's intervention in the Liberian war was said to have caused the country a whopping $8 billion, the death of 100 soldiers and another 100 missing. Nigeria contributed about 9,000 of the 12,000 UN Forces in the country, the only drawback was that Nigerian soldiers reportedly fathered and left behind 250,000 children in Liberia after the ECOMOG mission.

Unlike most of his other colleagues that abandoned their children in Liberia, my father came back to Nigeria with his wife and four children. Though a Christian, my mother did not hesitate in marrying my father who was a Muslim. My father even allowed my mother to give us Liberian names in addition to our Hausa names. Thus, my eldest sister, Fatima was also named Emine, while Zainab, my second sister, was Shelia. My own Liberian name is Jabbie while our last born Rabia was named Ella.

After his return to Nigeria, my father was not posted to Jigawa, his home state, but Madagali where he served for six years. I was therefore raised in Madagali, a beautiful town and Local Government Area in Adamawa State, adjacent to the border with Cameroon. Madagali had everything in moderation: good schools with devoted teachers, a well-equipped hospital, affordable foodstuffs, wooded areas with streams full of fish as well as rolling plains for Fulani cattle rearers. As the only son in the family and one whose father was always away on military assignments, I wandered freely across the vast expanse of beautiful hills and magnificent valleys of Madagali after school.

During my formative years, Madagali was a homely and sparsely populated community with mostly farmers who grew millet, corn, and yam while mangoes came in their full bloom in their season. I remember the farms as they were just before harvest time; heavy corn stubbles so rich that they bent the stalks of the corn plant with the millet equally brown, pregnant, and ready for harvest. I clearly recall roaming about rural Madagali, a restless boy caught between suburban boredom and rural desolation as I hunted grasscutters and squirrels in the company of my friends.

Behind me was the military barracks where my mother and sisters daily waited for my return, while the rolling plains with their cattle, sheep and goats laid in front. Occasionally, my mother would allow me to go on school excursions to the nearby towns and on two occasions to Cameroon with my French class. I became very familiar with some parts of Cameroon, particularly the bordering towns of Michika, Askira, Gwarzo as well as villages such as Gulak and Shuwa. This knowledge became handy to me in my military career when the Boko Haram insurgents took over Madagali and I was asked to use my knowledge of the place to guide the Nigerian troops in getting rid of them.

Like my grandfather and father, my military training was at the famous Military Depot, Zaria. Since the purpose of our training was to prepare us for the war front, our toilet facilities which was essentially pit toilet covered by a zinc and thatch fence was akin to that used at the war front. Our daily routine exercise which was meant to toughen us was in the form of push-ups, jogging, among others. We were also taught how to handle guns, fire, and clean them up. The first six weeks, involving rigorous training administered by our drill instructors was a real physical and psychological ordeal. From four in the morning until eight at night we were marched and drilled, sent on scaling of obstacle courses, and put through tough conditioning hikes under the intense stare of Zaria's ferocious sun. We were constantly shouted at, kicked, humiliated, and harassed. We were no longer known by our names but called all kinds of humiliating names such as "scatterbrain" or "mumu" or "idiot" by our drill instructors.

We were usually woken up at four in the morning by a fire alarm for commencement of daily activities.

Our first activity was general cleaning which involved washing of toilets and cleaning of dormitories. Afterwards we took our baths between 04:30 and 06:00am before going to the armory to sign for our rifles by 7am. We had to sign for the armory every day. From there we would move to the dining hall for our breakfast before moving to the parade ground for drills. Then we would march to the classrooms for lectures. We were taught how to use and service weapons. After the lectures, we would afterwards go for what we call 'puttee,' an exercise cum punishment, to prevent us from getting drowsy.

We did a lot of "forward rolling." There is no time limit for this exercise which we could be ordered to carry out all through the night. our instructors believed that the exercise would keep us strong and bold enough to face any attack no matter the timing. After being drilled and beaten by our instructors, we would be very dirty and then asked to go and clean up around 6:30 in the evening before proceeding for supper. After that, we would be asked to sit with our heads on our abdomens just to keep alert. By 8:00 pm, we would go for prep, mostly to be flogged, as you must not be found sleeping. Sleeping is a serious offence in the military hence, even if you were not reading, you must be seen with a book. After the prep at 9:30 pm, we would be allowed to go to our dormitories to sleep, only for the fire alarm to go off almost immediately. We had to respond to this by coming out again in our complete uniforms. This usually made many of us retire to bed in our uniforms, as a result, many trainees suffered from foot diseases. Though we had a medical bay, we weren't allowed there, to prevent people from using the place as an excuse to boycott training. One had better not be sick, what our instructors did to sick persons were worse than what they did to the healthy.

To lighten our burdens, most of our drills were accompanied by singing. My favourite song was the one I had sang countless times as a boy scout in my primary school days before I joined the army:

I remember when I was a soldier…
I remember, when I was a soldier…
I remember when I was a soldier…
I remember when I was a soldier.
Hippy, yah yah,
Hippy, hippy yah, yah
Hippy, yah yah
Hippy, hippy yah yah
Hippy, yah yah
Hippy, hippy, yah yah
Hippy, yah, yah
Hippy, hippy, yah, yah

We sang with gusto, chest puffed out and our backs, rod stiff as we marched along the dusty parade grounds of the Army Depot.

I endured the grueling training because I saw myself carrying out my grandfather's injunction of doing military service. Sometimes, we were made to roll on hot granulated stones under the sun on the parade ground. We also carried out rope climbing and anybody who fell was punished. To worsen matters, our meals were poor. Breakfast for the 6 months duration of our training was watery beans with pap while lunch was usually noodles with a thumb-sized piece of meat. Dinner was rice or beans, mostly without meat or fish. When we complained about the monotonous menu, our handlers said it was part of our training. "A good soldier must be used to poor or irregular meals in preparation for the war front where it may be difficult to get a decent meal," they reasoned.

We were schooled on the military codes we were expected to live by, such as never leaving our fallen comrades on the battlefield, never retreating, and never surrendering so long as we have the means to resist. "And the only time a soldier doesn't have the means to resist," one instructor told us, "is when he's dead."

The first ten weeks of basic army training were the toughest at the army depot. So tough was it that it changed us more radically than ten years of a formal education would have. We learnt that polishing our boots was as equally important as being able to speak good *turenchi*. We came to realise — first with astonishment, then bitterness, and finally with indifference — that being intelligent wasn't the most important thing in the army, it was your skill at 'bush attacks', 'drills' and 'obeying the last order'.

We joined the army with enthusiasm and goodwill,

but our instructors did everything to knock that theory out of us and replaced it with stoic endurance, resilience, and physical fitness. Before long, we saw that the classical notion of patriotism we heard from our teachers meant, in practical terms, physical drills made up essentially of saluting, eyes front, marching, presenting arms, right and left about, snapping to attention, insults and a thousand varieties of bloody-mindedness. In short, we discovered that we were being trained to be heroes the way they train circus horses, and we quickly adapted.

From a thin, tall teenager, the military training toughened me into a muscular handsome and tall young man with the sharply pointed nose and the light skin of my mother which made me resemble a mulatto. I was famous at the military school because of my family history of military service, and my natural disposition for adventure, knowledge, and friendship. My Liberian background and my frequent reference to my father's military adventure during the ECOMOG operation in war-torn Liberia earned me the nickname 'ECOMOG.' I had wanted to be known by the initials of my name; BJ from Bukar Jabbie, my friends preferred to call me 'ECOMOG'.

The six months training ended on the glorious morning we graduated as Privates. Two hundred and fifty out of the three hundred recruits that commenced the training made it. And as we marched past our Commandant and the representative of the Chief of Army Staff, we swore allegiance to our motherland.

At barely twenty-two years of age, I was more prepared for death than I was for life. I was almost completely ignorant of the ordinary things of life such as gardening, cooking, reading, politics and building a career. I had no degree and no skills, but I had acquired some expertise in the art of killing. I knew how to face death and how to cause it, with everything on the evolutionary scale of weapons from the knife to the 3.5-inch rocket launcher. The simplest repairs on an automobile engine were beyond me, but I was able to assemble and clean an AK 47 even if I were blindfolded. I could call in artillery, set up an ambush, rig a booby trap, lead a night raid. All in all, I had become a certified hunter of men.

The original plan was for me to be posted to the Kaduna School of Infantry to acquire more knowledge after graduating from Zaria. However, one early morning as I was polishing my shoes in preparation for a drill, one of my course mates, Bala Ali entered my room and said, "ECOMOG, Sergeant Kawu wants to see you." My heart started. Sergeant Kawu, our course director?

"Do you know why?" I asked.

"I don't know but I saw a vehicle bearing the insignia of Madagali Local Government packed in front of his office when I went to drop some message for him this morning. He most likely has some visitors from that area."

I hurriedly rounded off my task and headed for the Sergeant's office. Unlike the tradition of keeping junior soldiers waiting outside his office for a while before seeing them, Sergeant Kawu immediately ordered me to come in. As I saluted, he told me to sit down and went on to introduce an elderly man in a white Babanriga sitting in his office.

"This is Alhaji Sule Yahaya, the Chairman of Madagali Local Government which by the way, is my Local Government Area. Though you are not from that Local Government, your records showed that you lived there with your parents and attended school there. Am I correct?"

"Yes sir," I said.

"In that case, you should know the area very well?"

"Yes, I do." I replied.

"Are your parents and siblings still in Madagali?"

"No sir. My father is late, and my mother and sisters have since left the town for other places."

"I see," responded the Sergeant who began to explain that the Boko Haram insurgents have taken over Madagali town for the past three months and every effort to dislodge them had proved abortive.

"The town was seized by Boko Haram in June. This made the residents of Madagali, Gulak, and Michika to flee to the mountainous areas and Mubi town because government troops could not re-take the town from the insurgents after several attempts. These attacks have led to the loss of lives and destruction of property with the terrorists believed to be looking for food items. We strongly need a concerted effort of the military especially now that farming activities are picking up, further attacks may expose the communities to famine, said the Local Government Chairman.

"Actually, the problem is that we don't have troops that are familiar with the geography of that place. That is why your name came up. I know that you don't have any war experience yet, but you will be needed to help guide our troops when we commence "Operation Restore Sanity" in three days time. 100 of your course mates will be drafted to Madagali and you will be there to guide them through the area." Serageant Kawu instructed.

I became an instant hero when the news reached my course mates that out of all of us going to Madagali, I was going to play a critical role in the operation. Interestingly, while I should have been worried that I was being thrown into combat action so early, I was rather curious and excited at the prospects of my new aasignment.

We were assigned uniforms comprising rural guerrilla warfare uniforms, metal helmet, green bulletproof jackets, black rain boots, brown jungle boots, green waterproof coats, green hand glove, bags, scarves, wristwatches, knee, and elbow pads. Ready to go, we jumped into a column of twenty trucks for what was considered a final onslaught against the insurgents.

That was how I returned to Adamawa state after about a year's absence. On hand to receive us to the 'Land of Beauty' was a midday soft sun that peeked out of the azure sky bathing the horizon as our convoy drove into Jimeta. 'Jinta,' the original name of the town means

"I have received the blessings of this land with my two hands." From Jimeta we drove on to Yola South where the roundabout with the beautiful Fulani Milk Gourd still stood as it did during my last visit.

A written sign 'Welcome to Yola' welcomed us to the administrative capital of Adamawa. It was a lovely day as we moved past farmlands with farmers working busily and the cattle grazing solemnly. The scenery changed to palm tree-dotted mountainous peaks as we moved further north in the direction of the Cameroonian border. Mango trees and baskets of mangoes were all over the place as the roadside sellers bargained with prospective buyers.

As we descended into a valley, our vehicles became enveloped by a lovely ring of craggy mountains, beautiful date palms and more mango trees, only that at that point, the hitherto good road took a turn for the worse.

We got to Hong as I gazed with disbelief at different sections of the bad road where giant potholes made driving a nightmare. I saddened me to note that the same road which was in a very good shape just about a year earlier was now partially destroyed. All around us were bombed out shells and bullet pocked buildings including banks and churches which I was told were tell-tale of the dreaded Boko Haram insurgents' attacks.

As we progressed, the vegetation soon turned to rocky outcrops and mountains with dry vegetation and shrubs. These were interspersed with mud walls and thatched villages. Occasionally, we chanced upon dry riverbeds, a sign of a long dry season now anticipating the rainy season which was yet to begin in that part of the state. At Mararaba, we took a left road that led to Mubi. At Song, a drowsy and dusty small town a few kilometres before Mubi, we stopped for a lunch of semolina, okra soup and fish. As we approached Mubi, gun totting soldiers at several security checkpoints waved our convoy on. The soldiers were assisted by members of the local vigilantes in their maroon colour uniforms, bearing their own guns. Despite the bad roads, I noticed an ongoing afforestation project where thousands of gedu and ongoyaro trees were planted to combat desert encroachment. Just before entering Mubi, we chanced on the Mubi Army Barracks which was attacked by the Boko Haram insurgents the previous year. The barracks still had an artificially made barrier of a moat as its perimeter fence. After the barracks were sprawling cattle markets on both sides of the road.

Mubi is an enormous commercial nerve centre which continues to be a key international market serving Nigeria, Cameroun, and Chad Republic. At the town's Tike Junction, was another sad reminder of the Boko Haram insurgency. The remnants of a bombed Ecobank building, an incident which also took place the previous year where the insurgents were able to cart away millions of Naira from the bank's vault.

Twilight descended on us at the mouth of Madagali after our eight-hour trip from Zaria. The twilight in the rocky and scenic town was of a different kind. It was not the twilight of the Madagali of my youth. It was accentuated by darkness, colour of amber glow. It had the weak wattage of low voltage generator. First time visitors to war torn Madagali would find this feeling of twilight strange. The darkness, according to scientists, was said to have been caused by a large mass of soot and haze that had been spewed into the atmosphere from bomb explosions, bullets, and rocket fire since the war erupted many years ago. One would not need a scientist to understand that inhaling the soot for long could be injurious to health. I felt sorry for the surviving locals here, the real casualties of this senseless war.

We had just settled in our quarters when Alhaji Sule Yahaya came to give us background information about Madagali.

"Madagali is one of the areas with the highest Boko Haram presence in the Northeast," he began with visible urgency in his voice, after we had hurriedly exchanged pleasantries. "This is due to our proximity to Goza in Borno state as well as the Zambiza Forest." He paused, searching our faces for reactions at the mention of Sambisa, the infamous Sambisa. None of us uttered a word. He continued.

"The insurgents can be found in Gombe, Hul, Michikan, Chibok, Danbua, Bama and Kluka among other places now made inhabitable by those wicked boys." He paused again and produced a handkerchief to wipe the corners of his mouth before continuing. "When they first came into Madagali, they ransacked the whole place, killed people and took control of the entire town. Initially, they pretended to be our friends. They made us believe they were fighting for us, but in a sudden twist of events, they turned against us. I was surprised myself when they first came. Some of them walked into my house and started calling my family members by name. Even some of my children could identify them. Other Boko Haram members looked for vacant houses and occupied them and were reciting the Quran there. As side business, they sold perfumes and made caps, largely to make us comfortable, and so we stayed with them peacefully. When their commanders came in, they were the ones that finally completed the indoctrination of the people into real Boko Haram." He noted.

"But what is so special about Madagali that sparked the insurgents' interest?" Our Commander, Col. Ade Rasaki asked, sounding irritated.

"Eem, they found Madagali with its rich agricultural and cattle markets, a goldmine to fund their war," Alhaji Yahaya replied with the earnest innocence of a pupil in the presence of mindful teachers. "This is why the insurgents will do everything possible to continue to stay in this area, and we have continued to encourage the Federal Government to brace up to this war by making sure that as they are training and sending you people to us, they must properly equip you and take good care of your welfare. We have some embarrassing instances where federal troops were made to sleep in the open without any accommodation for a long time while being owed salaries and allowances running into several months by the authorities. I have witnessed a situation where a trained soldier was running to hide in one of my houses from a Boko Haram boy coming with AK47. It is most embarrassing and degrading," he added.

"You have spoken well. We thank you," our Commander began. We hope the authorities take our welfare seriously but that notwithstanding, I disagree that those small rats are better equipped than the Nigerian Army. Most of the stories about their superior firepower are false. The soldiers that abandoned their locations at the approach of the terrorists did not join the army to fight. They were just looking for jobs when they joined the army and that is why I am warning you," he turned to us with stern mien, "that as long as I am your commander, I will not tolerate any act of indiscipline, cowardice, or desertion. I'll always make sure to look after you and demand from the authorities, all that are due for you as combatants. Is that clear?"

"Yes sir," we mumbled haphazardly.

"I am not sure I heard you well," he retorted. Raising his voice, he asked again, "is that clear?"

"Yes sir!" we chorused loudly, sharply. He seemed satisfied, including the Chairman who wore an impressed look.

Then turning to the Chairman, the Colonel said, "Mr Chairman, the insurgents are not ghosts. They live among the people and the people know them and their informants. Soldiers are not magicians. We work with information and intelligence reports, and this is where we need help and cooperation from your people. As long as your people continue to accommodate these criminals and refuse to give us the necessary information about them, then the war will not end and it is to the detriment of your peace and existence," he noted, looking fiercely into Alhaji Yahaya's face who nodded slowly and promised to help sensitize his people on the need to cooperate.

After a proper study of the Madagali terrain, it was discovered that approaching the town from the southern end of Mubi would be too slow for our boys due to the destruction of the bridge over the River Maggar by the insurgents. I suggested we make a detour through one of my favourite villages close to Gulag for a quicker entry into the heart of Madagali. To avoid indiscriminate arrests and killings of people by our troops on the excuse of being Boko Haram insurgents, I volunteered to follow our soldiers on a house-to-house search to identify the real insurgents and save the innocent. In the company of some of my known friends, we would ask natives to come out for physical identification. This process reduced the number of casualties.

The method gave our troops a huge success, but it was a hectic job which took almost four years to accomplish. From undertaking this role, my health suffered a bit, but I was happy to have been promoted to the rank of Lance Corporal while in the town.

One sour point of our stay in Madagali was that we

terribly underestimated the capabilities of the insurgents, hence on the day we marched into the millet fields of Madagali on that rain-soaked month of May, we carried along our packs and rifles, the implicit convictions that the Boko Haram insurgents would be quickly dislodged and annihilated. Little did we know that the boys we had called small rats and *munafukai* and mad were, in fact, a lethal, highly determined, and resilient enemy. We soon learnt to hold a contrary view when our casualty status increased each week with little or nothing to show for the blood being spilled on both sides. Apart from breaking our confidence, it turned us into occasional cowards who, rather than fight, were eager to run away from the battlefield. At the end of the rainy season, what had begun as an adventurous expedition had turned into an exhausting, indecisive war of attrition in which we fought for no cause other than our own survival.

CHAPTER THREE

Two days after the discovery of bomb materials in the luggage given to me by my Brigade Commander, Lt. Col. Humus for his 'family' in Achilafia, I was court-martialed alongside several other soldiers at the Maimalari Barracks in Maiduguri. This was despite all my explanations that the luggage was not mine. I was initially arraigned on a two-count charge of theft of military property and attempted supply of dangerous weapon to the enemy. But after my Brigade Commander denied being the owner of the lethal luggage, a third charge of 'attempt to discredit a senior Military Officer' was added to the list of my crimes. While the punishments for the theft and discrediting a senior officer were imprisonment for four years, the supply of dangerous weapons to the enemy was a death sentence. From all indications, my case was the most serious of the thirteen suspects before the Military Tribunal. The charges against the other twelve soldiers ranged from theft of bullets and food items meant for Nigerian soldiers to absconding from duty and manslaughter.

My first appearance before the Tribunal was very

brief. The President gave the preamble after which I was sworn to 'speak the truth and nothing but the truth'. I was about to start rattling off my defence when the Tribunal President, Major General Etuk, called me to order and directed that I was going to be led in evidence in court-room fashion by the Military Lawyer assigned to defend me. One fact which the Tribunal was bent on establishing beyond any doubt was the source of the marterial for making the bomb. It was the belief of the Army authorities that I was part of a large ring of suppliers of lethal weapons to the Boko Haram and as such, needed to confess to the "fact."

My lawyer put up a strong defence by explaining to the prosecution that there was no way I could have been the source of the lethal weapon since I had been in the warfront for about two weeks prior to the discovery of the bomb materials. He emphasized that I was ferried to the Kano Orthopaedic Hospital in a near critical condition after being shot during the military offensive in Madagali and was therefore not in a good condition to be sourcing military weapons.

After what may be tagged as my evidence-in-chief, a few members of the Tribunal asked some questions for purposes of clarification. They wanted to know the kind of relationship I had with Lt. Col. Humus as well as my mission for going to Kazaure, among other questions.

After the Tribunal had adjourned, I was hauled back into the Land Rover that had earlier brought me from the guardroom in the barracks while a Hiace vehicle full of armed soldiers brought up the rear. As the heavy iron gates of the guardroom closed behind me that evening it dawned on me that all my beautiful plans for my sick leave had come to nothing. With the grim allegation of supplying lethal weapons to the enemy and the likely verdict of a death sentence on my head, I now realised that I was fighting a case of life and death. And much as I tried to keep the matter away from my family, I was shocked when, at the next mention of the case a few days later, I saw the dejected faces of my sisters, Zainab and Rabia as they waited to receive the land Rover driving into the venue of the Tribunal. My sisters, through my lawyer, informed me that my mother, who lives with my eldest sister, Fatima in Monrovia, was aware of my predicament and had sent message to me that all would be well.

Before my case was called, the Tribunal decided to give judgement in the cases involving the other soldiers. Twelve soldiers were accused of stealing bulletes and guns from the armoury. While six of them were discharged and acquitted, four were sentenced to 23 years in prison each for stealing high caliber ammunition meant for combating Boko Haram insurgency and the remaining two who are Corporals bagged 10 years each for the theft of bullets. The court said the sentences were subject to confirmation by the highest military body as provided by the Armed Forces Act.

Next was the case of 100 soldiers who were all kept in a truck outside the Tribunal Hall due to lack of space.

The authorities accused them of failure to capture the Sambisa Forest, a notorious hideout for Boko Haram terrorists in Borno State. Their lawyer argued that the charges against his clients were "untrue, false and malicious." The lawyer denied the claim by the army authorities that the soldiers abandoned their duties and ran away, explaining that sufficient weapons were not provided for them to fight the terrorists and therefore they ran out of ammunition. To prove to the court that the weapons provided for the troops were obsolete, he held up a large photograph of one of the bombs supplied to the soldiers to show it had expired since 1964, about 56 years earlier and could no longer be effective.

He requested the court to allow him to cross-examine one of the soldiers. During cross examination, the forlorn-looking soldier confirmed what his defence lawyer had earlier said about the expired bomb.

"Each of us were given five bullets, not five rounds, to fire, while in the forest. And while our biggest weapon was only able to cover just a distance of 400 metres, our enemy had anti-aircraft weapons that could cover a distance of more than 1,000 metres with other dangerous weapons. It is not true that we absconded, we only retreated to our base, waiting for ammunition for three days, in vain," he informed soberly.

Despite what many of us considered to be a good defence, the court found the 100 soldiers guilty on the two-count charge of "failure to perform military duty and disobedience to standing order." The presiding judge ordered their dismissal from the army for laxity and cowardice in the course of duty.

When my case was called, I was very optimistic that I had a good case. My optimism was further reinforced when I listened to the summing-up by my lawyer who again reiterated the point that it was impossible for a wounded soldier to be in possession of such a sensitive and lethal military hardware. He followed this up with a request to subpoena the Brigade Commander, Lt. Col. Humus for a cross examination in order to confirm that he was the actual owner of the weapons. The defence argued that the fellow who was to receive the luggage at Achilafia had been identified and should also be subpoenaed to confirm that he was a regular errand boy for Humus, a regular supplier of weapons to Boko Haram.

The prosecutor who was a military lawyer in the rank of a Colonel rejected my Lawyer's request to subpoena my Brigade Commander and his "courier", describing it as an abuse of court process that is tantamount to discrediting a high-ranking military officer before the eyes of the public. To him, I had no defence. My alibi of being at the war front or being on the sick bed before committing the offence were not tenable since I could have planned my crime with other accomplices. He also believed that my plan to use part of my sick leave to travel to see my mother was to be financed from the proceeds of the crime. He urged the Tribunal to find me guilty, as a deterrent to others like me who were busy supplying ammunition to the enemies through which activity many innocent lives had been lost. He concluded by asking for the maximum sentence of a death sentence for me. His submission was greeted with some audible gasps from members of the audience most especially my two sisters, huddled together in a corner of the courtroom.

Now that the prosecution and defence had completed their respective assignments, my fate was now in the hands of members of the Tribunal. According to the presiding judge, even though members of the Tribunal were determined to get to the truth, they were handicapped. As he put it: "Following the pleas of the defence lawyer that the court should subpoena Lt. Col. Humus as well as the contact who was identified in Achilafia, we applied to the Defence Headquarters for permission to bring the senior military officer to the court. But we were overruled on the grounds that our request, if granted would bring the military to ridicule in the eyes of the public. In view of that, the President said that the court had found the accused guilty and therefore sentenced him to death subject to confirmation by the Army Council. As he said this, my sisters' loud wailings resonated through the stunned courtroom.

With its red engine, dazzling black railings and fifteen green coaches carrying passengers and merchandise, the Kano to Lagos train appeared beautiful in the late afternoon sun. Under the hood of its 180-horsepower engine was enough strength to power about twelve coaches for passengers and three for merchandise.

Although the third-class compartment was full of civilians, it also contained six soldiers: four privates, one Lance Corporal and a Lieutenant. They were accompanying 10 caskets of the bodies of their late comrades, mostly officers, to their various destinations in the southern part of the country for proper burial. The officers had died after being referred to the National Orthopaedic Hospital, Kano following injuries from the "Yobe" front of the war. They had been embalmed for the three-day journey. Leading the team of soldiers on the difficult assignment was Lt. Tunde Okaka who was assisted by L/Cpl. Tony Adede.

It was odd for the army to use civilian transportation for the wounded and the dead, but the raging war of attrition in the northeast and the need to get the bodies of the dead officers to their various destinations in the southern part of the country made this option attractive.

Having been on duty the previous night, the soldiers were tired, but found the overcrowded third-class compartment of the train too uncomfortable to for a nap. The situation was compounded by the sweltering heat amidst baskets of foodstuffs, bundles of merchandise, smoked meat, and filth. A foul smell of stale perfume and decomposing foodstuffs hit the soldiers as they sat in the coach. Other passengers that could not get seats filled the aisles and passages as well as the canteen. Where space was available, they mostly spread out their sleeping mats and slept or played cards and chatted to kill time.

"We call the first-class compartment of the train America," said one passenger to a railway official. "Life there is okay." "The standard class we call China. Too many people but still good; Third-class we call Nigeria where life is only to be endured," he said as other passengers within earshot burst into laughter at the apt analogy.

The train was a moving village. Boisterous and noisy like a town that never sleeps. It was a wonder that amid the clamour of the train's crowded coaches, crying children, shrieking engine, and creaking wheels, some passengers dared to dose off. Just before dawn, many of the passengers were roused by the loud, grunting noise of the train as it hugged a very sharp bend. Outside the window were the remains of a previous train disaster, a crumpled mass of rusting couches and twisted rail lines. As the train negotiated the bend, it broke into a galloping run. Just then, an unpleasant stench of decomposing carcass enveloped the entire train. "There are dead cows near the rails," said one of the security men as the passengers frantically tried to close the windows to shut out the odour. But the afternoon sun was at its peak, the putrid smell of decaying flesh hung in the air for a long time.

It was both Okaka and Adede's first visit to the South in more than two years. Adede had informed his family that he was coming and eagerly looked forward to seeing them. He was sad that his best friend, ECOMOG with whom he had arranged to spend his leave, was not able to make the trip. It was just the day before that he heard that the luggage he had helped him to take to the motor park in Kano a few days earlier had earned him a death sentence. Since he knew his friend was innocent, he thought of how to help him. To clear his mind, he decided to go for a walk in the train. He took permission from Lt. Okaka and strolled from one coach to the other.

He ran into other soldiers in the train as he strolled. Though they were not in their uniforms, he still recognized and greeted him. They were wounded soldiers going home on sick leave and had taken advantage of the inexpensive train. The bandages around some of their heads were slightly blood-stained while some pairs of crutches were stacked on the overhead baggage rack. After the exchange of greetings, they felt awkward and remained silent for several moments as the train pulled out of the station and daylight streamed in to reveal the extent of the soldiers' injuries. Half of the legs stretched out in the aisle bore casts or metal braces secured with leather straps. At least, a third of the servicemen had cloth around their necks to support the slings that held their damaged or partially amputated arms. There were a few groans of pain now and then as the train swerved to negotiate another bend, the painful sounds reminded Adede of his time in the hospital. Again, he thought of "ECOMOG." He couldn't contain the clamour of thoughts in his head. Once back in his coach, he raised the matter with Lt. Tunde Okaka who was one of their instructors at the army Depot in Zaria.

"I personally drove ECOMOG to the motor park for the trip to Kazaure. That was when I saw the big luggage that Lt. Col. Humus asked him to drop at Achilafia."

"In that case you are very sure that Humus was the owner of the luggage in question?" Lt. Okaka asked.

"Yes sir," Adede replied.

The Lieutenant was quiet for a while. Moments later, he said, "Where are we delivering our last casket?"

"Ibadan, sir" he answered.

Lt. Okaka got up, brought out a packet of cigarettes from his shirt pocket, singled out a stick and lit it. He puffed, exhaled and for a while, watched the smoke slowly drift out of the cabin window before speaking.

"L/Cpl. Salisu is a good man from a noble family. His father and my father both served in the army around the same time. He has a rich military background, and I am sure, that he could not be involved in any criminal activity. I can't say the same for Lt. Col. Humus whose lifestyle is far above his legitimate income.

There have been rumors that he and some top-notch Military Officers have built mansions in Abuja and Dubai from the proceeds of their nefarious activities since the commencement of this war with Boko Haram. In addition to being very rich, Humus is also well connected in the Army Headquarters in Abuja, but we can save an innocent soldier. I also know a very influential former President of the country who is a retired General. He has zero tolerance for corruption. He now lives in retirement in Lagos. Once we deliver the last casket in Ibadan, we shall go and see him in Lagos. Hopefully, he will be able to help us. Cheer up boy!"

Lt. Okaka's words and offer to help L/C. Salisu was a big relief for Adede. He was full of thanks, and for the first time in the trip, smiled from his heart. Out of excitement, he called Rabia and Zainab from the train, to share the good news with them. The two ladies were ecstatic with joy and asked him to thank Lt. Okaka. Zainab then informed him of their own efforts in ensuring the reversal of their brother's court indictment. In conjunction with some human rights lawyers and NGOs, they have organised a Press Conference in Lagos and urged the Military High Command to free Salisu and prosecute Lt. Col. Humus who is the real culprit in the saga. They hope to follow up the Press Conference with visits to some media houses and Diplomatic Missions in both Lagos and Abuja during the week.

The slow-moving fifteen-coach train stopped at every station where, one or two servicemen hobbled off, to the warm embrace of family members and friends. Sadly, whatever joy those reunions on the platforms brought were overshadowed by the forlorn relatives who gathered at the last goods wagon laden with caskets waiting to claim the bodies of their slain relatives. This was after Lt. Okaka and L/Cpl. Adede, assisted by the four Private soldiers would have performed the very solemn ceremony of delivering the casket and other official documents from the army headquarters to the families of the late military officers.

And as he carried out this very solemn ceremony, Adede saw wailing women collapse to the ground and men cursing while gazing disconsolately at the sky. Faith leaders and local military officers tried to console mourners. In the background were military ambulances filled with flowers. Young servicemen draped in the green- white-green national flag accompanied widows bearing children, majority of whom were not yet old enough to walk. After a while, Adede could not bring himself to watch any of the scenes anymore. It had made him too self-conscious of being alive. Having survived battles that killed his friends and having now spent hours riding with caskets of dead and disabled-for-life soldiers, he realized that indeed, he had cause to thank God for his mercies. The war had now made him a better Christian especially after witnessing the brutal fall of his more experienced and proficient colleagues in battles and ambushes. His thoughts drifted to his friend, ECOMOG, who was now awaiting death for a crime he did not commit. He knew that he had to be thankful for God's special favours.

He also decided that if the good Lord could preserve him till the end of his military service, he would write a book on his experience even though at that point in his life, his thoughts and emotions were too fractured to set them down properly and coherently on paper. He knew he had an important story to tell, but he wasn't yet ready to tell it. He needed the distance that only time could give. He wanted the book to make people uncomfortable – in effect, to move them out of their snug theoretical positions into the actual world where real warriors dwelt. He promised to write about the war with unflinching honesty and painstaking attention to detail. He would make his readers feel the heat and mosquitoes, step on land mines, experience ambushes set up by the ubiquitous Boko Haram boys. He would tell the whole world about the Nigerian war commanders who not only pilfered their soldiers' allowances, but also stole their youth and their future. Not only would he write a book that would reach beyond its time and place, but tell a story of Boko Haram, revealing the underbelly of war itself. And if telling the truth about the war exposed the tragedy of a nation, so be it.

So engrossed was L/Cpl Adede in his proposed book that the did not realise that the Kano-Lagos train had arrived Ibadan. At that point the midday sun was at its fiercest. The relentless heat on the tin roofed train which had become half empty as many passengers including many of the wounded soldiers had disembarked along the route. The journey had taken approximately 24 hours. Only two of the original ten caskets of slain military officers were left in the goods wagons. As the train finally crawled into the Bodija station in Ibadan, the two caskets were handed over to the already waiting military officers and relatives of the deceased.

After the handing over ceremony, Lt. Tunde Okaka dismissed the four Privates but not before they had been given enough money for their return trip to their base at the Janguza Barracks in Kano. He and L/Cpl. Tony Adede quickly changed into civilian clothes and took a taxi to a nearby restaurant and awaited the arrival of Zainab and Rabia with whom they had resolved to see the former Nigerian President.

The meeting with the former President and Commander In Chief of the Nigerian Armed Forces went very well. First, he listened carefully to Adede's submission and later heard Lt. Okaka's addendum before turning to Zainab and Rabia. As he listened, he made notes in a small notebook. Occasionally, he went out of earshot and made phone calls which, I imagined, were to corroborate some of the things we had said. At one point, we overheard one of his telephone conversations where he berated the person he spoke to, apparently also a top military officer, for refusing to release Lt. Col. Humus for cross examination during the trial.

"And you call yourself a l-a-w-y-e-r?" shouted the former President. "Where in the army's protocol is it stated that cross examining a senior military officer would bring the army into disrepute?" he thundered as the conversation continued.

"It has been settled!" He declared to us as he reentered

the meeting room. "Your friend's appeal will be upheld, and Lt. Col. Humus will be presented for a thorough cross examination at the next trial," he said, struggling to recompose himself. L/Cpl. Adede and Lt. Okaka prostrated, and the two ladies knelt in gratitude.

CHAPTER FOUR

My cell at the Maiduguri prison was about six feet square-just enough room for a flat mattress, a pillow and two blankets. I sat down on the mattress. It was damp and coarse. The blankets stank of acrid body odour and urine. I covered my nose with the sleeve of my shirt, but this too reeked of stale sweat. A small opening on the posterior wall of the cell was the only window in the room. A pungent smell from an open gutter outside wafted through the window and assailed my nostrils. The floors and walls were covered by a slimy wetness and filth. Everything was foul and rotting and ugly. Thousands of mosquitoes buzzed about the room. I found it hard to breathe. The stench was choking.

As the day progressed, I started feeling the fury of the Maiduguri midday sun. The heat in my cell became unbearable and my sweat-soaked clothes clung to my body. Twice, I had sprinkled the bath water in the bucket on the mattress to cool it, but the heat persisted.

My mind flew back to the incident that had brought me to the cell. I could not help but shudder at the thought that it could come to this: a death sentence. From all indications, it had become obvious that Lt. Col, Humus was a sponsor of the

Boko Haram Movement. This has confirmed the rumours that some members of the Nigerian Army were collaborating with the group. Now that Lt. Col. Humus had washed his hands off me, only providence could save me from death.

Even after sentencing me to death, the military authorities were still interested in knowing whom I was taking the lethal weapons to just as they wanted to uncover the identity of other collaborators in the Army. And despite my pleas of being innocent of the charges, my jailers continued to interrogate and torture me in the belief that I would confess to a crime that I did not commit.

As soon as I was arrested with the bomb parcel, the driver of my hired taxi was taken to another facility while I was brought to the Maimalari barracks. On entering the jeep that brought me to the prison, I barely had time to cover my head before the beating began. The heavy boots of the soldiers, *koboko*, belts and rifle butts found their way to my back, neck, skull, face, stomach, legs, anywhere they could find. My hands were bound behind my back with compact, rustic handcuffs which bit sharply into my flesh as I was violently shoved into the back floor of the jeep. Like laser lights, a searing pain shot through my body as if a bomb had exploded in my skull. Before I knew it, another blow hit me on my face between my two eyes. Much as I tried to protect myself from the blows, I was powerless. My face and eyes began to swell while my arms and legs went numb. There was no power left in me. I lost my voice from screaming and began to pant. When the soldiers noticed that I was gasping for breath, the beatings ceased. Sufficiently pleased that I was well subdued, the interrogations commenced. My last interrogation took place in a different facility. To get there, I was handcuffed, blindfolded, and driven in a jeep. When my handcuffs and blindfold were removed, it took my eyes a while to adjust to the harsh and bright light of my new cell. I had to massage my wrists for a while to bring some life into them.

It was a large room, well-lit with several fluorescent lamps that shut out the darkness of the night. For a moment, I thought it was daytime, then I remembered that I had been taken out of my cell after the last evening prayers. I reckoned that the time of my arrival at the interrogation facility would be about ten o'clock in the night. There were several maps on the walls of the interrogation room to which arrows of different colors had been stuck. Standing and lining the four walls of the room were six-armed soldiers. The heavy presence of armed soldiers in the room made me realise the enormity of 'my' crime. In the middle of the room, some chairs and tables had been arranged in a semi-circle in front of which was another desk and chair. While five stern looking soldiers sat in the semicircle arrangement, I was hauled to the lone desk and chair.

"Sit!" my interrogator, a short stocky soldier in dark glasses who sat in the middle of the semi-circle, ordered.

As I sat weary and hungry, I saw the semi-circle group of soldiers scrutinizing me with curiosity. Some showed pity, others, despise and anger.

There was a pause as the man at the extreme end played back the recording of the last interrogation. Before then, I had thought that somebody was writing the notes of the conversation in longhand. I did not know we were being recorded. As I listened to the play back of the recording, I found it difficult to recognize my voice. I was surprised that despite my ordeal, I still spoke in a very calm, controlled, and reassuring manner.

Obviously satisfied with what he heard, the record operator signaled that the interrogation should resume. My interrogator now removed his dark glasses to reveal a pair of tired but alert eyes. He cleared his throat, leaned forward and in a stern and slightly menacing voice said, "Tell us all you know about the bombs found in your luggage."

Unlike the first interrogation where physical force was unleashed on me, the torture this time was by electric shock. Unknown to me, the chair I was sitting on had been rigged with electricity wires. As soon I repeated my innocence about the lethal baggage, an electric shock of unquantifiable quantity was sent into my body, and I let out an ear-splitting scream.

The question was repeated. This was followed by another searing and painful electric current shock as soon as I declared my innocence. Just then, I was brought out of my reminiscences as someone rapped on the door to my cell and pushed in an aluminum tray under the door. I looked at the tray and saw that it contained the same once-a-day-meal—some-half-cooked rice with stew, one piece of meat and a sachet of water. In spite of the poor quality of the food, I wolfed it down. Minutes later, I was still feeling hungry and was looking for a way of attracting the attention of a friendly warder who sometimes helped me get one loaf of bread to augment the meal, when I heard quick marching sounds approaching my cell from outside. Before long, the door to my cell opened and the Controller of the Prison, two warders and two armed soldiers appeared. My heart missed several beats: it was time for my trial.

"Pack your things and follow us," the Prison Controller said.

I was a bit puzzled, but I obeyed, as I tossed my towel, toothbrush, toothpaste, and a few other personal items which I had kept for my two-week stay into a black nylon bag and followed the group.

After being in the cell for about two weeks, it was a relief seeing the outside world again. It seemed as though I hadn't seen the sun for years. It appeared beautiful despite its harshness and radiating heat. The air also, despite the heat, was a refreshing change to the stale and pungent air that had drowned my breathing for two weeks.

I became more confused because rather than being put in the usual Land Rover that often took me to Maimalari Barracks venue of the Military Tribunal, I was led to the prison car park where the Controller of Prison handed me a letter and said "You are free to go" before driving off.

Left standing alone in the sparsely filled parking lot, I pondered on that command "You're free to go." I couldn't believe it. Just like that? Someone who was just a few minutes away from the gallows? Yes, I had been praying for a reprieve, but I never imagined it would come this quick, this easy. It was as though an unseen hand came to pull me away with electro-magnetic force. I had thought there would be a re-trial where I would have the opportunity to confront Lt. Col. Humus and debunk his lies against me. But to be told to go just like that sounded like a Greek gift. Experiences have thought me to be wary of low hanging fruits. This freedom looked like one. I was circumspect and glad at once.

The mere feeling of walking outside without restriction was just wonderful. I was eager to see my sisters and friends, but I didn't know where they were. I didn't want to walk quickly. I wanted to savour my freedom. I took a couple of steps, filled my lungs with the air of freedom and my ears with sweet silence. Someone called out my name as a taxi screeched to a halt before me and my sisters alighted gingerly. Tears rolled down their cheeks as they ran towards me and threw their arms around me.

"We were waiting for you in the barracks thinking they would bring you for another trial," Zainab said as L/Cpl. Tony Adede, my friend and course mate, joined us.

"Never knew it would be this quick," he said as we hugged each other.

Rabia, my younger sister was ecstatic with joy as she kept stroking my shoulders, neck, and head. "I have been counting the days when I will see you again" she said. "At a point, I was so worried that I might never see you again. We are so very proud of you, Bukar. You are a true hero".

We went to the hotel which my sisters had arranged and spent the remaining day celebrating my return. For the first time in weeks, I ate a very delicious food, joked, and had fun, as we always did whenever we were together. I could not tell my sisters what I had gone through. It would have been too painful for them. I knew I would still recount my tale to my friend, once I had rested sufficiently and gained some energy.

After a while, Zainab phoned Fatima, my elder sister living in Monrovia with her husband. Then my mother who also stays in Liberia with Fatima came on the line. When my mother heard my voice, she burst into tears. I too, began sobbing, heaving, sniffing, and struggling to control myself.

"You must come and rest in Monrovia. You need a change of scene after all the ordeals. You hear?" she asked.

When she noticed my hesitation, she said "Fatima will send you a return air ticket and you can stay with us. Her husband is a very nice man who has been looking forward to meeting you," she added.

Later that evening, Tony told me how he was able to convince Captain Okaka to intervene in my matter.

"Captain Okaka then advised we see a former President and retired Army General for help. Zainab and Rabia had also mobilized some Human Rights Lawyers and NGOs to publicise the matter. They joined us to go to see the General. At the end of our meeting with him, he assured us that your appeal would be upheld and that Lt.Col. Humus would be subpoenaed for cross examination so that you can be cleared," Tony said over dinner in the hotel as I looked at my sisters with pride.

"But the cross-examination never happened because I was just asked to go home," I said.

"I was surprised," Tony said. "The information we got was that Zainab, Rabia and I should meet in the Maimalari Barracks, venue of the Military Tribunal this morning for the appeal. We were waiting for you in the barracks only to be hurriedly summoned to the prison to fetch you."

"So, what happened? Why the change of plans?" I asked. "When I called Captain Okaka, he said that Lt. Col. Humus's godfathers at the Headquarters in Abuja realised that the truth would finally be out if he came to court, and quickly arranged a soft landing for him in exchange for your own outright discharge and acquittal."

"And what was the soft landing?" I asked.

Tony was quiet for a while as he chewed a piece of *suya*.

He then sipped from the glass of beer in his hand, smiled wryly and said, "you won't believe this. The soft landing is an overseas course in intelligence gathering."

I shot up on my feet, livid with anger. "An overseas course for somebody who should be shot. What kind of joke is this?" Tony shook his head.

"We need to mobilize the NGOs again until the man is arrested. We can't allow this kind of thing to continue. Only God knows how many similar cases are currently going on in the army," I protested, still on my feet.

Tony too stood up and gently pushed me to sit. "Sit and take it easy ECOMOG. As much as I am not happy with the way our bosses at the headquarters handled this case, I don't want you to overreact and endanger your life. These top guys can be top danger. I don't want what happened to Col. Yusuf Abu to also happen to you."

"Yusuf Abu, you mean the officer who commanded the Army's 190 Tank Battalion and was killed alongside 12 other soldiers in an ambush by Boko Haram in Katarko, Yobe State last month?" I asked.

"That was the official version. What I heard from other credible sources was different."

"What did you hear?" I asked Tony with a hot longing for clarification.

"What I heard was that the man was killed by our own men in an operation that was made to look like an ambush," Tony replied.

"Ha, come on, Tony. I don't believe that" I replied. "Why would anybody want to kill such a well-trained officer whom I learnt, also served with the Peace Keeping Forces in Darfur and Liberia?" I asked.

"He was found to be very popular with the soldiers and was regularly commended over and above the rest of the top rank, as if he was the only officer that could fight. You will also recall that last year, after a brutal massacre regarded as one of its worst attacks, Boko Haram captured Babangida, in Borno State. A month later, Abu led an operation to successfully retake the town. As a reward for his bravery, he was promoted from Lieutenant to Colonel. This may not have gone down well with his colleagues who thought that Abu was being favoured because he was the son of an Army General. With the way he was going, he would have succeeded in ending the war very quickly and they didn't want this especially those making money from the war. So, they had to cut him down."

Despite my position, Tony stuck to his 'conspiracy theory' about Abu Ali's death.

"If you also add to the whole situation, the suspicious withdrawal of one officer and forty-nine soldiers from Katarko on Friday morning while Boko Haram attacked at night, you will realise that the boys had advance information of the troop's reduction."

"I was made to understand that the troops were withdrawn because they were to carry out attack elsewhere in the theatre. The only controversy is why the suddenness of the withdrawal that fateful day," I said.

"Is it not standard practice to have replacement on location before pushing men elsewhere?" Tony asked.

Not willing to continue the argument, I said, "Fortunately, there is a plan by the authorities to carry out an inquiry into the circumstances surrounding Abu Ali's death. Hopefully, the truth would be out."

"Amen," Tony said. "My main concern is for you to maintain a low profile and not to try and play any hero. Now that God has saved your life from the court case, my advice is to just go about your work quietly. Remember that there are many Lt. Col. Humuses in the Army who are not happy with the way you have exposed and even disgraced one of them and they will not be happy with you. It is also dangerous for your colleagues to see you as somebody to fear. They can arrange to eliminate you," he added.

I thanked him for his concern and promised not to probe the matter even though inside me, I still felt bad about the way Lt. Col. Humus was allowed to get away without any reprimand.

After dinner, Tony suggested that we visit some of our colleagues at the Maimalari Barracks, especially those of them who had been very helpful during my ordeal. As we moved from room to room to greet our friends, I soon relaxed as the pains and bitterness of my previous experience started to wane. We visited some of our officers including one of our former Course Instructors in Zaria, Major Emeka Orlu. Major Orlu who had a master's degree in Psychology was known to be very intelligent and outspoken. He too was not very happy with the way the Boko Haram war was being prosecuted and he didn't mince words when we engaged him in a conversation about it.

"It is sad that the Nigerian Army is announcing that the attacks are being carried out by remnant Boko Haram terrorists when all reasonable persons can see that Boko Haram is still a formidable force. It is a pity that the Nigerian Army is more concerned with pleasing the political class than facing the truth. And while it may be the duty of the Nigerian Army public relations department to make the Nigerian Army look good, it is also necessary for the Nigerian Army to take practical steps to end this insurgency by improving the state of its equipment and telling the government the true situation. The truth is that from September to November this year, we have lost count of the troops that perished in this Boko Haram war of self-denial." He reasoned.

"One of the reasons why the Boko Haram terrorists have an upper hand was because it is the dry season, a time when the ground allows smooth movement of vehicles and considering that they have a better understanding of the local terrain, they could easily access troops' location and escape. This is in addition to the pressure on them around the Sambisa front, hence they seem to have pooled forces to concentrate on the northern Borno axis," I noted.

"The major cause of troop casualties now is poor equipment. Now, the equipment in the theatre is mostly worn out and obsolete. Provision of adequate equipment is the only major solution for now. Troops' confidence is a function of sound and functional equipment. Remember that a man without equipment is, at best, inefficient and machines without man are almost useless. Therefore, the only way to minimize the casualty rates among our troops is for them to be adequately and well equipped. Obsolete equipment such as Vickers MBT have become so worn out that they often do not get to action most times troops are under attack. This is why the semi-serviceable T-72 tanks are being moved everywhere in the theatre. The artillery Shilka guns are even the worst. Boko Haram terrorists fear the effect of Shilka guns, but I still wonder why almost all Shilkas are not serviceable in the theatre. Even more worrisome is the fact that the Nigerian Army has not procured more Shilka guns. These Russian-made weapons have relatively less complicated purchase protocol compared to those from the West. Unfortunately, for every battle we engage in, the equipment keeps wearing out, and to worsen issues, the equipment is not procured with their fast-moving spares." He said, breathing heavily from talking at length.

"But we now have more AK47guns," Tunde chipped in.

"AK47 is a personal assault rifle, needed after long range weapons have done much of the job, but unfortunately the long-range support weapons are inadequate. You boys know what I mean. We need more mortar tubes as well as artillery weapons like Shilka guns among others," the Major countered.

So how did we achieve the initial upper hand of cutting down the terrorists and recapturing territories from them?" I asked.

"That was when the newly procured T-72 tanks were supplied to the theatre" Major Orlu explained. "Chadian troops also assisted in mounting pressure on Boko Haram terrorists at the same time. This resulted in Boko Haram splitting their forces to several fronts at the same time, spreading thin at the theatre. Do not also forget that two years ago, we had mercenaries that fought alongside our troops. They came with armoured fighting equipment. Above all, they had night fighting capabilities. Those mercenaries really assisted us, and their withdrawal signalled the gradual regrouping of Boko Haram terrorists. Recall that their withdrawal was sudden and not in phases." We all kept quiet and dispersed with sorrow written on our faces. The facts were incontestable.

My four-week sick leave was reconfirmed the following day. I followed my sisters, Zainab and Rabia to Kano for my preparations for the trip to Monrovia. While waiting for my departure, I stayed with Tony Adede at the Jacunza Barracks in Kano soaking up love from my other course mates in the barracks. I also went out and enjoyed all the other sights, sounds, and smells that I had missed. In the evenings, I spent time hanging out with my friends in the ancient city – eating *kilishi* and drinking coffee in the barracks' "mammy market." As I strolled around the well-lit and expansive confines of the barracks in the company of my friends, I inhaled the peace and simplicity of freedom.

CHAPTER FIVE

"Jabbie, welcome to Liberia, the Land of your birth," my brother-in-law, John Rodney said as he called my Liberian name. We hugged each other after I had disembarked from the plane at Monrovia's Roberstsville Airport. "Emine could not come because of the baby," John said as he put away the placard upon which he had written my name for identification since we had never met. Initially, I was a bit confused when I heard the name "Emine" until I remembered that it was Fatima's Liberian name.

"I understand" I said. "I was not even expecting you. I thought I would take a taxi and find my way to your house since you may still be at work," I said, as the thunder rumbled overhead. On our way to the car park, the heavens opened, and rain came down in torrents. We made a dash for John's car.

"We are in the rainy season, and it could rain continuously for 24hours," my brother-in-law said. "If only it is possible for us to trap all the rainwater and export it, Liberia would be far richer than many other developed countries" he added.

We left the airport for the one-hour trip to the city of Monrovia. I relished the beauty of the thick and extended vegetation of green forest on both sides of the road.

Liberia was still recovering from its fourteen-year civil war that reportedly resulted in the casualties of about 250,000 Liberians. On either side of the road were buildings damaged by mortar shells. The blue berets of the peace-keeping UN troops could be seen everywhere. Just outside the airport, we chanced on the Military Barracks that housed the UN troops. Amidst the barbed wire fortified building was a big billboard with the screaming headline: WE BRING PEACE!

"I thought the UN soldiers have left Liberia," I turned to John, a Liberian civil engineer in private practice.

"They wanted to go but we begged them to stay a few more years while we sort ourselves out. Even though the war formally ended about six years ago, my people are very stubborn and may resume hostilities if foreign soldiers suddenly depart. While it is true that a sizeable number of arms had been seized from the combatants, I still believe that a lot of arms are still hidden in the forests ready for use.

"But I learnt that some Liberians are already complaining that the UN soldiers have overstayed, accusing them of causing inflation in the country because they have higher purchasing power with their salaries paid in US dollars" I said.

"Well, that may be what you soldiers call collateral damage, only this time, on the socioeconomic front," he replied, as we passed some moneychangers.

"They also accused them of rape, violence and armed robbery," I said.

"Yes, you are right," John said. "Every time a UN soldier is convicted of a crime, he is aided to escape from the country by his superiors before judgement can be meted out," he said. "Many Liberians are of the view that it was time Liberia began training her own army and police rather than depending on international peacekeeping forces. I agree with them but, that notwithstanding, we need the foreign soldiers to stay for a little longer."

One hour after leaving the airport, we got to John's house in the Sinkor section of the city. A bustling mid–town district, Sinkor is home to many diplomatic missions and hotels. On hand to receive me were my mother and my sister, Fatima. I had to learn to start calling her Emine, her Liberian name. Emine was carrying Janete, my 10-month-old niece. It was a very emotional reception as I had not seen Emine for over five years since she returned to Liberia to complete her nursing education and later got married just before our father died in a motor accident in Nigeria. Since I was only about five years old when my father brought my mother, sisters and I to Nigeria, everywhere in Monrovia looked strange to me.

Barely an hour after a lavish dinner of jollof rice and fish, my uncles and aunties started pouring into the house to welcome me. I had some difficulties recognizing who was who as they all looked alike with their pointed noses and light skin. I was just about to make this observation when my uncle hugged me passionately and shouted "Jab! Jab! You are now a big boy. Look at how you resemble us? You are more of a Johnson than a Salisu. Do you still play football? I remember how you used to play football all day long even as a toddler and how any attempt to pry the ball away from you often resulted in serious crying." He brought out an old photograph from his jacket's pocket, it was me in a sports wear cradling a football that was almost as big as my head. I remembered the photograph because I had a copy which I used to carry in my primary school in Madagali for a long time until I lost it.

"I still played football until a few years ago when work made it impossible to play again," I replied to my Uncle Timothy.

"Football?" My mother asked. "He is now a soldier just as his father. His football has been replaced with a gun," my mother said and shook her head sorrowfully.

More visitors and relatives trooped in and out of John and Emine's house to welcome me but in fact, to confirm what they saw as the spitting image of my mother, a delightful piece of news which had already spread round family circles since my arrival a few hours earlier. My mother must have informed her family members of my coming. "Jabbie is kinda a Liberian less a Nigerian," I overheard some of them say in Liberian English which I found difficult to understand unlike my sisters who often spoke it effortlessly with my mother or among themselves anytime they wanted to communicate secretly.

I allowed my eyes to wander round the room and noticed that amidst all the excitement of my visit, one young lady didn't seem to be part of the fun. She sat quietly in one corner from where she only smiled at the jokes and banter that flowed through the room. She was pretty with dark curly hair some of which protruded from the yellow scarf around her head. I had thought she was part of the family, but nobody introduced her to me. She was enjoying everything, the warmth, the close intimate atmosphere of family and friends all together in one room.

Intrigued, I sidled up to Fatima, sorry, Emine, "Who is that girl?" I asked.

"Your wife," she said, and changed quickly from laughter to seriousness.

"My wife?" I asked, alarmed but managing to laugh. "Who married her for me and when?"

"Has mama not told you?"

"Told me what?" I asked

"After your last war injury, she thought it was time for you to get married…and…"

"How can I marry a woman during the war?" I interjected. "By the way, I am too young for that."

"Daddy married mummy at your age during the Liberian war," Emine shot back.

Her response dissolved my anger, so I kept quiet for a while. I stole another look at the lady who had now stood up and was talking to somebody. She was tall and looked angelic in a tight-fitting bright orange frock which accentuated her hips and bust with…..

"Isn't she lovely?" Emine said interrupting my thoughts. The lady was obviously giving me a sneak preview of her physique and daring me to reject her.

"What does she do for a living?" I asked, breaking into a smile.

"She's a final year nursing student at the Monrovia School of Nursing. I usually see her anytime she came to my Department at the John F. Kennedy Medical Centre on Tubman Boulevard. She's a good and hardworking girl. I have told her about you."

"What's her name?"

"Jewel. Jewel Roberts. She's just 21."

Three days later, I took Jewel out on a date. Though I saw her every day in my sister's house where she normally came after work, I took my time before asking her out, as I did not want to rush into things. Since I was not familiar with Monrovia I asked her to choose where we would go for our date. She suggested a restaurant that sold local Liberian food, but I turned it down since I was not keen on Liberian food. When I again turned down her suggestion of a fast-food joint, she asked me the kind of food I wanted.

"Do you have any Chinese Restaurant?" I asked "Yes, but they are usually very expensive."

I wanted to change my mind but since I wanted to impress her and since I had some money from my leave and sick leave allowances, I stuck to the idea of a Chinese restaurant.

"There is a new Chinese Restaurant on Broad Street in downtown. We should check it out." She said and I agreed.

Since Jewel usually finished school at 5pm, we agreed that I should meet her at the hospital which is not far from Emine's house. I strolled down the road and took the turnings on the road as Emine had described. Though I still walked with a slight limp because of my war injury, I arrived at the hospital at exactly 5pm. Jewel appeared very shy and awkward as she later walked beside me to the Hospital's main gate and to the bus station.

"You looked scared," I said. "Are you not allowed to have visitors at work?"

"I am not scared, just a little nervous," she replied.

"Nervous? Why should you be nervous? At least, my sister has told you a lot about me."

"Yes, but I still do not know you well enough. You are still a stranger to me."

"Yes, especially when I am also a soldier," I said as I burst into laughter. "Are you afraid of soldiers?"

"Not really. Soldiers are also human beings. One of my cousins is a soldier and a very nice person."

The bus arrived, and we boarded. It was very rowdy and a little difficult getting seats.

"It is the rush hour," Jewel said as she managed to get a seat. "You can sit down because of your injured leg, while I stand," she said.

"No, am okay," I replied. "You are the one who should sit down," I said as the bus bumped along the pothole riddled road on its way to Broad Street in downtown. We passed a bridge, then a market before coming up beside the grey walls of a secondary school. The bus stopped a couple of times to pick more passengers. Due to the bumpy nature of the trip, I had to hold on to the railings in the bus. On one occasion when the bus listed and it appeared as if I would lose my balance, Jewel quickly held my hand and gave me a large smile.

"I am sorry. I shouldn't have brought you out in a bus. Next time we shall go out in a taxi," she promised.

By the time we reached our destination, the sun had gone down, and the atmosphere had become relatively dull as twilight was setting in. It was as though someone had deliberately smeared a thin dark paint across the sky, but Jewel was not in the least worried. On the contrary she looked delighted as she locked her hands in mine and guided me through the congested sidewalk full of office workers going home, shoppers and market women.

On either side of downtown Broad Street were green grocers, butchers, tobacconists, fish shops, with dealers in fruits and flowers hawking their wares in wheelbarrows. The pavements were full of people; it was like a big carnival going on. Further up the street was a brand-new, glittering shopping mall which housed the object of our trip. It was just after the sad incident of the Ebola epidemic when the whole country had to be locked down. With the terrible scourge behind them, Liberians now made a great point of enjoying their newfound freedom.

Similarly, after months of living in a war zone with the sounds of artillery, bombs and rockets, as well as the cries of the dying and the wounded in my eardrums, I was also like the Liberians, enjoying a life of peace and freedom. While my military training had equipped me with all that I needed to kill and avoid being killed, it had robbed me of the basic knowledge of life. I was taking my time to look around and listen to beautiful music that boomed out of many loudspeakers by the sides of the street. I was also admiring the beauty of the colourful lights from different shops and restaurants around me. Jewel was not having it.

"Jeez, I didn't know that this place would be so crowded today. I don't know where all these people came from. We need to move faster before the Restaurant closes." She worried.

As we entered the glistering Chinese Restaurant, I felt awkward seeing the beautiful cutlery, crockery, and the bright overhanging lamps, even as light music wafted from invisible speakers embedded in the roof. When I told Jewel that I had never eaten a Chinese meal before, she decided to give me a small lecture.

"A typical Chinese meal has two things, a carbohydrate or starch like noodles, rice or buns, and accompanying stir fries or dishes of veggies, fish and meat. They use a lot of fresh vegetables and mushrooms, water chestnuts, bamboo and even tofu. Each dish focuses on creating a balance between three aspects – appearance, aroma, and taste. They pay a lot of attention to aesthetics, in other words, the appearance of the food with diversified colours. Sauces and seasonings like fish sauce, five spice powder, oyster sauce, soy sauce, vinegar, root garlic, fresh ginger and others are used generously to offer a complex play of flavour and aroma," she said.

"Whoa! How did you know so much about Chinese food?" I asked.

"My mother works in a Chinese company. Initially, she was hired as a cleaner but when the directors of the firm saw how clean she was, one of their wives taught her how to prepare Chinese food. She, in turn, taught me."

"You mean you can prepare Chinese food?"

"Yes, at least, some common ones and…"

She was interrupted by a waiter who came to take our order.

Not familiar with Chinese foods, I asked Jewel to place the order. She ordered springs rolls and Peking soup for starters, and a combination of Basmati rice, chicken, and beef sauce with mixed vegetables as our main meal. We had strawberry ice cream for our dessert.

As we ate, Jewel and I sought to know more about each other, but I was careful not to reveal too much detail about me, about the ongoing war back home and my neck-deep involvement in it. I didn't want to frighten her. I was also careful to avoid the issue of marriage. Apart from the fact that I wasn't mentally ready for it, I was just getting to know her and didn't want to raise her hopes. I changed the topic of our discussion. "How is life in Monrovia? I thought it was supposed to be a vicious place with a high crime rate, but it looks like a good and peaceful place to be."

"During the war, things were very bad with a lot of insecurity and poverty, but the situation has now improved, though we are still a poor country. Don't leave your belongings. And don't run around displaying affluence or showing off. People are generally friendly and prepared to help but at the same time, they may tell you pathetic stories and end up asking for money. When you tell them you don't have, they leave you alone. Just as in any city you will get scammers or a bit of crime but as long as you are careful you don't have to worry."

"Yes, I agree with you even though, a few days is not enough for me to reach a verdict. However, from what I have seen so far, Liberians appear to be warm, friendly, and sociable. I love the energy around here.

"Liberians are good. They often go out of their way to make foreigners comfortable and welcome. Liberia is a very poor country, everyone knows that. Here, bribes are often given to the police, just as in many African countries. Burglars also break in especially if you left your things unattended. However, violence is a thing of the past," Jewel said as we finished our meal.

After dinner, I asked Jewel if we could go and dance even if it was just for one hour. "I haven't danced in ages," I said.

"But where do we want to go... and about your injury? Are you allowed to dance?"

I told her that I saw a Club's neon sign on our way to the restaurant and that my doctor had even advised me to exercise the leg very well to encourage healing.

We found both the Celavi Night Club and The Empire too expensive and finally ended up at Angels, a smart new smoky but comfortable night club down an alley off Broad Street. As we entered the dimly lit club, a strong smell of cheap alcohol and cigarettes hit the nostrils while the pulsating beat from a musical band floated around the club. After paying the mandatory entry fee of 5 Liberian dollars, I found myself in the happy company of young and not so young Liberians as a pretty but very thin vocalist rendered some old classical songs such as "Cera Cera" and "Farewell Jamaica" among others.

And when she started singing Michael Jackson's 1983 famous song "Liberian Girl," the enthusiastic crowd took up the song in unison.

Liberian Girl...
More Precious Than Any Pearl
Your Love So Complete...Liberian Girl
You Know That You Came
And You Changed My World

Stirred by the persistent percussions of the guitar and the rumbles of the drums, I was instantly on my feet half dragging Jewel to the dance floor. Music after music, we were on the dance floor as we wriggled, jumped, twisted, and clapped to the series of melodious songs dished out by the DJ. I ignored Jewel's admonitions that came over the din of the noise for me to slow down and be mindful of my injury. Having spent all my youth in the army, it was my first time in a night club, hence I was down for whatever. I had never been so happy in my life. In the heat of the fast-paced songs, the DJ switched to soulful R&B playlist as the lights dimmed to give effect to the blues. I took Jewel in my arms, and we waltzed through a most wonderful night.

Two days to the end of my leave, Jewel came to my room in Emine's house. It was a Saturday, her usual free day. It was not the first time she came to see me, but because I would soon be returning to Nigeria, the visit would be her last and a very emotional one. We had spent most of the ten days in Monrovia together, trying to know each other better. Though the issue of marriage was not directly discussed, some veiled references had been made to it. When I reminded her that I would soon be going back to Nigeria, she said that she would also be in Nigeria to visit me. "How would you find your way?" I asked curiously. "Your mum has promised to bring me along when going back to Nigeria during Christmas," she replied. When she noticed that I did not say anything, she then asked, "or you don't want me to come and see you?"

"No, I am not against your coming. It's just that we are still at war, and I may not be given any leave again this year."

Not convinced, she said, "Perhaps, you already have a wife in Nigeria?"

"Me? A wife?" I burst into laughter. "Where is the time? I was dragged from Secondary School where I was top of my class to the Army Training Depot and from there, straight to the warfront. I never had a normal adolescence, never knew, until now, how it is to toast a lady, or even fall in love. I never knew how to use a set of cutleries to eat or even engage in a civil discussion about politics and history which were my favourite subjects in school. I learnt everything in the last few days spent in your company. The dinner at the Chinese restaurant was the first time I would eat in a restaurant or even dance in a night club, yet you are talking of a wife? My gun has been my wife. That is what every soldier is taught. We eat and sleep with our gun. We have also been taught to take care of our guns, like you take care of a wife so that she can also take care of you."

Jewel was moved. She inched closer to me on the couch where we sat, hugged me and caressed my head. "My poor, little boy, tell me about the war. I hope you are enjoying it and it would soon come to an end"

"Nobody enjoys a war. Forget all the glamorous things you see on television or in the movies. War is not a picnic. It is a matter of life and death. It is even worse when you are not fighting a conventional war. We are fighting a guerilla war with opponents who have been brain washed for martyrdom. Our opponents are also more familiar with the terrain than us and have more sympathy from the local community in the theatre of war. The fighters were selected from the class of the hopeless, those considered to be worthless and so, are ready to die and are working to be killed while we are trying to keep ourselves safe."

Jewel sighed and affectionately ran her fingers through my hair and said, "So, it's like the Vietnam War, which I read about in our history class. I read about how America had to finally pullout of Vietnam to avert a disgrace despite its military strength. "Exactly! Just like America and just like Sri Lanka. In the case of Sri Lanka, the war with the Tamil Tigers lasted 25 years while America had to pull out of Vietnam when the numbers of body bags going back to the US were becoming increasingly alarming. Nigeria commenced the Boko Haram war with the expectations that it would be a short war which our troops could easily win. However, things have turned out differently for many reasons, some of them self-inflicted. Apart from inadequate training as well as provision of poor equipment, some of our troops who had sympathy for the insurgents were busy selling information and equipment to the Boko Haram boys. In addition, Nigeria is currently terribly divided along ethnic and religious lines. Even the ethnic groups and religious groups have been further subdivided into sub-ethnic groups and sub-religious groups. All the gains and teachings that our forefathers and great nationalists fought for have long disappeared and the only language out there on the streets is how to break up the country under the guise of 'restructuring."

"In that case, if there is no hope for your country, why don't you relocate to Liberia? At least, you are half Liberian, and your sister is married to a Liberian," Jewel said as I interrupted her.

"And I can also marry a Liberian...ko?" I said, laughing
"What is 'ko?'" she asked.

"That's a way of seeking affirmation in Hausa for 'ok?' or 'not so?' or 'right?'"

"Yes and yes" she said smiling and hugged me. "When we get married, you will teach me Hausa...ko?" Jewel said, making the point that she was a good learner.

"E."

"What is that?"

"It means 'yes'" and we both burst into laughter and hugged each other tighter, before lapsing into a long silence as if preoccupied with our secret and private thoughts.

For me, my main problem with Jewel was the idea of another trans-cultural marriage. Having witnessed my parents' marriage with its many challenges which are traceable to their different cultural backgrounds, the idea of getting trapped in another cross-cultural marriage was not too pleasing to me.

Although I had also seen so many same-culture marriages hitting the rocks, I still wanted to locate the causes of the usual tension between my parents on the vast cultural differences between the two. While my father was brought up as a conservative Muslim, my mother was a liberal Liberian Christian who cherished her children's independence and creativity more than a belief in dogma and what she termed "prehistoric religious beliefs." The effect of this kind of confused religious background on me and my siblings was that we were neither Muslims nor Christians in the real sense of it. And while this dilemma did not matter during my secondary school days, it greatly mattered in the highly religiously divisive

Nigerian Civil Service and Military establishment, not to talk of the larger society itself. Many times, I had to claim one of the two religious beliefs to suit the occasion.

My other problem was even more urgent and crucial. In their effort to make me comfortable, John and Emine had given me a room in the basement of their four-bedroom bungalow which they shared with their three children. I suspect that Emine had carefully selected the location of the room to give me enough privacy which she hoped would encourage intimate moments with Jewel. It must have been her hope that such intimate moments would eventually dovetail into the "marriage" plans she and my mother had so much looked forward to, between Jewel and me.

Ordinarily, this shouldn't have been any problem since the few days I had spent with her, it was obvious that Jewel was a 'marriage material', to use my army barrack terminology. In the army depot, my colleagues and I used to categorize our girls into 'marriage' and 'non-marriage' materials depending on their behaviour, background and other qualities known only to us. Thus, the girls that our commanders allowed us to 'import' into our rooms from the slums of Zaria during special occasions such as Sallah and Christmas celebrations were not 'marriage materials'. Neither were some of the refugees in the Internally Displaced Person's (IDP) camps who try to sell their bodies for some basic commodities such as sanitary pads and body creams.

Jewel, by all standards, was a beautiful lady with a figure that should set any straight man on fire. At least, she was miles above those 'quickies' that we used to let off tension at the Army

Training school and the War Fronts. That her physical closeness to me as well as her passion for my love did not elicit the type of sexual response that those below her on the spectrum of attractiveness and love did was a thing of serious concern to me.

Jewel had barely entered my room that Saturday morning when it started to rain. The day had begun with a clear sky. It suddenly became cloudy over breakfast time and just after Jewel's arrival by ten o'clock, it began raining. As it often happens during a typical Liberian rainy season when it could rain continuously for 48 hours, the rain was still coming down by midday and by the time we had our lunch an hour later, the downpour had increased. With the downpour came a chill that seared the skin and penetrated the bones despite the tightly shut windows. We moved to the bed and dived under the duvet and clung to each other. Moments later, Jewel was ready for the love making which I initiated, but I could not get an erection. Tried as much as I could, I remained limp. That was when I remembered the army surgeon's remarks about the bullet having missed my sciatic nerve which according to him "supplies your prick." I think he was wrong. The bullet must have hit the nerve. I was still in a state of shock when Jewel announced that she was going home.

Chapter Six

When we came under enemy fire one Friday morning, I crouched with my other colleagues in the corridor of the premises of the Internally Displaced Person's (IDP) Camp at Kaya, about one kilometre to Gulag, the administrative headquarters of Madagali LGA. I had been posted to the IDP Camp after my return from my sick leave. Our duty was to guard the unfortunate group comprising mostly women and children who had been displaced from the comfort of their homes by the insurgents. Hardly had I settled down to what I thought would be a routine and dull duty post than the facility was attacked by the Boko Haram boys one early morning. We immediately returned fire with our machine-guns, rocket launchers and AK-47s.

The previous day, we had been busy sorting out the crowd of refugees who had trooped to the IDP camp. There were terrible scenes of panicked soldiers beating and trampling the displaced civilians who were seeking help and shelter. Some of the queues were about one hundred metres long, winding out of the hills and valleys full of millet and corn toward the frontage of the old St Mark's Catholic Seminary which had now been turned into an IDP camp. The refugees stretched along the roads for as far as we could see, in processions that seemed to have no beginning and no end. Barefoot civilians, lost children crying for their parents, parents for their children; wailing and disheveled women, wounded men covered with dried blood and filthy dressings, some walking, some lying in heaps in the backs of trucks, motorbikes, and oxcarts creaking on wooden wheels. They were packed densely and stretched down the roads, solid, moving masses that stood helpless in the heat and rain. There was so much human suffering in these scenes that I felt numb and frightened at the same time. In the heat of the mayhem are members of the Humanitarian Agencies like Red Cross, Mercy Corps, Action Against Hunger, among others dashing about the refugees distributing drugs, food, clothes, and blankets.

As we remained crouched and fired back at the insurgents, the old walls of the abandoned Catholic Seminary which had been turned into an IDP camp trembled from the concussion of the rockets fired by the insurgents. The noise of the shooting was deafening. Cringing in the corridor of the old building, we were not sure of the strength of the insurgents and how long we could hold them up. Neither could we fathom why a group of so-called religious jihadists who claimed to be good Muslims could be attacking a group of innocent women and children.

"They are looking for food," shouted one elderly woman refugee. "Rather than fight them, let us release some bags of rice, millet and provision to them so that they would leave us alone," the old woman pleaded from where she huddled with the other frightened women and weeping children in the seminary's chapel.

While the woman's assertion could be true, as soldiers our order was to repel the enemies and protect the refugees and not to succumb to intimidation. We refused to release any food. Rather, we continued firing as the tension around us slowly built up. It was a deadly tension that seemed to overwhelm us all as the endless screams of the frightened civilians came to us in waves. But we had no choice but to keep firing. The sounds of the guns from both sides were now so regular and strong that they soon merged into a single strong thunderous outpouring. Occasionally, amidst the rattle of the machine guns and the whistling and hissing of bullets and shrapnel, we heard the occasional whimpering and crying of some of our men and refugees as they were hit.

Unfortunately, we could not afford to look at one another not to talk of helping anybody, out of fear of seeing the unimaginable. By then, the usually fresh bucolic air of the countryside had become hazy with smoke from the guns and the shells. From the superior firepower of our opponents, it was obvious, that we were not fighting, we were defending ourselves from annihilation. We squatted behind every corner, behind every concrete pillar of the old building as we kept firing at those coming at us praying that they would not get us before we got them.

A few minutes earlier, we had contacted our airbase in Yola and just right on time, our planes appeared and began dropping bombs on the positions of the insurgents. We were relieved to see them being blown up like rag dolls. Thrice, our planes dive-bombed them and returned to base. The firing from our opponents ceased and we were glad that our position was safe even though the tension had almost worn us out. We grabbed hold of our hand grenades and heaved them out in front of the corridors before leaping out to check on the refugees. We found some of them wounded, with another handful dead. While some had died from the bullets and shrapnel of the enemy, others especially the aged had succumbed to shock and heart attack. We handed over the care of the refugees to the Red Cross and the Médecins Sans Frontières.

Just then, our reinforcements arrived as about thirty young replacement troops from our Yola base joined us in their fresh uniforms and well-stocked weapons. With the assistance of the reinforcement that had just arrived, we secured our positions. We fanned out into the surrounding bush, behind a tank that led the way, guns at the ready, we went in search of remnants of the Boko Haram boys who had caused us so much pain. I noticed a movement ahead of me, as I aimed to shoot, I saw a ragged blood-stained figure on his knees begging me in Hausa not to kill him. I was about to shoot him but something in his dishevelled beard and hungry appearance touched me

"Let us shoot the bloody bastard *shege banza*" my partner, L/Cpl. Hassan hissed angrily and aimed to shoot, but I held up my hand to stop him.

The lone figure was still on his knees begging. "I am hungry," he said. "We have not eaten for three days."

Hassan held his peace. He lowered his gun and asked the fellow his name.

"Bala, Maiduguri Bala," he croaked.

On further interrogation, Bala informed us that there were others like him in the bush. He promised to call them out and cooperate with us if we can assure them of the safety of their lives. Before long, more pitiable figures emerged from the surrounding bushes and craggies of the Savannah Desert with their beards and dirty *galabiyas* blowing in the wind. They begged for food and water and promised to help us to track other Boko Haram members. As we all gazed at the haggard and woe-begone remnants of the insurgents, it was difficult to believe that the kind of superior fire power that bogged us down and almost eliminated us a few minutes ago came from the same captives. It was a herculean task for our Platoon Commander Lt. Akpan to convince the other troops to allow us to take the twelve ragged criminals as Prisoners of War (POW)rather than eliminating them on the spot as some of our men had wanted.

"There is no morality in war," one of us, a fresh soldier shouted.

"If not for our air force and our arrival, these idiots would have made mincemeat of you people," he argued.

He was supported by another soldier who said he even doubted their story of being starved. Where did they get the strength to shoot us for so long if indeed they were that hungry?" he queried. The debate went on for a while, but Lt. Akpan stood his ground.

"Apart from strict adherence to the principles of the war convention," he said, "don't also forget that members of the humanitarian groups are watching us. In recent times, Amnesty International among other International Human

Rights Organisations, has rated us poorly. We must do all we can to not worsen our international image."

Another soldier suggested that we should not allow the so-called humanitarian groups to intimidate us because according to him, their activities since the beginning of the Boko Haram war has been suspect; "Sir, you would recall that the Nigerian Army recently accused some of these so-called humanitarian organisations of supplying foods and drugs to the terrorists. Even, this same Amnesty International is fond of fabricating allegations of human rights violations against us. In another case, another well-known humanitarian agency was declared "persona non grata" when a large sum of money believed to be for the use of the insurgents was found with the agency. They should therefore not be taken seriously," the soldier said.

The constant pleas for mercy by Bala and his men seemed to pay off and calm nerves for the moment. They were allowed to follow us unharmed back to the IDP camp. As I watched the haggard-looking men drag themselves back to the IDP camp, I could not but wonder if the same people would not turn against us again once their stomachs become filled with our food. They appeared incapable of causing any harm, thus one could say they are under some yet unknown spell that has turned them into animals devoid of any human feeling. They trudged along looking forlorn like culprits cut in the act. They cut the image of bearded apostles of hope. Though I was conscious of the current public aversion against the idea of assimilating those of them who have repented into the larger Nigerian community, I still believed that it was the right thing to do because, while some forces had turned them into animals, another force could also reform and reintegrate them into human beings. At that point, I took out my food pack, took out some pieces of army rationed sausage rolls, cut them into bits and gave them to the prisoners who wolfed them down. It reminded me of myself as a little boy doing the same to the "gala" sausages that my mother used to give me. I found that strangely comforting. Back to the IDP camp, I was drafted into the team that would debrief the POWs before their final transfer to Yola. As the Platoon Commander explained to me, one of the reasons for my inclusion in the team was the fact that since I grew up in the area, I would be able to understand the POWs more than other soldiers. In addition, in case of the need for reconnaissance, I would be very helpful since I was very familiar with the terrain.

My job according to the PC was to assist with the interrogation of the POWs. Having just been lucky to have been rescued from an unjust detention coupled with brutal torture, I saw my new job as a challenge. It was my turn to serve humanity by ensuring that no one suffered deprivation of his personal liberty for a day longer than necessary because of the vagaries of war or other circumstances. I was also determined to see that no innocent person was unnecessarily punished. I was aware of the limitations of my powers since my job only finished after rendering a report at the end of investigation. It was not my responsibility to effect their release. It was by chance that I saw the result of some of my reports resulting to the release of some of the suspects whose cases I investigated.

As we commenced the interrogations, the POWs appeared

very shy and nervous despite their viciousness in the battle. It was as if they had a split personality. They had also been severely starved from the way they greedily scooped the *koko* and *kunun zaki* which some of us thought were badly prepared. It seemed odd seeing these men—our enemies—at such close quarters. Their simple and humble appearance made you wonder how they could be so vicious. They really ought to be busy on their farms or tending their cows and goats and teaching Koranic classes instead of going about slaughtering women and children. It was strange seeing them look so weak when just a few hours ago, they were shooting with a ferocity that made a professional soldier green with envy.

From the interrogation, we learnt several ways by which Boko Haram recruited its members. While some hardliners volunteered on religious grounds, others joined the sect to protect themselves and make a living. The most gruesome method of recruitment was simply to raid a community, then conscript all their able-bodied men while their women and girls were shared among the commanders as sex slaves. We also learnt that whenever there would be an attack, the Boko Haram would have informed other members living in different camps about the upcoming attacks. Communications were done using Thuraya satellite phones where there was no mobile network. They also travelled by motorcycles to convey messages. Members and sector commanders usually gave an update of the amount of the ammunitions in their possessions. When not enough, more supplies of weapons and IEDs were supplied and used in launching attacks.

We learnt from a young recruit, who could not have

been up to sixteen years, that during attacks, members of the group are selected and asked to do *istishadiyya*, sacrifice for martyrdom and get rewarded in the hereafter.

"But do you believe in such a thing?" I asked one of the wide-eyed teenagers.

"*Haka ne su ke ce*, that's what they said," he replied, noting that where to attack, how and when are strictly adhered to, as failure to obey commands given by a commanding leader known as "Amir" was met with severe punishment.

"We normally train very hard and if any of us is found wanting, all of us will suffer for it. We were the *Yaran Mayu*, the young forces, teenagers blessed to have been specially chosen. This has become the life if we must live through the day. We have forgotten what love tasted like when the blood from our helpless parent's bodies flowed from their slit throats, oozing from the gashes that seemed to smile back at us, while we were forced to watch as their hands were bound behind them, kicking and screaming and grovelling, their bodies thrashing like animals being slaughtered for festive occasions. Our mallams celebrated with shouts of joy and sporadic gunshots, the birth of a new dawn was celebrated". The wide-eyed teenager informed.

Another teenager related a typical ambush using land mines in Hausa.

"We all milled around with the children, playing innocently with toys locally made of bamboos and bathroom slippers. Dashing around and pretending

to enjoy it as we call out to each other. As soon as the
vehicles crossed the invisible line we had marked on
the dusty road behind the village, we rushed to the side
waving at the *Batures*, the white people in the vehicles.
The *Batures* looked at us with veiled amusement and
waved back sheepishly. The youngest of us triggered an
electromagnetic pulse from a device embedded in her
own toy and all the vehicles grounded to a stop. In a
swift move, the military men peeled away from their
vehicles and formed a cordon, noisily cocking guns.
They kept their eyes on us as we swamped them with
curious carelessness. A senior officer stepped out.
He was not wearing any rank. They hardly wear their
ranks in the fields these days as we were informed, for
security reasons possibly, but his air of importance was
so obvious. He squatted near one of the vehicles as
we milled around him, he barked an order to another
soldier, maybe the mechanic, to go into the first vehicle
to see what was wrong, and get it fixed. The senior officer
looked relaxed but impatient nonetheless, this obviously
was not planned.

The soldier carried his rifle over his shoulder and
got into the vehicle. After trying the ignition many times,
he stepped out, opened the bonnet, and began to tinker
with the engine. He returned into the vehicle and tried
the key one more time, but again nothing happened,
only a soft kikiki which was just the physical key turning
inside the steering barrel. A soft little click no one really
heard, because normally it was drowned out instantly by
the sounds of an engine bursting into life.

I looked long and hard into the thicket in the distance, and as prearranged, timed to the exact second, I turned and smiled at the officer who was in charge, looked back again into the thicket and nodded. I knew at that instant, that like the key in the vehicle, it was going to be the same thing with the click of a trigger, ahead of a gunshot, but not that morning, as a flash of light accompanied a muffled crack. Instantly, we were all sprayed with red liquid as pandemonium broke. The *Batures* were no longer smiling, no one was smiling, the children were no longer smiling as each went up in a cloud of explosion."

From the interrogations, we were also able to put together the experience of a typical example Boko Haram captive, Ali Mohamed who was just 10 years old when Boko Haram fighters attacked his village in the middle of the night. His father and uncle were ridden with bullets right in his presence, and their houses set ablaze. The Boko Haram fighters killed the men of the village, carted away as much food as they could carry, and took the women and children as prisoners. His mother was repeatedly slapped and beaten for crying too loudly as she mourned the death of her husband. Some of the fighters distributed the women including his mother and his two older sisters among themselves as new wives. Anyone who protested was publicly beaten or killed. He could not make sense of it. He was consumed with anger and hatred but knew it was only impotent rage. Ali Mohamed and the other boys were taken to a different camp where those who were fourteen years old and above were forced to under training as fighters, while the younger ones like himself were given chores of gathering firewood and washing the clothes of the fighters. Ali lived in this new camp for four years until they were rescued by Nigerian Army. He is now living in an IDP camp and has no idea of what became of his mother or his sisters. We couldn't prise too many words from him in either English or Hausa. He is now withdrawn, but prone to occasional outbursts of aggression at the slightest provocation. Ali Mohamed is constantly wary and starts at any loud noise. Attempts at enrolling him in school failed as he always beats up the other children if they as much as looked at him.

As we rounded off our interrogation, we wrote the report for our Commanders as well as the International Humanitarian Organisation. Our report cross-referenced the International Organization for Migration (IOM)'s estimates that the Boko Haram insurgency has directly or indirectly impacted on the 17.2 million people living in the north-eastern region of Nigeria. The IOM estimated that at least 3.6 million persons have been directly displaced, with children accounting for about 62%. In addition to these displaced children, we also had high numbers of children resulting from rape, or who were born to women and girls who were forcefully 'married' by the insurgents. These children are stigmatized, shamed in the community, and not accepted even by some of their biological mothers.

Our report made it clear from the outset that Nigeria has a tragedy on her hands. It stated that hundreds of thousands of children who were either displaced or orphaned, including those of Boko Haram fighters, had been exposed to massive trauma.

Some of these children were still undergoing psychological distress is the form of daily humiliation, stigmatization, and rejection especially for the girls who returned home as mothers of children, with no clarity as to the identity of their fathers. This was always going to be a source of social exclusion in a conservative environment like north-eastern Nigeria where there was now a generation of young and fertile minds who have lost their innocence and childhood, seething with rage against the larger society.

After the POWs were interrogated, they were locked up for the night in preparation for their onward movement to Yola the following day. That was when we were able to have some rest, have food and drinks before bathing and replenishing our weapons and artillery. We had to be ever ready for any eventuality. As I took out my knapsack, the photographs of my mother, sisters and Jewel dropped on the sandy floor. As I gazed at the photographs, memories of my last leave in Monrovia rushed back to me. I had a swell time in Monrovia but the pain of saying goodbye was so heart-rending that I promised not to go for leave again. I still remembered my mother as she counted the days towards the end of my leave. She used to be unhappy as the day grew less and less. Even for me, the days passed so quickly that I avoided thinking of them by going out with Jewel.

One day, when my leave was about two days to go, my mother called me to her room. She carried my sister's daughter as petted her to make her sleep. She was sitting up as I entered the room.

"Is it not possible for you to be posted somewhere else apart from the war front?" she asked.

I was silent for a while. I watched her still beautiful face glowing under the subdued light of the kerosene lamp which was on due to the incessant power failure that characterized post-war Liberia.

"Yes, I could be posted to the kitchen to be peeling potatoes or the office as a messenger but that was not what I was trained to do. Will that kind of position make my late dad and grandad happy in their current celestial abodes? The safest place for a ship is in the harbour, goes the saying, but that was not what it was built for." I spoke. My mother was quiet as she tried to hold back tears.

"I wanted to say something else to you."

"Yes mother, what is it?"

"Be careful of the women you meet at the war front. They are usually very vulnerable and will be ready to do anything to please you. They are no good, those women out there. That was why we got you Jewel. She is a well brought up girl, the type that can give you peace in your marriage. Don't mess her up."

"Don't worry mother. We don't have that many

women at the war front. We only have refugees, and they are busy trying to survive just like us to have time for any form of romance."

"Those are the ones I am talking about. The poor, the sad, and the vulnerable women. We had many of them during the fourteen-year war here in Liberia. They were cheap and very much available for the soldiers. That was why so many fatherless children were produced during the war. They have now become a source of problem to our society. Your father was a good man. He came looking for me in my father's house after meeting me when I used to help my mother sell food at the entrance of the Army Barracks. He was not like the other soldiers who were out for cheap sex. Your father wanted a real wife. That was why he married me properly and took all of us back home to Nigeria after the war. You must emulate him by getting yourself a good woman as a wife and not just a whore or sets of whores."

I promised her.

"And make sure you take good care of yourself. If you need to change from the war front to a safer place, let me know. I can still reach some of your father's friends who can influence a better place for you." I thanked her as I moved to the door where I turned back and hugged her.

"Go well, my son. I shall pray for you every day," she said as I stumbled out of the room, scared of letting her see my tears.

Part of the fallout of our interrogation of the Boko Haram POWs was the overwhelming evidence of how the humanitarian agencies were pampering the insurgents in a classical case of 'feeding the enemy'. Some of the POWs confirmed that some aid workers went as far as using helicopters to drop food and medicine for them behind Federal Troops anytime they found it difficult to reach them. On several occasions, the aid workers often loaded foodstuffs and by some accounts of the insurgents, some quantity of ammunitions in dilapidated trailers which would expectedly break down in the middle of the bush at a convenient place for the insurgents to come out and cart away the booty. Based on our report, the Nigerian Army declared some of the aid agencies 'persona nongrata' and even went as far as restricting them from operating outside of government-controlled areas based on the Terrorism Prevention Amendment Act, 2013, which criminalizes engagement with groups the government listed as terrorists. Military authorities have reinforced this ban with threats of arrests. The Office of the National Security Adviser also banned the transportation and use of fertilizers considered "dual use items," which could be diverted and used by insurgency groups to make explosives. Only certain types of NPK liquid, organic fertilizers, have been approved for use in Borno, Yobe, and Adamawa states.

The military also required humanitarian organizations to vet local businesses they hire to transport or provide food and other relief items in communities where they work, to ensure they have no ties with armed groups. Aid agencies have introduced internal vetting measures, including proof of mandatory registration with the Corporate Affairs Commission, operation of valid bank accounts with established institutions, and checks on various platforms that gather information on organizations or individuals financing terrorism in Nigeria.

We gathered also that the military has come down hard on organizations for using vendors accused of flouting military regulations and has recently proposed requiring all humanitarian organisations to use only eight military-approved vendors. The agencies told Human Rights Watch that they have concerns about the eight vendors' capacity to meet their needs, and about the military or political control of the vendors's approval processes.

We learnt further that in August of the current year, UNOCHA and the International Non-Governmental Organizations Forum – a member organisation which provides a collective platform for international aid groups – worked with the EFCC on guidelines to facilitate the movement of cash used in the field for the payment of salaries, humanitarian transfers, and other miscellaneous expenses. This stemmed from persistent accusations by government officials that humanitarian organisations were funding terrorist activities. Under the guidelines, the aid groups were to notify the EFCC of cash movements and the commission will, in turn, inform the military. But aid groups were said to have reservations due largely to the military's lack of awareness of the detailed process and guidelines. For instance, aid groups providing life-saving assistance, including medical care complained of the military's decision to limit the amount of fuel available to each agency, which, they said, drastically affected their operations, leading to total shut down in some cases.

We had expected them to protest the military's measure by the internationally connected agencies, but we did not expect them to go as far as organizing a press conference as they did to accuse the Nigerian military authorities of using the Terrorism Prevention Amendment Act to threaten to arrest and restrict activities of aid organisation with allegations that they were engaging with terrorist groups. The military was also accused of violating conditions for the usage of military escorts, in such manner as to compromise the aid agencies' independence and neutrality.

Our report cited the comments of the country director of one aid agency to underline the thinking of the group towards the military thus: "operationally, the activities and programmes of the agency are not neutral because everything is under the control of the military. The military is imposing a non-neutral response on us because we only go where they approve or want us to go," they were not happy with the situation as they saw it because, as another director claimed, "our independence guarantees our safety. Whatever action indicates humanitarians are on a certain side of the conflict, makes us vulnerable and puts us at risk."

But as we noted in our report, there were also reports of the military's alleged courting of partisanship. "The army does not want to hear of neutrality," said a humanitarian worker. "Saying to the military that you are neutral is saying that you are supporting Boko Haram."

Much as I wanted to support the position of the army regarding the activities of the humanitarian organisations, I was convinced that some of the accusations of tardiness on the part of some army commanders were true. Apart from delays in giving permission to these aid agencies to perform their duty, it was an open secret that most of the foods and drugs supplies handed over to our bosses for onward distribution to the refugees never reached the beneficiaries. In fact, some of the bags of rice, millet, sugar, and milk were re-bagged and redirected to the open market where they were sold at exorbitant prices. It was because of this kind of criminal activities that compelled some junior soldiers to join a civilian revolution one cloudy day in the month of Ramadan.

CHAPTER SEVEN

Our morale was badly dampened after our nearly tragic experience when the Boko Haram insurgents attacked the IDP camp we were guarding at Kaya. On that unforgettable day, we were heavily outgunned by the insurgents. Were it not for the quick arrival of the reinforcement from Yola, my team of ten soldiers would have been totally wiped out. From the accounts of my colleagues from other military formations, the story seemed to be the same in all sectors of the war front. The situation had got so bad that rather than fight, some soldiers would rush back to pack up their camps and flee on learning that Boko Haram fighters were advancing. We had lost the initiative and had been dispirited owing mainly to inadequate support from our bosses. As professional soldiers who should be ready to stay and fight it out under any condition, but climate and the fighting terrain were hostile. For weeks we had to operate like primitive men on remote desert outposts surrounded by endless stretches of sand and clusters of *dongayaro* tress that gave little or no cover from our enemies who, unlike us, were very familiar with the terrain. This made us sitting ducks and easy targets for their long-range rockets and land mines. The sun scorched us in the dry season, the dry and sandy northeast wind pelted us during the harmattan, the rain mercilessly pounded us during the rainy season. At night, the visibility was poor due to the dust and smoke of burnt rockets and shells. This compounded our problems as we squatted behind concrete and sandy barricades and braced for attacks that could come at anytime, from anywhere.

The reality was that there was a large population of Boko Haram terrorists and sympathizers in the territory assigned to us. We could only brag about defeating them. We lacked the capacity to do so, given the kind of approach we used in prosecuting the war. From our estimate and without the help of foreign forces, it may take more than ten years to chase out Boko Haram from the hinterlands. This is the usual problem when you are fighting a guerrilla war. Unfortunately, some politicians and other armchair commentators refused to face the reality. Rather, they kept comparing the current war which has been ongoing for eleven years old to the Nigerian Civil War which was prosecuted within three years. They forgot that querilla wars usually took longer to prosecute than conventional wars.

I recollect vividly my military history lesson at the Army Depot in Zaria where we were given the examples of some international civil wars where the guerilla methods were adopted. The Vietnam war, which was principally between North and South Vietnam, for example, began in 1959 and did not end until sixteen years later in 1975 despite eight years of US involvement. The war killed 58,220 American soldiers and wounded 153,303 more. Another 1,643 were missing in action. North Vietnam lost 1.1 million soldiers while 250,000 South Vietnamese soldiers died. Both sides lost more than 2 million civilians.

Another example given by our history teacher was the Sri Lankan Civil War, which was orchestrated by the rebel group, the Tamil Tigers that fought to create an independent Tamil state called Tamil Eelam in the north and the east of the island. The war, which lasted twenty-six years, began in 1983 and ended in 2009. Apart from thousands of casualties on both sides, thousands of people were displaced and there were many cases of sexual abuse. Just like the Boko Haram, the Tamil Tigers fought a largely guerrilla war during which many churches and mosques were bombed along with several other places.

In addition to the comparative analysis of different guerrilla wars, our history teacher also gave us a lot of information about Boko Haram which had been declared the most dangerous terrorist organization in the world. It is believed that in the last decade, the group had killed an estimated 20,000 people and forced millions from their homes. According to Amnesty International, Boko Haram's army has grown to around 15,000 members, with the stated goal of creating an Islamic caliphate. To achieve this, the group forcibly recruited young men from poor rural villages in northeastern Nigeria, as well as Chad and Cameroon. The average age of recruits appeared to be about 30, although the recruitment is reduced each year and the group often targeted teens and even children. The Mercy Corps study reveals that Boko Haram's recruitment strategy depends on the poverty level in their targeted areas. The group offered money and loans as inducement to potential recruits, only to show up a few days later demanding immediate repayment. Borrowers that couldn›t repay were forced to join the group.

Most of this information tallied with what we discovered after interviewing the POWs we arrested in Kaya. That was when we confirmed that the Boko Haram also used social pressure tactics, in much the same way as ISIS and other Islamic terrorist groups. Almost all the POWs cited a friend, family member or business colleague as a factor in joining Boko Haram. Our interrogation also confirmed that efforts at fighting against Boko Haram's recruitment methods were starting to take hold. When the group was formed in 2002, it enjoyed broad public support as an alternative to Nigeria›s corrupt government, which was blamed for impoverished conditions in the first place. But hypocrisy and increasingly violent methods soon associated with group later turned the tide of public opinion. Western-backed counter-terrorism campaigns highlighting these elements were starting to work, dissuading at-risk youths from joining the insurgency. The very fact that

Boko Haram has resorted to forced recruitment suggests that its ideological influence was declining.

Regarding recruitment of new members, our findings confirmed that some members joined the sect because Boko Haram paid them to kill Nigerian government officials, steal cars in the group's name and sell them to businessman or government officials, or to rob banks, in order to source funds for further operations. Some immigrants from contiguous countries also joined for economic purposes. Some northern Nigerians, including politicians, got affiliated to Boko Haram because they are related to members, or to some of the one thousand followers of imam Muhammad Yusuf said to have been killed during clashes in July 2009. The history of violence between Muslims and Christians in the Middle Belt and civilian deaths during battles with Boko Haram might have led some partisans to seek revenge against Christians or the Nigerian government by aligning with Boko Haram. Perhaps the most frightening discovery we got from the POWs was that some Boko Haram members could have been radicalized by some Nigerian imams. These imams created acceptance in mainstream society for many of the issues that Boko Haram and Ansaru used to appeal to recruits. Boko Haram has attacked polio vaccination workers and a media agency that was said to have associated the Prophet Muhammad with beauty pageants. Also, Ansaru attacked Nigerian troops preparing to deploy to Mali. Both Boko Haram and

Ansaru have taken advantage of anti-American and anti-Western sentiment and have adopted al-Qaeda's ideology in their public relations strategy. Abubakar Shekau, the infamous leader of Boko Haram, specifically mentioned he would respond to the "Innocence of Muslims," an anti-Islamic film that caused violent protests throughout the Muslim world in September 2012.

Apart from being outgunned by the Boko Haram, we also suffered from irregular or non-payment of our due allowances. Matters had gone so bad that more and more soldiers were now becoming courageous enough to write protest letters directly to the Commander-in-Chief of the Armed Forces, like the copy Private Dogo showed me he wrote anonymously:

President Muhammadu Buhari,
Commander in Chief of the Nigerian Armed Forces,
Presidential Villa,
Abuja.

His Excellency,
Your Excellency, corruption in the Army is REAL, and it is killing us. Every man and woman who decided to join the Army knows the risks. While we expect to die in the hands of the enemy, we don't expect to die in the hands of the Nigerian Army, due to corruption and criminal negligence. Just the other week, about 14 of our colleagues died in the hands of Boko Haram when they attacked the Army camp.

The circumstances surrounding their unnecessary death warrants a full investigation by his Excellency. Sir, you will be shocked of the outcome. The bodies of the slain heroes are still lying here and there in Yobe State. The story of this incidence has hardly been officially published by the Army or Nigerian media.

Your Excellency, our 'ogas' have been stealing the little money they were meant to pay us. For example, instead of our N24,000 welfare allowance, including N12,000 given us by the Chief of Army Staff, our Commanding Officer (CO) only paid us N12,000. Right before the increment of Operations allowances, our previous CO used to give us at the end of every month one pack of sugar, 12 sachets of Chocolate and 12 eggs. However, the moment the current CO took over, he stopped everything.

Your Excellency, we are treated like animals. Most of us are afraid to talk because of the dire consequence. As the Commander in Chief of the Armed Forces, your Excellency, kindly investigate. There is corruption in the Army. Brave soldiers are needlessly dying.

Thank You.

By Patriotic Soldier,
Operation LAFIYA DOLE,
Damaturu,
Yobe State.

As I read the letter, not only was I shocked by the allegations of corruption, but I was also disturbed by the audacity of a mere Private to write an open letter to the Commander-in-Chief. Apart from the fact that the offence might warrant a court martial, the action showed that the new and young soldiers were more daring than the former.

During one of our weekly meetings, our Platoon Commander, Lt. Akpan warned us to desist from writing letters to the army command in Abuja. He reminded us of the Army protocol in such matters. "Your Platoon Commander should be your first point of call. It is the PC who will then decide whether to forward the complaint to the next senior Military Officer if he cannot tackle the problem. Anybody caught abusing this protocol will be severely dealt with," he warned.

Our PC also told us that while there could be instances of corruption in the army, he believed there was a good deal of exaggeration about the whole issue. Lt. Akpan decried insinuations that money meant for procurement of military hardware was usually misappropriated just as the invoices for the procurement were inflated. He debunked stories of "ghost soldiers," noting that the actual number of soldiers was inflated, and that Commanders were collecting the salaries meant for the "ghost soldiers." Other rumours that did not go down well with the PC were that some Commanders intentionally sent soldiers to the war front with obsolete weapons for them to be killed so that their allowances and salaries could be collected by their commanders. The PC noted that the most painful accusation against the army is that of Human Rights violations championed by Amnesty International who accused the army of setting fire to entire villages where Boko Haram had many sympathisers.

"Like all generalizations, each contains an element of truth, still we should not use the same broom to tar every one of us. Despite these rumours, we still have several devoted and hard-working officers in the Nigerian Army. In addition, we should not forget that the insurgency war has combined the bitter forms of warfare such as terrorism, fraticide and ferocious guerilla warfare. All these have blurred the military's moral view and has made our forces to accept ruthlessness as a necessity if not a virtue. Whether committed in the name of principles or out of vengeance, atrocities are now common. Although our forces are not innately cruel, but on seeing the way the Boko Haram has been killing our soldiers and helpless civilians, they learned rather quickly that the war front was not a place where a man could expect much mercy. You saw, for example what happened recently at the IDP camp in Kaya. How would one explain an attack on defenceless, homeless people all because the insurgents claimed to be hungry? We would have all been dead by now if not for the timely arrival of our men from Yola. Why will such kinds of atrocities be taken lightly? This is why men who are treated callously are also inclined to be callous. Even at that, we were very magnanimous in Kaya. Instead of killing those criminals as some of you suggested, we captured them as prisoners. Those of them that have repented are being rehabilitated and reinstated and we are also getting vilified for this by outraged masses. It is clear that people would have various notions of events despite the intentions. So, I urge us to remain focused and discharge your duties as instructed. We shall overcome."

With that said, he turned to leave, and we saluted him. As we later went for our lunch of rice and beans with fish in one of the abandoned seminary's classrooms, I turned to my colleague and course mate, L/Cpl. Hassan and told him that I agreed, to a large extent, with our PC's position.

"Though I cannot confirm that all was well with our welfare, and that our superiors were not pilfering our salaries, I also know that some of us have our shortcomings. Just as those officers whom we regularly criticized; we have also not been very fair to one another. We use religion, ethnicity, and social backgrounds to judge and deal with one another. Sometimes, comradeship which should be one of the war's major redeeming features is pushed to the background. Some of our troops, especially the lazy ones among us could not withstand the stress of guerrilla-fighting which we had been taught at the Military Depot. These include a constant hair-trigger alertness, constant perception of being under attack at any time as well as the ability to distinguish civilians from combatants. All these created emotional pressures in some of the troops to the extent that a trivial provocation could turn them into animals who could be very destructive even to themselves and their mates," I noted. I was surprised when Hassan, who was well known for his strong hatred for the Boko Haram insurgents and a lot of sympathy for our troops whatever their shortcomings, agreed with me.

"The problem with some of us is our overbearing greed for survival. Of course, survival is a basic human need but as soldiers, we have sworn to defend our country and so, we should be ready to take some risks. Sometimes, what we call self –preservation if taken too much to the heart, can turn a soldier into a coward or a mindless destroyer. I am usually saddened when I hear stories of some of our boys running away at the mere mention of Boko Haram. The other day, I was discussing with a Private who had just been posted to our platoon and was surprised when he said to me; 'Oga, I am not a young man like you. I only joined the army late. I have a wife and children at home, and I want to see them again. I will therefore do anything to stay alive, even if I have to run away from those nasty criminals,' I was shocked and disappointed at once."

The statement of that Private must have impacted on us very deeply as Hassan and I continued our meal in silence. Moments later, with a mouth full of rice and beans, I said, "much as the Boko Haram insurgents have been behaving like lunatics with their indiscriminate killings and bombings, I still believe that our current approach in executing the war with these *Munafukai* is also not right. I am against our current practice of killing and killing as many of them as possible. The pressure on unit commanders to regularly produce corpses of the insurgents to be shown on Televisions and the Newspapers to assuage the expectation of Nigerians that we are winning the war is sickening. It is even affecting the behaviors of some of our soldiers some of whom have now developed a severe contempt for human life," I said.

"What else can we do? We are soldiers. We are trained to kill," replied Hassan as he scrapped the remaining grains of rice from his plate.

"We can try the multi-dimensional approach we were taught in history class."

"What's that?" Hassan asked.

"A combination of diplomacy, war and community outreach," I said.

"Hmm… that will be difficult. These criminals are beyond redemption. They are sick. Anyway, that is not our job. Maybe the humanitarian organisations can look into that…" Hassan said before he was interrupted by another colleague who bumped in on us.

"The signal just arrived that we should proceed to Sokoto State to guard a village currently being evacuated due to an invasion by suspected bandits, cattle rustlers and Boko Haram members."

"Bandits? When did our job extend to chasing bandits? Are we not supposed to face the Boko Haram insurgents squarely? I asked.

Hassan burst into laughter.

"Are you not a soldier? Who told you that you have a choice? Your duty is to obey orders."

That was how we departed for Sokoto early the following morning in the two trucks provided for the journey. The trucks rolled along several rural roads as we passed hot dusty villages and farms with their ubiquitous small huts flying past as peasant farmers tended their millet and guinea corn among other crops. In the distance was an enormous and vast expanse of land that stretched into the horizon. One soldier even suggested that Nigerians from other parts of the country with inadequate land could be relocated to the region. Kaduna, Zaria, Funtua and other smaller towns passed in quick succession as the trucks headed for Sokoto.

Just after Funtua, the hitherto smooth ride became disrupted as we now travelled on a dusty rough sequence under construction. All around were green cornfields extending far into the horizon, rolling into the distance as far as the eyes could see. To keep our spirits up, one of us intone:

Oh, my home
Oh, my home
When shall I see my home?
When shall I see my native land?
I will never forget my home

At Faskari Local Government Area, we chanced on a busy market where lorry loads of millet, corn, and other farm products were being offloaded. Cows, goats, donkeys, and camels completed the merchandise on offer. Just before Gusau was the famous Kwatarkwashi rocks which is considered a major tourist attraction in the place. Gusau, Kadauri and Talata Mafara and other smaller towns and villages were soon behind us.

Along the way, we met groups of fleeing locals, in their hands, on theie heads and shoulders were mattresses, tables, pots, pans, clothings, blankets, and as much personal items as they could grab. Some of the items were loaded on donkeys and mules, while the more prosperous natives had theirs on their motorbikes and vehicles. Many of them appeared pitiful and weary, their heads bowed in misery and despair. Hunger was etched on their faces. Children clung desperately to their despairing mothers. The boys held their fathers' hands. Some were carried on their fathers' shoulders as they stumbled forwards, occasionally casting occasional furtive glances behind them and their surroundings as they passed us silently.

Just before twilight, we arrived our destination, Taura Village, which I later learnt, was another hour to Sokoto city. The whole village was almost empty. I wondered at the sense in protecting an empty village. The answer came later that evening at a meeting which our Platoon Commander arranged with about ten community leaders who were left in the village.

"Our village is the remaining buffer zone between the bandits' hideout and Sokoto city," Alhaji Adamu

Sokoto, the community leader said. He informed that even though Sokoto city had a garrison of soldiers, it was believed that a buffer zone must be created to keep the city safe.

"We have a lot of Fulani cattle rearers here. Apart from being criminals who work hand in hand with the Boko Haram insurgents, these bandits are also cattle rustlers. They sometimes steal as many as 100 cows from the Fulani which they take to neighbouring states for sale," he replied when we asked him why the bandits found his village very attractive.

"The bandits are about 1000 in strength. Their leader's name is Sani Barawo. A journalist who once visited the bandits' hideout in the Karama Forest not far from Gusau confirmed the figure. The journalist also confirmed seeing young boys of about 14 years of age who were under the influence of drugs carrying AK-47s, he informed.

Alhaji Sokoto told us that when the farmers and businessmen around the area realized that the farming season was fast approaching, they arranged for a peace meeting with the bandits because if there was no peace between them and bandits operating in the area, they would not be able to cultivate their farmlands. It was the belief of the communities that such a meeting would enable them to have an understanding with the bandits so they could be allowed to go to their farms and resume trading in the markets while the bandits are allowed to move freely. When they held that meeting, the communities felt the need to invite somebody in the media. That was how the Journalist was contacted so he could witness the event and report it to the world.

According to Alhaji Sokoto, most of the 1,000 bandits had AK-47s which costs about N750,000 each. "When you calculate the total cost, you can then understand why the bandits needed money so badly that they had to go into the illegal business of cattle rustling."

"How about the bullets?" the PC asked.

"I understand they buy each bullet for N2,000. Most of them carry about 300 each in their bags," the Chairman replied.

"Did they tell you how they got them?"

"Our borders are porous. They live in a forest from which you can reach as far as Libya, North Africa, Niger, Chad, and Mali without coming to the main road," Alhaji Sokoto said.

We were shocked by his revelation that we were very quiet for a while. After a while, the Chairman spoke again, "It is equally believed that the peace meeting between the bandits and the community have started paying off as many of the family members of the bandits who recently went to the village market returned home safely unlike in the past, when they were molested. Government has been advised to initiate a dialogue with the bandits for a lasting solution, but they are adamant."

"I don't see how a whole government should dialogue with criminals. They should have been arrested and prosecuted," the PC said

"Why not?" Alhaji Sokoto replied. "Don't the military people also dialogue with dissidents? How about the repentant Boko Haram members that the Army is trying to rehabilitate? I don't see anything wrong with dialoguing with the criminals if peace is achieved," the Chairman replied.

He made us to know that one of the reasons why the bandits were attacking the community was because the community was releasing information to security agencies about how to attack them. This led to a lot of recriminations on both sides for a long time. The matter had been building up over the years.

"Now, because of the agreement reached with the communities, the bandits no longer kidnap, commit armed robbery and rustle cattle. They are confined to one area," the Chairman said.

"If that is the case, why do you still need the army to protect the community?" Lt Akpan asked, almost sarcastically.

"You know without any source of income, the bandits will be soon become broke and the youths under them who had been used to spending money recklessly may be uncontrollable. That is why their leader said that there is a limit to which they can control the youth under them because when the youths are pressed, they can go back to their old ways. And that is why the government must come in quickly and use experts to address the situation."

As I listened to the conversation between my PC and

the Community Chairman, a large dose of anger welled up in me. I couldn't fathom how a whole government would be so afraid of criminals to the extent of trying to bargain with them. I found it difficult to make any meaning out of such a meaningless situation.

It was as if the PC was reading my mind when he spoke, "If you say the government should come in, can you be specific?"

"Let the government quietly facilitate a peace agreement between them and the local communities. It is very important. And let the government have their confidence so they could give up the arms in their possessions. Their major fear is if they give up the arms, other groups and local communities may attack them. Negotiating peace without surrendering the guns does not make sense. That kind of peace will not last."

"But do you see that working?" the PC asked.

"It will work if you engage experts. Let us look at the amnesty programme in place in Katsina. The state Governor recently said most of the leaders that were part of the programme were killed. If leaders were killed and amnesty died, certainly you should know that there is something wrong with the agreement. You know these leaders; they may use that amnesty to exploit the youths. And you know the youths, the moment they know, they would say "so you people are benefiting, and we are not part of it. They would go after them and that is why they killed most of them."

The community leader also advised us on how to

tackle the insurgents. Although the Boko Haram used religious fanaticism to recruit most of its members, tackling the terrible state of corruption in the country is the main antidote to the Boko Haram menace in the country. "

"The other solutions include the even distribution of the nation's resources to those who need them most, as well as impartially prosecuting government officials and Boko Haram members who break the law."

Things remained quiet for us in Taura village for about a week. The bandits, cattle rustlers and Boko Haram insurgents did not bother us, so we took things easy. Just like Alhaji Sokoto predicted, it could be that the dialogue between the community and the bandits worked. Maybe it was just luck. Except for a few villagers who were still coming to tend to their crops and animals and some aids workers, everything was quiet. On our arrival in the village, we had sent out a patrol to secure our position. We also did a survey of our encirclement to know the range which our machine-gun fire could cover. And since our main job was to keep the village safe, we spent the first few days digging a protective trench at the village entrance. With the help of some villagers, we identified potential breeches in the village encirclement and secured them. We identified an abandoned but still solid Health Centre building which was strategically overlooking the village entrance as our base. Since I had no intention of being blown to bits in bed, I dragged my sleeping gear to a room behind a big concrete pillar where I bunked for the night.

"Haba, Bukar, don't tell me that you are scared of ordinary bandits?" Hassan taunted.

"You are married with two kids and as such, you're ahead of me. Abeg, let me also leave somebody behind," I retorted. We both burst into laughter.

Since we were not on sentry duty that night, Hassan and I stayed up and spoke about our plans for now and the future.

"So, when are you going to bring home this your Liberian beauty?" he asked me as we drank from the canned beer we had been given at the IDP camp in Kaya.

"Very soon," I replied as my mind drifted to my last day with Jewel in Monrovia.

CHAPTER EIGHT

I was restless throughout that day after I got confirmation from my sister that Jewel was on her way to see me in Nigeria.

"She would board an aeroplane at Monrovia airport anytime from now for her flight to Lagos," Zainab had said when she called me earlier that morning. "She would thereafter take another flight from Lagos to Kano where I will receive her," she added.

I was happy that my girlfriend and future wife would come to visit me as she had promised. I applied for my annual leave and waited, breathless, for the approval. I was restless , but the cause of my restlessness was not the fear of not getting approval for my leave since I had been assured that the leave would be granted. Neither was my restlessness caused by the fear of Jewel's safe arrival. I also didn't have anything to hide from Jewel having kept away from other women in absolute obedience to my mother's injunction not to mess up my girlfriend.

The only woman who had come near me during my war posting was Safiya, the daughter of Aminu Mohammed, the leader of the Boko Haram insurgents whom we captured at Kaya. After Aminu's arrest and debriefing, the middle- aged insurgent had relayed to his daughter how I had saved his life when he was first captured. Somehow, the daughter who later introduced herself to me as Safiya had tracked me down through some aid workers to say her thanks.

Safiya worked at the IDP camp with foreign aid workers as an interpreter. She visited me several times after our first meeting while I was still stationed at Kaya. On those occasions, she would bring me some food and provisions which I shared with Hassan. I had no emotional attachment to her, but Hassan said he observed that the lady appeared obsessed with me.

"She's in love with you," Hassan had said.

"How did you know? I thought that you are just a bloody soldier and not a romantic." I had asked him jokingly.

"Can't you see the way she normally dresses when coming to see you? From the way she looks at you with admiration and love, all you need to do is to propose and she will just say yes." Hassan dramatized as he spoke. We both let out loud pearls of laughter.

"Throwing yourself at someone just because the person saved your father's life is not love. That's infatuation. There is no way I can marry the daughter of a Boko Haram insurgent. Never!" I noted loudly in disgust.

"You mean, the daughter of a former Boko Haram insurgent?" Hassan asked, cynically.

"Whether former or current, Boko Haram is Boko Haram," I said.

"Look who is talking?" Hassan began, "are you not one of the chief advocates of the rehabilitation of repentant Boko Haram insurgents?"

"All the same, I am not interested. I can't give her what she wants. My heart is already with someone else, Jewel."

Though I didn't like Safiya, she had been very good to me. Apart from the hot meals, fruits, fresh vegetables, and canned beer which she brought to me, she also brought some books and journals having known that Hassan and I enjoyed reading books.

"I collected them from our foreign aid workers. They came with a lot of books for the refugees," was her reply when I asked her how she came about the books. It was through her that I also discovered that some of the foreign aid workers were sympathetic to the Boko Haram insurgents. "Apart from the food and clothings which the law allowed them to send to the insurgents, those humanitarian organizations sometimes also sent them money."

"Why?" I asked.

"They said to meet their urgent needs."

"How about ammunition. We also heard rumours of ammunition being discovered in the food containers sent by some of the humanitarian organisations," I probed.

"I am not sure about that, but one can't rule out

these things. The BH boys have sympathizers in the most unusual places. The other day, one of the foreign workers who hailed from Europe told me how one of her brothers converted to Islam and joined the ISIS. Some aid workers are also middlemen for some arms dealers."

"Really? But I thought they were being well paid? How much?"

"Yes, they are well paid, but money is never enough for some people. From what I heard, the money for the arms which is in dollars is usually paid into the workers bank account in their home country. All they do is to collect the arms from the supplier here in Nigeria and smuggle them to the insurgents as food and clothing items."

"This is serious," I said. "But I thought that all these marterial are usually inspected by our troops before they are handed over to the insurgents."

"Yes, that was the rule, but it was never obeyed because money usually changed hands between the foreign workers and those of the Federal troops expected to inspect the stuff," Safiya said. I found her disclosures mind boggling.

Just like Jewel, Safiya was a beautiful lady. I liked her figure despite the *doduwar riga* which covered her from head to toe. She was slim and dark like her Fulani father, the repentant Boko Haram insurgent. Among other things, she had the seductive habit of squeezing her face when you asked her a question. She told me it was her defence to escape punishment from her dotting father anytime she couldn't answer a question from him. And the way she curved her eyebrows when smiling, makes you want to make her smile again and again. She spoke Fulfude, the language of her forbears with such oratorical elegance that even her employers, those who speak in foreign languages have started learning the language from her. And as the words of the language which I could hardly understand elegantly roll off her pink and serpentine tongue, they touched in me, feelings that were once hidden but now open and clear. Though I found her very attractive, I was able to keep my emotions in check knowing full well that my heart laid somewhere else beyond the sand dunes and the bombs and bullets of the Sahara.

Puzzled at her love for books and how well read she was, I was moved to ask the very important question: "Why did your father join the Boko Haram group and at the same time, sent you to school. I thought Boko Haram is against western education?" She told me that people join the Boko Haram movement for many reasons and that she was the reason her father joined the sect. "

"It is not everybody that joined the sect did it for any ideological reason. My father wanted me to get a good education, unfortunately he didn't have money to buy the books and uniform as demanded by the Teacher Training College I wanted to attend. Just then, the Boko Haram people were looking for men who were familiar with the terrain here. When my father who was a hunter heard that they were offering money for new recruits, without informing anybody in the family, he quickly joined the sect."

"When was this?"

"Going to five years now. He just came home one day, took me to the Teachers College and paid my fees for the entire three-year program."

"Just like that?"

"Yes, just like that."

"You didn't ask him where he got the money from?"

"He said it was from the sale of his millet. He was also a farmer."

"That to me is Boko Haram in reverse. Encouraging the love of western education by joining a sect that abhorred western education," I said.

"Yes, it is. It was much later that we realised that he had joined the sect. There are many people like that who joined the sect because they needed money and not because they believed in the sect's ideology. Some other people even joined because they wanted protection while others did so because of family ties."

"You have a point there. I also don't that believe that Boko Haram is fighting Western Education. If it is, then the insurgents won't be dropping bombs in Kwamam and Bambulu west of Maiduguri where you find peasant living in slums and then leave the GRA intact. Not a pin exploded in GRA where the real 'Boko' people live. All they do is to burn the slums where the poor people who have nothing to do with Western Education live and kill and slaughter them and not touch anybody in the Government Reservation Area (GRA), the University or any tertiary institution. They burnt public primary and secondary schools in the villages leaving the ones in the cities. Which one is more Western, is it the University or the village primary schools? They even went to the market and burnt the place while leaving the supermarket. Which one is Boko, is it not the supermarket?"

"That was why I said that the motives of Boko Haram are many," Safiya said.

My relationship with Safiya further got a boost when I informed her that I grew up in Madagali.

"That's my hometown," she said, excitedly. "I was even there when the Boko Haram invaded and ransacked the town."

"Really? My family had left the place then. I learnt that the Boko Haram were in the town for a long time and almost wrecked the place."

"It was very serious. They were there for three months. At that time, it was Madagali and Adamawa State that had the highest concentration of Boko Haram in the Northeast. When they entered the town, they told the inhabitants that they didn't want to destroy the town so as not deny the people of their means of livelihood since they have the biggest market between Maiduguri and Mubi. They saw the place as a rich source of food and other marterial for life and living. There was a filling station every fifty metres to daily supply their vehicles with petrol. They assured the people that they would not prevent them from running their business but would only use the place as their base. They asked the community leaders to inform their people not to get worried since they would not harm them. However, some of the people, especially the rich ones, having known that Boko haram could not be trusted started running away from the town. That was when the insurgents concluded that since all the rich and good people had left Madagali, it meant that the remaining citizens were the useless ones. They called the community for a meeting and asked them to declare their religious stand. They accused the community of turning their 'land of believers' into a 'land of infidels and hypocrites.' They said that they had thought that the people would be their followers but that they were rather disappointed that they had turned against them. They therefore gave the people of the town two days to take a stand on whether to join their sect. That was when one young Islamic scholar, whom I knew very well, stood up and said that the reason the people of the town did not join them was that the sect was not fighting a religious war the way it should be fought. As he put it: "We know this religion very well and what you are doing is not in line with Islamic religion. That is why we are not joining you. I am challenging you on this matter. If you say it is for religion then you come and sit down let see what the religion said so that we can fight this war according to the dictate of Islam." So, they said "Ok, we will show you that you don't know anything about religion." In the presence of everyone, they cut the boy into pieces with a matchet. Then out of the few boys who were standing with the killed Islamic scholar, one came forwards and said, "The young man you killed was my teacher. You cannot kill a teacher in front of his students…" before he could finish, they hacked him to pieces. From then, they decided to kill the whole community which they had herded into a big fenced central primary school. This made it difficult for peole to run away. From there, they moved to the next town and gave them 24 hours to decide whether to work with them or not. As the people were leaving the meeting place one of the leaders of the Boko Haram came and when he learnt that the community had been given one day to make up their mind, reversed the order and asked the people to go back to the venue of the meeting. And as they called the people back, they opened fire on them. As they were shooting, others were running away but even those people were killed. About 300 people were killed on the spot with machine gun. Those who managed to escape ran out of town into Cameroon."

"What? Are you serious?" I asked petrified

"I saw everything with my two eyes," Safiya said. "When the military arrived, they did their intelligence work and were able to identify those who invited the Boko Haram to the town. It was even a cousin of mine who led the Boko Haram to the town. He was the first one to be killed by the army. He was also the one that led Boko Haram to my house to pack my books. He carted away the Islamic books to his house and put all the western ones outside and set them ablaze. He did all that in our presence even though he knew all of us. Then from a short list in their hands, the military called out names of other Boko haram collaborators, traced them and shot them. That was how all those who connived with the Boko Haram to destroy Madagali were shot dead. After that the military set their rules over the town and imposed a curfew from 4pm to 6am."

"After all that, were you not ashamed that your father joined the Boko Haram?" I asked Safiya.

"I was scared but not ashamed because I know why he joined the sect. I know that he joined to give me good education and that he would not kill people for frivolous reasons. On the contrary, my siblings and I later became grateful that my father joined the sect."

"Why?"

"Because we knew that we were protected. The Boko Haram has many sympathisers within the communities here. That is one of the reasons why it has taken it so long for the Federal troops to get rid of them. Not only are they protected by the community, but they also get advance information in case of any impending attacks by Federal Troops. Therefore, once people know that you have links with the Boko Haram, they don't touch you," she added.

"So, in a way, you have also been giving information to the Boko Haram?"

She was quiet for a while as she squeezed her face in that seductive way that I so liked.

"Well... Well... I can't say no, and I can't say yes. In these areas, such things are well known but at the same time done quietly. It is a matter of life and death. Even some people give information to the Federal troops, but it is very dangerous. Anybody caught is summarily beheaded while the village the person comes from is set on fire."

As I spoke with Safiya where we usually met under the mango tree near our base at the IDP camp, she wanted to open the food warmer she had brought for me. "You must be hungry. Can I serve your food now?" she asked.

I told her to wait a while for Hassan to finish his sentry duty so we could eat together. We continued our discussion to while away time.

"As you have young men from your community who joined the Boko Haram do you also have those who joined the Nigerian Army?"

"Yes. We have many of our boys in the Nigerian army. I even have a cousin who is currently serving in Borno state. Families are happy when their son joins the Nigerian Army. They usually believe that they and their businesses are secured."

"Which is better, to join Boko Haram or the Nigerian Army?" I asked.

"It depends on which one approaches you first, but I think, the Nigerian Army is more lucrative."

"Lucrative? Really? Why do you say that?"

"You know I told you that this part of the Northeast,

especially Madagali which borders Borno state and the Cameroon Republic, is very rich in agricultural products and cattle which may be the eason why both the Boko Haram and the Government forces don't want to leave the place. While the Boko Haram is always prowling around here, the Federal forces will be pretending to be protecting the place. You know this place also has a lot of cattle and being close to Cameroon, an international border with a booming rice and sugar market."

"So what has Cattle, Rice and Sugar got to do with soldiers?"

"Your people, especially your *Ogas* are into the business of exporting Rice and Sugar across the Cameroonian border. They took advantage of the insecurity in the region to take over the distribution and sale of the goods. They buy cattle cheaply and take them in trailers to the south. Nobody can stop them with their army passes. They even encourage cattle owners to bring their cattle for easy passage to Mubi from where they take them in trailers to the East where there is a ready market for them. I also understand that some of your men who are close to Lake Chad also make a lot of money from the fishing business there."

"Really?" "How do they do that?"

"The same way they deal with cattle. Since many of the fishermen have abandoned the fishing business due to the insurgency, all that some of your army officers do is to pay fishermen to harvest the fish which they bag and take to the south for sale."

Because of my closeness to Safiya, I tried to learn as much as from her as possible about the Boko Haram, and the international aid groups which she worked for. One day, I asked her to advise us on how bring the war to a quick end. She was quiet for a while before talking.

"Hmm! That would be very difficult. You know that I have already told you that the community here is very much in support of the Boko Haram. You will need to station a lot of your men here for a long time to monitor and appease the people. I am not sure if you have enough soldiers to do that. You may need to seek for international support."

"You mean an International Peace Keeping Force?"

"Yes."

"As good as that may sound. It also has its own problems. My father served for along time with the ECOMOG force in Liberia, so I know something about International Peace Force."

"The other option is to train your people on how to fight inside the bush like the Boko Haram. From what I have seen, many of your soldiers are not used to this place. And its like they are not trained to fight with rough things. Many of them are just coming from classrooms without any experience. All they know is book work not the real practicals."

"I don't agree with you that the classroom is not a place to train soldiers. We need to learn the theory of combat first before going to war. At any rate, we had good teachers, experienced, and well versed in the latest use of weapons," I said, a bit irked that the young girl was trying to rubbish my profession.

"I know. I am not in any way condemning your classroom work. What I am saying is that your soldiers need some war experience before coming to the war front. Take for example that strange incident when some Nigerian soldiers were said to have been chased into Cameroon by the Boko Haram members. The question we should be asking is how possible it was for the Boko Haram that were outside your men's position which is in Nigeria chase Nigerian soldiers to Cameroon? It was embarrassing that the Nigerian soldiers were eventually disarmed by Cameroon soldiers and eventually escorted in a big truck to their headquarters in Cameroon. After the Nigerian soldiers had been checked and cleared, they were then put into trucks and driven back to Nigeria where they were dropped in Mubi and given back their arms. The actual truth was that the Nigerian troops lost their way during battle and strayed into Cameroonian territory. It was such a shameful incident and confirmed what I said earlier on that your colleagues still need some professional exposure before being brought to the war front."

I was quiet for a while, thinking, when Safiya again spoke.

"Let me tell you another big secret," she said. "The Boko Haram boys also have lots of Nigerian Army uniforms with them."

'How did they get them?' I asked, alarmed.

"They have tailors. All they do is to buy the material and sew them."

"But what do they need them for?"

"Ha! You are asking me that kind of question? They use it to confuse your boys a lot. When they wear the uniform, your people will see them and move to them thinking they are together. That is when the boys would strike. They also used the uniform to do business just like your people. The business of Cattle and Fish."

Our conversation was interrupted by Hassan who had just completed his duty post and came to join us for dinner. Dinner over, Hassan thanked Safiya for the meal and excused himself. He winked at me and gave me a broad smile and a thump up sign. When I turned back to Safiya I noticed that she was smiling.

What's funny?" I asked

"It's you and your friend. You are always behaving like two little boys."

"Boys? You are calling a man with a wife and two children a boy?"

"Hem hem? I never knew that he is married. How about you? How many children do you have?"

"I am not yet married. How about you?"

"I am not married."

"That's unlike an Arewa girl."

"I was betrothed but he could not wait because of my schooling."

"How old are you?"

"Twenty, next week."

"Next week! That's wonderful. So, we are going to have a big party here?"

"Maybe, but I am not sure you will still be here then" she said.

"Why did you say that? I will still be here. At least, we have not been informed that…"

"I know. You will soon be moved to another location," she said, sure.

"How did you know?" I asked, puzzled.

"I have seen the signal. My office gets this kind of information ahead of you people so that we can plan. That's the protocol," she said as I kept staring at her in shock.

Just as Safiya predicted, a few days later, we received the signal to move to Sokoto state to provide security for a village under the assault of bandits. Safiya came to see me the night before our departure. We met in a one-room air-conditioned *portacabin* close to her office at the IDP camp arranged by her. The facility according to her was used to counsel refugees. In her hand was a medium sized package which she handed over to me.

"I understand that your next station is a village. You will find this very useful," she said.

I opened the package to find various delicacies such as pieces of fried chicken, fish, fruits, and cans of beer.

"Thank you very much," I blurted in gratitude as

the ghostly light from the overhead light threw a brilliant glow on her lovely face. Suddenly, all my military restraints dissolved as I held her head in my hands and planted a timid kiss on her forehead. She looked intensely and strangely at me for an instant before lifting herself on tiptoe, rested her hands on my shoulders and kissed me, not on the forehead as I had done, but fully on my lips. I trembled with delight at her sudden kiss and at the warmth of her full breasts on my chest as I put my hands on her hair and began smoothing it back. It was fine and brilliant and smelt of perfumed olive oil. My heart was brimming with happiness as a desire to have her swept over me. She too must have felt the same desire as the yielding mood came over her. Still holding my head between her hands, she quickly freed one hand to check if the door was well locked before drawing me closer. That was when I slipped one arm towards her back to release her brassiere. And as the naked pair of breasts touched my hairy chest, she moaned with pleasure and pulled me closer. Suddenly, the desire that had hitherto swelled up in me gradually eased off and I became limp. Safiya who was obviously expecting more from me continued to draw me closer, but I could not reciprocate.

"Any problem? We are safe here..." she began but stopped when she saw that I had already turned away as a wave of shame and ridicule enveloped me.

"I... I am sorry..." was all I could mumble. Then I thought of an excuse. "I just don't think it is right for us to do it," I said. She continued staying in my arms for a while as if to allow her racing heart to calm down.

"You don't like me? Am I not beautiful enough for you?" she asked. "No, not that." I replied. "I... I just don't want us to..." I stuttered. She left my arms, used her hands to smoothen her now ruffled hair and clothes and opened the door before mumbling a horrifying good night.

And as I watched her go, I trembled with annoyance as the reality of what I had done sunk in. Why did I allow myself to get distracted? I had thought all along that it was just an innocent flirtation and that my military training would keep me above the storm of passion and that I would be the master of my mood? Despite all the promise I gave to my mother and Jewel, I had failed. On top of it, I had made a mess of myself. This was the second time. It was now obvious that my war injury had badly affected my libido.

Back in my bunk, a terrible feeling of guilt and sadness welled up inside me and I found it difficult to forgive myself. At just 24, I was now a certified xxxxx. I felt locked out. However much I might plead, however much I try, nothing will be the same again. I sat like a wretched and condemned man as the past turned away from me. I had opened the Pandora box and I was frightened of what I saw now and what I will see in the future.

CHAPTER NINE

It was raining as the commercial vehicle I boarded at the Sokoto Central Motor Park departed Sokoto for Kano. I sat in my civilian clothes in front of the 7- seater 'Hiace' bus with the driver, a lively elderly man who entertained during the entire duration of the trip with tales of his occasional brushes with bandits, Boko Haram insurgents and men of the Nigerian Army.

"The other day I ran into the bandits between Bungudu and Gusau in Zamfara state just outside the notorious Sambisa Forest. When they asked for money, I told them I didn't have any then they asked me to park my vehicle by the roadside and come out. I pretended to park, suddenly I accelerated my vehicle and sped off. They started shooting but I was too fast for them."

'Isn't that dangerous? They could have shot one of your passengers," I said.

The elderly man laughed and declared, "My vehicle is bullet proof." Pointing at one red gourd which he tied to his steering, he said, "One powerful mallam gave me this thing to protect the vehicle against bullets and it hasn't failed me once," he said slapping his right thigh with delight when he noticed my bewildered looks.

Lowering my voice, since I wasn't sure of the identities of the other passengers in the vehicle, I asked him about the Boko Haram insurgents.

"Those ones are mad people. The way they kill people especially soldiers, women and children anyhow is too much. One day, I took some passengers to Maiduguri when the Boko Haram terrorists ambushed a convoy of Nigerian troops on the Maiduguri-Damboa Highway. They killed at least 10 soldiers and wounded many others on that day. The terrorists had planted mines on the road near the Sambisa Forest on that day. I remember quiet well, it was a Sunday. We were stopped by a military convoy after the soldiers' vehicle mistakenly drove over the mines and then the terrorists opened fire on them. I was still at the scene when a military ambulance came at about 1 p.m. to evacuate the corpses. All vehicles were asked to stop until they evacuated all the slain soldiers," he said in his normal voice as if he didn't care who was listening.

"Much as I sympathise with our soldiers, some of those their *Ogas* are very greedy. Some of them don't even want the war to end because of the money they are making from illegal businesses. My vehicle was once hired by a Colonel to transport fish from Baga to Kano after the usual fishermen had been frightened off the place with indiscriminate bombings by the military," he said as the vehicle passed through Dange-Shuni on to Tereta. It was a very busy market day in Talata Mafara when we reached the town about two hours after departing

Sokoto. And even though some passengers wanted to have some food there, the driver refused insisting that he would not stop until we reached Gusau, the capital of Zamfara state. After a hurried lunch of Semovita and Okro soup at Gusau, we continued our journey as we passed Tsafe and Sheme in quick succession. After the initial rainfall which fell immediately when we left Sokoto, the weather had remained bright and clear during our journey except for a mild shower that fell in Marabar Kankara and later at Dayi, a dusty roadside hovel some distance to Gwarzo.

Then as we approached Gwarzo, a few kilometers into the ancient and historic city of Kano, the sky broke loose. With the rain, the usually congested Kano traffic was now clear of the ubiquitous motorbike riders popularly known in the city as *yan acaba*. The previously hot weather which had thrown the city into an unprecedented heat wave the previous week had remarkably gone down. The rain also prevented the usually boisterous almajirai from ploughing their begging trade on the streets. Instead, I could see them on a roadside clearing playing soccer, their begging bowls littering the margins of the makeshift football field like miniature spectators. And as I observed their frail, supple limbs dance over a football in movements that would have made Austin Okocha green with envy, I had the mind of calling the attention of the Green Eagles' coach to the highly skilful young men in case he needed fresh feet for his already aging team.

I arrived my uncle's house in Janbullo, Kano where I planned to stay for the period of my seven days leave just as the muezzin was calling for the jumat prayers. I had applied for the two-week leave, approved for all members of my rank but my Platoon Commander approved just seven days. "You are even lucky to have been given any leave at all in this very difficult time when we need all available human resources to prosecute the war. I only approved the leave because of your hard work and diligence."

And as I came out of the *Keke* that had brought me to Janbullo, I slung my duffel bag on my back and started walking, I came across a young man of about my age and his son who could be about two years old. They were taking a leisurely walk just ahead of me. I liked what I saw and wished I had also had a son I could stroll with hand in hand. I remembered my challenge and felt a stab of anxiety mixed with fear at the possibility of achieving what I considered a feat. I felt bad that despite all my promises to my mother and Jewel, I had strayed. I had thought that my relationship with Safiyatu was platonic and that it would end in that way, but I was shocked that despite my steely resolve to stay away from any romantic liaison with her, I had fallen like a pack of cards.

I must have been naïve for ignoring the warning bell had been sounding in my brain ever since my discussion with Safiyatu strayed in the direction of marriage. I could vividly remember her remark after I had told her about my fear of getting married during the war.

"Some of the best weddings have taken place in war time. That of the former Head of State, General Yakubu Gowon and his wife, Victoria is a good example," she had said.

Then in a thinly veiled reference to our relationship she said, "As a muslim, you will need a muslim wife who will help you practice your faith in an orderly and peaceful religious environment where you can bring up your children in the fear of Allah."

I couldn't even believe that I missed many of the signs of an impending romance especially when during one of our short meetings at the *portacabin* to keep away nosey parkers' she had said concerning the choice of the secluded space she had briefly leant on me while bidding me good night. In that moment which was the first touch between the two of us, her perfumed body had sent through me a sudden pang of lust. For a moment under the excuse of brotherly love and the cover of the surrounding silence, I had hugged her in return. That could have been the day my steely composure would have crashed were it not for her passionate and sonorous voice that had brought me back to life. I could recollect how she still held me though, probably to allow my emotion to gradually calm. She then patted me on the back as you would do to a baby being encouraged to burp.

My remorse must have been very deep on that when, without thinking, I blurted out, I'm sorry, mother..."

'What did you say?" She queried.

"I said am sorry for getting out of control," I quickly corrected.

"Its okay. I thought you were apologizing to your mother."

Matters had not been helped by my friend Hassan who, eager for me to settle down, had referred to what he called Safiya's 'grace and wifely carriage' which he said, I should be proud of. "She will be a better choice for a wife being of the same culture and religion as you unlike that your Liberian girl," he added.

"While your assessment may be correct, I am still very wary of marrying the daughter of a Boko Haram terrorist."

"Reformed Terrorist, you mean? Don't forget that the Federal Government is already committed to the rehabilitation of repentant terrorists."

"I know, but I wonder how the army authorities will take it if they discover that some soldiers have started getting married to former terrorists."

"Army Officer marries Boko Haram member's daughter. That will make a big front cover story in our newspapers," Hassan said as he burst into laughter.

I was soon in my uncle's house where he lived with his wife and the last of their four adult children.

"Where is Jewel?" I asked surprised to see only my sisters, Zainab and Rabia in the sitting room.

"Didn't you hear the news?" Rabia my youngest sister said in sad mood.

"Which news?" I asked.

"Jewel is not coming again. Her leave was not approved," she said.

"What?" I shouted as I sank sadly into a cushion chair. "But I was told that..." Zainab's raucous laughter interrupted me.

"It's a joke," Rabia said. "I don't want you to have a heart attack. Her flight was postponed. She will now arrive in Kano tomorrow morning."

"That's better," I said with a deep relief.

Seeing that my uncle was preparing for the mosque, I also went into the bathroom to perform my ablution. Though I had been heavily influenced by my mother's Christian belief which all my sisters also practiced, I had always wanted to practice my father's religion. As a small boy growing up in Madagali, I still recollected how my father had taught me how to perform my ablution. He taught me to wash my hands up to the wrist, rinse my mouth, and sniffed water into my nostrils. I then scrubbed my faces with both hands from forehead to chin and ear to ear, washed my arms up to my elbows, and wiped my head from the forehead to the back of the neck once with a wet hand. Finally, I had to wet my fingers and wiped my ears inside and out wiped around my necks and washed both feet up to the ankles Then I repeated the whole process two more times.

My father also told me how difficult it was for him to practice the religion of his father during the Liberian war because the attendance at the mosque in the ECOMOG barracks was very poor. The first time my father entered the mosque, he was shocked to find only five soldiers praying. Every other soldier who was not on duty was either in the club house or in the cinema house. Things improved when we arrived Madagali where my father had time to teach me about Islam. The mosque in the barrack was very close to our house and I felt very proud to be able to walk there by myself. I desperately wanted to be like my father, just as he had wanted to be like his father.

It was not too difficult for me to get back into the muslim prayer routine. As my uncle got ready for the mosque on that afternoon in Kano, I performed my ablution, purified myself, put on some cologne, dressed in nice clothes like my father used to do and set off for the mosque. It was a beautiful day.

After Jumat service, I took a taxi to the National Orthopaedic Hospital in Dala and asked to see the doctor who had attended to me when I was referred to the hospital with the bullet injury about a year before.

"Is he expecting you?" The Nurse in front of the doctor's office asked.

"Yes," I replied. I lied. Minutes later, I was in the presence of Dr Isa Mahmud, the Consultant Orthopaedic Surgeon. He remembered me once I told him whom I was.

"I hope your wound is okay now?" he asked.

"Yes sir," I answered before telling him the problem that had brought me to see him. He listened attentively before talking.

"Are you sure that it wasn't the stress of the war? You know how it is with all the shooting and anxiety at the war front?" he said in a fatherly tone.

"I don't think so sir. I... I mean my other friends don't have the kind of problem I have." I replied.

"Your injury seemed to be far away from the sciatic nerve," he said as he went over my case note and x-rays again.

"Yes sir. I recollected that when the bullet was removed, the attending surgeon said that the bullet missed the sciatic nerve."

The surgeon was quiet for while before speaking, "while it is true that that nerve damage plays a big role in erectile dysfunction up till now, the impact has not been well understood. A recent Spanish study of 90 men found that nearly 69% with sexual problems had nerve damage, mostly peripheral nerve damage."

As he said this, my heart skipped.

"Were these also as a result of gun shot?" I asked.

"Not really but gunshot also causes nerve damage. In the past, we used to put more attention on heart disease and stroke as the common causes of sexual dysfunction and impotence but now, we have more evidence that nerve damage is also culpable."

I was getting a bit uneasy and despite the air-conditioned room, sweat was dripping down my back.

"I'm sorry sir if I appear too inquisitive... and..."

"Not at all, you are free to ask any question."

"Have you ever confirmed any direct cases of sexual dysfunction and bullet wounds?"

"Yes. In fact, out of the four main causes of sciatic nerve injury associated with sexual dysfunction such as gunshot wound, femur fracture, laceration and contusion, gunshot wound is the commonest."

I felt like fainting. He must have noticed my sudden depressed looks when he said: "Okay. This is what I will do. I will send you for a nerve test. It's called Nerve Conduction Velocity Test (NCV). From the result, I will be able to take a final decision."

Since he had given me the permission to ask questions freely, I quickly said, "what kind of test is this Nerve Conduction velocity Test sir?"

He smiled. "I can see that you are very inquisitive person. That's good. It's the mark of a good soldier."

I smiled.

"Let me answer it this way. A nerve in the body works somewhat like an electrical wire in your house. If you want to see if the wire is functioning properly, you need to make sure that electricity can run through it. If there are any problems along its length, you will know it by a failure of the electrical current to go through. Like testing current flow in a wire, nerve conduction velocity test (NCV) is an electrical test, carried out by a doctor, to detect abnormal nerve conditions. It is usually ordered to diagnose or evaluate a nerve injury in a person who has weakness or numbness in the arms or legs and ..em.. em genitals."

I winced.

"The test also helps to discover how severe the

condition is and how a nerve is responding to injury or to treatment. In this test, electrical signals are sent down specific nerves of the arms or legs, where an electrode placed on the skin detects the electrical impulse 'down stream' from the first. The nerve is stimulated with a tiny electrical current at one point. A nerve stimulator placed over the nerve supplies the nerve with a very mild electrical impulse. This electrical activity is recorded by the recording skin electrode. When this happens, you will feel a tingling sensation that may or may not be uncomfortable. Between the brief shocks you will not feel discomfort. The distance between the skin electrodes and the time it takes for electrical impulses to travel between electrodes is used to calculate the speed of the nerve signal. A decreased speed suggests nerve disease. A healthy nerve will transmit the signal faster and stronger than a sick nerve."

"How long will the test take?"

"Usually, NCV testing takes less than 30 minutes depending on the number of nerves tested."

"How safe is the test?"

"Very safe. The small amount of current delivered to the nerve is always at a very safe level." He explained. He scribbled on a piece of paper and asked me to follow a nurse to another part of the hospital for the test.

An hour later, I was back with an envelope which I handed over to him.

"You said that your erection failed on two occasions?" he asked, looking up from the paper in his hands.

"Yes sir."

"Was it with the same woman or different women?"

"How are they to you?"

"Well, casual friends," I replied.

Again, he went through the report and then looked straight into my face, "the result confirmed a nerve injury which may be responsible for the erectile dysfunction. We normally classify the degree of severity as severe, moderate, or mild. We usually manage the mild cases with drugs while the moderate and severe categories are managed surgically. Your condition falls under the moderate category and so will be managed surgically,"

"You mean, I will need an operation?" I asked, terrified.

"Yes. We call it surgical exploration of the sciatic nerve to correct or stich the part of the nerve that has torn in order to make it functional again."

Rather than improve my restlessness, the visit to the surgeon now worsened it. Apart from confirming that I had problems with my erection because of my war injury, the visit to the doctor added another burden of the need for a surgical operation to correct the problem. With the impending arrival of Jewel the following day, I was now in a dilemma regarding what to do. I badly needed somebody to talk to, but I didn't consider my sisters appropriate for that task. I decided to seek the opinion of my uncle, a younger brother to my father.

"Hello Bukar," he greeted me from the verandah of the house where he was having his supper with his wife.

We spoke generally about my military service and politics just to allow his wife to leave us alone. That was when my uncle changed the topic to more personal issues.

"Zainab and Rabia informed me of the visit of your girlfriend from Liberia tomorrow."

"Yes, uncle." I replied. "Actually, I didn't want her to come because of the nature of my job. I was given only a seven-day leave."

"I can understand. You will be very busy at this time but all the same, you also need to take care of your personal life. How long have you known this lady?"

"Not too long. I got to know her during my last trip to Monrovia. I met her through Fatima."

"Do you like her?"

"Yes. To a large extent, I do."

"In that case, you should marry her as soon as possible. How old are you now?"

"Twenty-four, sir."

"That was about the age your father also got married."

"Yes, but I don't want to get married during the war. I won't have time for my wife." I declared.

"But your father married your mother during the war and…"

"Uncle that was different. They were both living in Liberia then."

"You should also bring her to come and live with you in Nigeria then."

"My worry is this cross-cultural marriage, and she's a Christian…"

"Just like your dad and mum."

"It wasn't easy for them, and I don't want to go through that kind of stress.

"You will get by. Once there is love, everything will sort themselves out just like it did for your parents.

I was quiet for a while wrestling with the decision of whether to let my uncle into my secret. I finally summoned the courage to tell him.

"The doctor told me to inform my girl friend so that both of us can work things out together, but I am afraid to tell her. I don't know her that well and I don't know how she would take it when she realizes that her future husband is impotent."

"You are not impotent. May Allah never allow you to be, but I agree with you that you should not let the lady know your problem."

"So, what would I do? Once she arrives tomorrow, she will expect us to be intimate especially with the pressure from my mother for me to get married."

"I can understand," my uncle said as we discussed far into the night.

The following morning, I went to Kano airport in the company of Zainab and Rabia to welcome Jewel. As the passengers disembarked from their Lagos flight, I craned my neck searching for her. Because of our previous encounter which took place some months back, I was not sure if I would recognize her again.

"Here she comes," Rabia shouted as Jewel, bedecked in a green jump suit, broke loose from the motley crowd of arriving passengers and ran to where I was standing with my sisters and threw her arms round my neck.

"Oh Jabbie, I have missed you," she cooed.

Despite all my anticipation of her arrival, I was momentarily taken aback as I did not know how to respond to Jewel's burst of emotion. Zainab came to my rescue and quickly hugged both of us together. That gave me enough time to give her a warm embrace as well as an affectionate kiss.

"You look radiant. I like your dress. Its simply gorgeous." I complimented Jewel as we walked hand in hand to the car park after she had cleared her luggage.

It was a bright sparkling morning. It had rained the previous night as could be deduced from the several water puddles on the ground. But now the sun was shining, and the surrounding green roof tops of the airport building as clean and fresh as though they had been scrubbed and polished. As usual, the airport was as boisterous as ever with arriving and departing passengers mingling with family, friends and relatives who had either come to welcome or see them off. Also visible were the ubiquitoes traders who offered wares ranging from newspapers to dresses, caps, shoes, and other items among which is a specially made *Kilishi* that made me salivate.

As I continued admiring her glossy hair which shone brilliantly in the early morning sun Jewel turned towards me and said, "You looked tired and weary"

"I am a little," I answered.

"I hope you are not ill or wounded again?"

"No, tired, that's all," I said wondering how she was able to see through me despite my efforts to mask my emotions. Her reaction brought to fore my dilemma on whether to confide in Jewel about the issues with my libido. While a part of me wanted to tell her everything with the hope that she would support my efforts in seeking for a solution to my problem, another part of me was opposed to the idea. The fear of this part of me is that with that realization, Jewel may eventually abandon me.

"Jammie, my darling, what are you thinking about?" Jewel's voice rattled me out of my deep thoughts.

"I was thinking how lucky I am to have a wonderful girl like you," I said and cuddled her.

"Thank you. Same here, she said, beaming in her usually beautiful smile.

"How long will you be here for?" I asked.

"Depends on how long you want me."

"One year," I said jokingly, thinking she would revolt but I was shocked when she said yes to it. "I am ready. I can even stay for ever. You know that I have finished my examinations so, I am free like the wind," she added.

I was still tying to get over what she just said when her next statement almost threw me off my balance.

"When are you going to meet my parents? I have told them about you."

"That will be a nice idea," I said, regaining composure.

"So when are you coming to Liberia?" she asked.

"Soon," I said as we entered the car and left for Janbullo.

CHAPTER TEN

My inability to get intimate with Jewel for the first two days after her arrival in created tension between us. I explained that I was tired from battle and needed to rest for a few days. I needed to buy time for the native medicine which the *Mallam* gave me take effect. During our discussion on the day before Jewel's arrival, my uncle had impressed upon me, the need not to disclose my problem to Jewel.

"The news may frighten her and make her to break off her relationship with you. As bad as that will be, it is still better than for her to remain with you but start a secret relationship with another man who would satisfy her. Apart from endangering your life, she may pass another man's baby to you as yours."

It was my uncle's belief that instead of subjecting myself to an unnecessary and costly operation to correct my problem as the doctor had suggested, we should try the traditional form of treatment which he believes, is far better and safer than western medicine.

When Sani was still bedwetting at the age of 14 years and all the drugs and injections given him by the doctors at the Teaching Hospital refused to work, it was Mallam Askira who solved the problem," he said.

As good as my uncle's proposition sounded, I was still a bit skeptical about using traditional medicine to solve my problem. Since I was drafted to the Boko Haram war, I had encountered all kinds of *Mallams, Juju men*, prophets and soothsayers who had disappointed many of my colleagues with their spurious claims of success with *amulets, igbadis, ayetas, asakis, bullet proof vests and other* protective portions apart from fake visions and prophesies. There was even one *mallam* who came to my Platoon on one occasion claiming to have the power to make all of us 'bullet proof'. Despite all my pleas to the effect that the Ak 47s and machine guns of today could not be stopped by any local potion unlike in the olden days, some of my colleagues believed the *mallam* and patronized him. Unfortunately, many of them were mowed down by the Boko Haram machine guns.

Notwithstanding this and other similar tragedies, some of these *Mallams* and Prophets were still patronized by our soldiers depending on their religious beliefs. In fact, some Brigades and Platoons placed some of these charlatans on monthly stipends in addition to official cars to ease their movements from one army formation to the other. It was when the army authorities realized that many soldiers had more trust in *mallams and soothsayers* rather than their military training that they issued official warnings against these practices. Unfortunately, the warnings went unheeded. I believe that the activities of these set of people must have contributed largely to our high casualty rate and the prolonging of the Boko Haram war.

With my mistrust in the efficacy of *mallams*, I found it difficult initially to agree to my uncle's suggestion of patronizing his *mallam,* but with Jewel and I sharing the same bedroom, I came under pressure to perform, and I needed an urgent remedy to my problem after rejecting the surgical approach as recommended by my surgeon. I therefore agreed to my uncle's plans. Even when it was almost midnight, my uncle still called his *mallam* and within thirty minutes, we were before Mallam Askira.

"You will take this medicine three times a day. You can put it in your tea or koko. The important thing is to make sure you take it," the elderly man said, handing me two sachets of some black powdery stuff. He then asked me to remove my trouser and then brought out a small gourd and a sharp blade.

"You will take this medicine three times a day. You can put it in your tea or koko. The important thing is to make sure you take it," the elderly man said, handing me two sachets of a black, powdery stuff. He then asked me to remove my trouser and then brought out a small gourd and a sharp blade.

"What is that for?" I asked, petrified at the sight of the sharp blade.

"I want to make some incisions through which some powerful medicine will enter your body," he responded. "The incisions would be on your thigh, and not on your penis, so relax," he assured upon seeing how scared I looked.

"Is the blade sterilized?" I asked, not wanting to be a victim of any infection.

"Yes, it is, but to satisfy you, I will repeat the sterilization," the old man said as he brought out a paraffin lamp, lit it and used a fork to hold the blade to the flame for a few minutes. Thereafter, the *Mallam* made some incisions on the inner parts of my right thigh. I flinched as the razor bit into my flesh and blood oozed out of the fresh wound. He repeated the same on my left thigh and then opened the small gourd in his hand and sprinkled its contents, some black powdery stuff on the wounds chanting some incantations in the process. As I later put on my trousers, I asked the mallam how soon the medicine would start working.

"In two days," he responded.

To keep from any form of intimacy between Jewel and I, I kept her busy with my affection and sight seeing for the next two days. Apart from the Kano Zoo, I also took her out to other interesting cultural sights such as the Emir's Palace, the Kurmi Market, and the Gidan Makama Museum among other important sights. While on a visit to the Bayero University, we both blended with the other students who were our age group as we moved about the campus.

"Bukar. Bukar Salisu." Someone was calling my name. Someone who knew me too well. As I turned towards the voice, a bearded young man came forwards smiling.

"Are you not Bukar Salisu?" he asked.

When I nodded in affirmation, he said, "I am Yaya Muhamad. We were classmates at Madagali High School, remember me? We used to share the same desk."

I peered at the face underneath the beard and my memory box picked his face.

"Hey! Yaya! Is this you?" I screamed as I gave him a hug. You have changed. This your beard didn't allow me to recognize you." I added.

"Yes, that's me. I easily recognized you. You haven't changed a bit. Heard that you joined the army.

"Yes, I did."

"No wonder, you are looking so fit and young," turning to his friend, he said, "this is the great Bukar Salisu. He used to come first in class, in fact, he used to teach me mathematics even though History was his best subject. We all thought he was going to become a professor, but he suddenly abandoned us for the army," he told his friend as a way of introduction.

I introduced him to Jewel.

"So, what are you doing here? I thought you should be somewhere fighting the Boko Haram boys?"

"I'm on leave. You too, what are you doing here?" I asked.

"I have just finished my master's in Mathematics. I am about to commence my Doctorate."

"Really? That's wonderful. Yes, I remember how we used to discuss mathematics back at Mad. High. I am glad you have really mastered the subject. Very soon, you will become a professor of mathematics," I said in earnest happiness.

"Ha! See who is talking. You are the one who should have become a professor since. If not for you, I would have since abandoned the subject." He noted as we bid farewell with the promises of seeing again.

Jewel cast an admiring look at me and said, "so all you had been telling me about your brilliance during your high school days is true after all? Nice!"

"You can see what the army has turned me into. As you just heard, I was the one who taught that friend of mine mathematics. Now he is on his way to becoming a professor while I am in the bush fighting and scheming to stay alive."

No, Jabbie, don't say that. You have chosen a very noble profession, one that will make you defend your fatherland, and you are doing well in that regard. While your friend may become a professor, you will soon become a General," she said as we both broke into laughter.

"Seriously speaking, I also want to go back to school." I said after recovering from the laughter spell.

"School? Is that possible again? Will the army allow you?" Jewel asked.

"Yes. The army has a programme for those who want to go back to school," I replied.

"That will be nice. I want you to go back to school and even if possible, leave the army and become a professor. The life of a soldier is too risky."

"But somebody has to do it," I said as we continued our sight seeing.

After the University, Jewel and I went for Lunch at a Lebanese Restaurant on Zoo Road from where I took her shopping at the new Ado Bayero Shopping Plaza. And as we mingled with the crowd, Jewel nudged me and whispered see that young couple and their two children?"

I looked and saw the young family just ahead of us.

"Yes, what about them?"

"They look so lovely and very beautiful. That's the model I wish for us; a boy and a girl."

Jewel continued talking but I was not listening – my heart was beating heavily as the import of what she was saying hit home. Matters were not helped by the fact that, that evening would mark the second day after my visit to *Mallam* Askira. For the past two days, I had been taking the black powdery substance as the *Mallam* had directed. With the little package hidden in my pocket, I was able to sprinkle some of its contents into either my food or drink without Jewel noticing me. Now that the two days of the medication as directed by the *Mallam* were over, I had no more excuse not to deliver tonight. I did not know that I had gone so deep in my thoughts until Jewel brought me back to life.

"You didn't say anything Jabbie?"

"Oh...it's fine." I stuttered.

"What's fine?"

"What you said," I replied.

"What did I say?"

"Em ...em.. about the family with a boy and a girl..."

"And what else?"

I nervously smiled at her as I tried to recollect what else she had said

"I said it would be nice for us to also have such lovely children now that we are young," she said when I couldn't recollect what she had said.

"Insha Allah" I said

"What's 'Insha Allah'?" she asked.

"By God's grace"

"Yes, by God's grace. But we also need to do our own bit, like coming to see my parents and formalize our union so that everybody can know about us."

"That would be fine," I replied my heart beating wildly, quietly.

The news of the gruesome killing of more than fifty Nigerian Army soldiers when the Boko Haram insurgents attacked the Nigerian Army Garrisson outside Mubi was on the front page of many newspapers the following morning. Different versions of what happened were being relayed over the news media, what was confirmed was that the insurgents succesfully deceived our men by wearing Nigerian Army uniforms were let into the barracks by our own men. Once inside our facility, they unleashed one of the worst forms of carnage ever reported since the start of the war. The incident sent panic around the Army High Command in Abuja so much that the Minister of Defence had to relocate to the Command Office at the Maimalari Barracks in Maiduguri where he immediately called for an emergency secret meeting of all sector commanders.

The moment I read about the incident and the issue of fake Nigerian Army uniforms, my mind went to what Safiya had told me that evening as we sat under the Mango tree under the moonlight at the IDP camp in Kaya.

Though I knew she was very close to the Boko Haram leaders, I never knew that the information was true. Even at that, how would I have passed it on to my colleagues without incriminating myself and Safiya. Now that this major calamity had happened, I searched my mind to know what else she had told me that may could seriously harm my colleagues. Secret supply of arms to the Boko Haram by some unscrupulous international aids agencies, leakage of intelligence reports to the insurgents by some of our sector commanders, airlift of weapons to the insurgents by some international terrorists' organisations... the list was long.

What was discussed at the secret meeting soon became an open secret in a matter of hours. The Defence Minister who had been dissatisfied with the way the army theatre commander had been running the war front ordered his immediate removal. The Commander felt that he should not be singled out for blame for the military's failure but that other sector and platoon commanders should also be changed. Luckily for him, the other middle level officers supported his position.

Another request by the officers was that if the Army top brass were interested in getting to the bottom of the rot in the army, the meeting should be enlarged to include all the officers and men of the Theatre Command. It was suggested that every effort should be made to also involve leaders and stakeholders in the community in the search for a solution to the problem.

"The various shortcomings in the sector were the handiwork of some community leaders and in some cases, some politicians as well as members of the international aid agencies. Unfortunately, the Army High Command as well as the average Nigerian did not understand this big challenge and have continued to blame every shortcoming of the region on the soldiers. It was time the whole truth about the nefarious activities of these devious Nigerians be exposed," an enraged officer suggested. So concerned was the Minister about the terrible state of things that he agreed to all these suggestions. In the meantime, as a a way of getting every able-bodied soldier back to the front, Minister of Defence ordered for a revocation of all forms of leaves with immediate action.

I was still with Jewel in Kano enjoying my leave when I received the signal from the Army Headquarters in Abuja:

SECRET:
THE NIGERIAN ARMY HEADQUARTERS ABUJA.
NIGAA/98027/6/BC/490HQNEC'G'270ZXTT(Art),

CANCELLATION OF LEAVE FOR OFFICERS
AND MEN

1. *In view of the current developments resulting in the increasing rate of attacks by the insurgents on Army Formations in the Northeastern part of the country,*
2. *All forms of leaves to Officers and Men of the Northeastern Command should cease henceforth.*
3. *All Officers and Men of the Command who are currently on Leave should as a matter of urgency return to their posts.*

(Sgd) for COMMANDER,
N/EASTERN COMMAND

Copy to:
All Sector Commanders
Platoon Commanders

The Minister of Defence who had relocated to our command base kickstarted the meeting between the Junior soldiers and the Community leaders and stakeholders by calling on the State Governor who was the Chairman of the occasion to read his Welcome Address:

"*Fellow citizens, in the last couple of days and weeks, our state has faced resurging attacks from insurgents. The latest of these attacks happened yesterday while the most horrific took place last night in Konduga. Fellow citizens, including an infant and nursing mother, were set ablaze. Before these recent atrocious incidents, many communities had also come under various degrees of murderous attacks in the north, south and central parts of our State.*

I share the grief of fellow citizens who have either lost their loved ones or confronted the agony of watching loved ones on hospital beds. I feel the trauma of hundreds of thousands of fellow citizens who have lost everything and have been forced to live on makeshift shelters and rely on food and non-food aid as internally displaced persons and refugees in neighbouring countries.

Beyond sharing the griefs and pains of fellow citizens, I assure you, that we have never for one second, ignored our constitutional and moral obligations towards you, the good people of our state. As your Governor in the last nine months, I have lived, slept, and woken up with a constant reminder that where I deliberately fail to do my utmost best in trying to secure lives, Allah will hold me accountable at His appointed time. Fellow citizens, security of lives and property is the number one essence of government. We are continuously giving support to our gallant and patriotic armed forces in both logistics and mobilization of community intelligence. We are constantly increasing, equipping, and motivating thousands of volunteers who make unquantifiable sacrifices in joining the Civilian JTF, hunters and vigilantes to defend our communities across the 27 local government areas. Fellow citizens, we are more than determined to continue deploying and sustaining all lawful and necessary measures in our desperate search for enduring peace in our State.

However, as we redouble our combined efforts, we must acknowledge that as human beings, our strength is limited. I know we have ceaselessly sought divine intervention in our individual and group prayer sessions. This time around, I will like us to seek Allah's intervention, not as individuals and groups, but as an entire state. In our prayers, we should be kind to remember thousands who were killed in this unfortunate crisis, and those who gave their lives fighting it. We should also be charitable in giving help, particularly food, to our neighbours because majority are in need. Fellow citizens, we should fervently pray for our armed forces and volunteers, who right now, are in battle fronts risking their lives to keep us safe.

These gallant fighters and those who died fighting, are the true heroes of our state. We shall remain endlessly grateful to them. These gains for humanity, are what the Boko Haram insurgents hope and are determined to reverse. We cannot let them succeed. We must fight and pray for good to triumph over evil."

In his own short opening remarks, the Minister of Defence said:

"Some of our major partners in the war against the insurgents are donor agencies and Non-Governmental Organizations. Because they are well funded, they can penetrate nooks and crannies of government, agencies, and parastatals to funnel out information which are sent to their home countries. They have access to sophisticated monitoring equipment. More importantly, the agencies identify critical, but most times disgruntled actors who supply them information at nocturnes. In the process, they

*also claim to get information of certain conspiracies between top
military officers and the insurgents through which the insurgents
get critical information with which they launch their offensives.
These NGOs also claim to get information that some of our
corrupt military officers, in association with officials of government,
sit on billions of naira meant to buy military hardware, thereby
subjecting fighting soldiers to needless casualties in the hands of
well-equipped insurgents. As part of our determination to rid
the Army of corrupt and dubious personnel, we have used some
of thes information from the NGOs and Donor Agencies to
prosecute some of these bad eggs among us. However, we want
to admonish the media and the NGOs to make sure that the
information being passed to us are genuine and not just to tarnish
the good name of the Nigerian Army."*

It was obvious from the chaotic way the meeting
commenced that militarily and psychologically, the
tide was turning against us in the war with the Boko
Haram. The moment the Minister of Defence finished
his opening statement, several hands went up for
recognition to speak. It was glaring, from the way they
spoke, that the junior soldiers were already disillusioned
with the way they were being treated by their superiors.
They stressed that they had lost confidence in the senior
officers and could no longer trust their leadership.
Unfortunately, this loss of confidence in the senior
military officers was not limited to the military but also
to the various communities in the region. As one elderly
community leader noted, "It is distressing that the war

against terror in the Northeast has now become a one step forward, two steps backwards. Action and inaction of the command structure has left many expressing discontent. How many more have to die before we say enough is enough?" he asked.

Hardly had the elderly community leader finished speaking than a middle-aged woman who was still sobbing over what she referred to as the loss of her husband and two children also took the floor.

"Exactly a week ago today, the Boko Haram people opened fire on a funeral procession on the outskirts of this same Maiduguri, killing at least sixty-five people. Six of them were my family members," she said in between tears.

One of the youth leaders in the community also presented a poignant and depressing message, "Despite the supposed beauty of the North of Nigeria, perhaps, the seamy side of its underbelly is the menace of the Boko Haram. Statistics has shown that more humanitarian service workers, the paramilitary, allied forces, and the military on tours of duty in the North have died more than in any part of the country. Of this number, several more have died from suicide bombings, shrapnel, improvised explosive devices and kidnappings gone wrong than actual combat. This is not a feat they are especially proud of or comfortable with, but one for which they have had to fill the resultant gap with less experienced personnel. Morale was down and flat like the chart of a bad stock analysis. Boko Haram has become a scourge, it has become the dreaded name whispered before the sun sets; it has become the end of several promising lives; it has become the perpetual politics on the lips of those who continually gain at the detriment of meaningful developments." He concluded his presentation with a poem which he said he had seen on the internet written by an anonymous poet:

Tears and Bloood
Of innocent Nigerian's trying to make ends meet
The Sahara is littered with bodies of poorly equipped
soldiers killed by superior enemy
Of Volunteers shot from behind with 7.62x51mm bullets
From Mambila to Baga
Voices of innocent Nigerians crying for help

The voice of the terrified and trapped Girl made me shed tears
I refused to play it to Mum for the Nation is already
flooding with tears
I can hear hoarse voices calling the resignation of the Army Chiefs
That Failed their people woefully
The Passengers along Damaturu-Maiduguri Road are
still asked to raise up their hands before passing the military
checkpoint

'I thought we'd passed this stage'
Asked a heavily pregnant Woman with raised hands
A day will not pass without sad news
Even the narrators of the story are living in phobia

they well know they are not safe
from the hands of these overzealous havockers
We are back to the days of clinging to our prayer beads
Chanting 'Ya dafi'u'.

Another young soldier who was worried about the perceived corruption in the army also delivered his own message: "Your Excellency, with deep respect and honour, I plead for your urgent intervention to avoid the rot in the Army. It is so sad to note that despite your administration's effort in bringing reforms in our hard-earned democracy, the army authority has flagrantly refused to key into Integrated Payroll and Personnel Information System (IPPlS) even after many years of directives from you and finance ministry. IPPlS is a unified platform for payment of salary and wages directly to government employees' bank accounts with appropriate deductions and remittances. The failure of the army authority to enrol in IPPIS has not only caused discontent but also disaffection and low morale in the profession, particularly among non-commissioned cadre who do most of the job but are the most downtrodden. For your information sir, our last month's salary was short paid to some soldiers as some were over paid. Till now, those who were short paid have not received the balance. Nigerian Army lacks financial prudence as both payment of salary and allowances are always characterized by fraud.

Your Excellency, according to the Management

of the Armed Forces and Financial Administration (MAFA) policy approved a few years ago, the operation allowance of one hundred and fifty thousand naira (150,000) per month you endorsed for troops/soldiers engaged in internal security across the country is only on paper as the Army High Command are paying just fifty thousand (50,000.00) which is just a small fraction of the amount approved by the federal government. The most pathetic of this ugly trend is that soldiers' wives whose husbands were killed in active service have become perpetual beggars in Military Pension Board (MPB) in Abuja, as the death benefits of their late husbands are hardly paid. Some of the widows have been subjected to sexual molestation by the MPB staff. We pray that you will kindly come to our aid."

Some of the Military spokespersons said that some of the activities of some of the NGOs and international donor agencies have persistently sabotaged the efforts of the Military. One of the spokesmen issued a statement laced with a charge against Amnesty International's operations in the Northeast, particularly in Maiduguri, the birthplace of Boko Haram. The Army accused "hitherto well respected" Amnesty International of having "deviated from the core values, principles and objectives of the original Amnesty International domiciled in the United Kingdom." It claimed that it had "credible information that the Nigerian branch... is determined to destabilize the Nigerian nation... through fabrication of fictitious allegations of alleged human rights abuses against the Nigerian security forces and clandestine sponsorship of dissident groups to protest, as well as unfounded allegations against the leadership of the Nigerian military." It went further to say that AI had "tried over the years using Boko Haram terrorist conflicts, Islamic Movement in Nigeria, some activists and now herders-farmers conflicts" and that the NGO was "at the verge of releasing yet another concocted report against the military, ostensibly against the Nigerian Army." It thus said it had "no option than to call for the closure of Amnesty International offices in Nigeria." The Army equally accused UNICEF of training Boko Haram spies in the Northeast, a development that led to the brief suspension of the organisation's operations.

At the meeting, a journalist who claimed to represent the international media also presented a report by the highly influential Wall Street Journal over its allegation that over 1000 soldiers were secretly buried at night in unmarked graves at the Maimalari Barracks, Maiduguri. But another military spokesperson quickly debunked the allegation, noting that "The Defence Headquarters has noted with dismay an article purporting that the Nigerian military maintains secret graveyards in the North-East theatre of operation. The armed forces of Nigeria have a rich and solemn tradition for the interment of our fallen heroes. Therefore, it must be unambiguously clarified that the Armed Forces do not indulge in secret burials, as it is sacrilegious and a profanity to the extant ethos and traditions of the Nigerian military."

As part of the recommendations on moving the region forwards, a representative of the International Donor Agency called on the government to seriously invest in social re-engineering with concerted efforts to ensure effective psycho-social rehabilitation for the youths who must have been heavily traumatised by the war.

"What is needed is a co-ordinated, systematic and planned efforts as well as investment which will help these traumatized youths overcome their challenges and pent-up anger. They need help to move beyond anger and gesture towards compassion, understanding and societal re-integration. Unfortunately, while several non-state actors have raised funds from all over the world for the psycho-social rehabilitation in the northeast region, only a handful, have been effectively engaged. Ongoing efforts are further hampered by those who would rather line their pockets than see budgeted funds go into streams of activities to promote healing and rehabilitation. It is unconscionable that even within the IDP camps, children and women are still being traumatized and denied of their basic amenities. One would hope that the government at both state and federal level will identify and make scapegoats of some of these heartless people. We need to ensure that the funds voted for the reconstruction of the northeast region is judiciously utilized and that the reconstruction effort is not limited to physical rehabilitation alone. It necessarily needs to include psycho-social rehabilitation and social re-engineering with public awareness and sensitization campaigns. Sociologists, psychologists, and psychiatrists have an invaluable role to play in this regard."

In his closing remarks, the Governor, after enumerating ongoing collaboration with the military, mass recruitment, equipping and deployment of thousands of volunteers in the Civilian JTF, hunters and vigilantes, said his call for prayers was a strange but necessary decision made based on popular wish of the people of the state.

"Even though this decision is based on the popular demand of our people, some observers may rightly argue that it is a strange call. But then, our state has been befallen with a strange evil since 2009, and sometimes, strange ailments require strange approaches. As your Governor, I hereby declare a day of devotion to pray for the return of peace in our state. I intend to fast on that day, and I appeal to every one of us in the state who can, to join in that simple, but pricelessly rewarding spiritual endeavour. I also appeal for the sacrifices of all other well-meaning friends and associates of our dear state who can, to join us in fasting *insha'Allah*, for the restoration of peace in our State and rest of Nigeria," he noted.

After the exercise was concluded, the Minister of Defence went on to announce some decisions taken by the Military High Command which includes the removal of Major General Jeunkuko Bimbola as the Theatre command under whose watch many lives and properties were lost. He was replaced by Major General Mohammed Timotu. The people broke into spontaneous applause over the change. They hoped that incessant attacks on military bases occasioning loss of lives, as well as the incessant seizures of military tankers would cease. Maj. Gen. Timotu is reputed to be a combatant commander who had been in the frontline for long with vast knowledge of the terrains, with good rapport with the locals and CJTF, in addition to possessing a keen knowledge of the geography and culture of the place. He was also seen as a relentless and ruthless commander and not one of those commanders who will be spending the whole day sleeping in air-conditioned hotel rooms while insurgents had a field day attacking military bases.

It was on such note of optimism that the meeting ended.

As we all trooped out of the venue of the long and exhausting meeting, twilight descended on us and on the sand dunes and valleys of the Sahara Desert. I suddenly felt lonely. In my solitude, my mind went to Jewel and my second failed encounter. Despite Mallam Askira's scarifications, incantations, black powder, and assurances that all would be well in a short time, I could not have an erection. I could still recall Jewel's sad expression when I again rolled off her with a limp and dry penis. Instead of looking for another excuse, for my second failure, I wanted to confess everything to Jewel but remembered my uncle's advice and decided to keep quiet. "God knows how much I really want to make you happy. God knows…but… I can't. It is beyond me. God is my witness. Please, forgive me." I apologised to her within myself.

That evening Jewel had waited for me without sleeping. I had gone for a discussion with my uncle. She waited for me, trembling with anticipation and anxiety praying that the man she had so idolised and loved would finally make her a woman that night. After my previous failed attempts which I had blamed on tiredness, she was sure that I had rested well enough for that night. When I later joined her in bed, she stretched out her hand in the darkness and felt the strong muscles of my shoulders, my taut abdomen which military drills had made firm and strong like a rock. She was happy when I cuddled up to her and undressed her. She was happy when I undressed too and whispered lovely things into her ears. With the imminent expectation of a wonderful love making ahead of her, she reached for my manhood, but she did not find what she expected. Instead of a rock- hard organ, her hands only held a limp piece of flesh. She was devastated. Her discovery was an anti-climax, and I felt the brazen shame of helplessness. But Jewel persisted in the foreplay. She continued to cuddle me, massaging what was in her hand with the hope that it would gradually come to life. However, try as much as she could, I could not perform. After all the giddy anticipation of the past two days, my limpness has now put her in a state of turmoil. She must have sensed there was a bigger problem to my excuses of tiredness for she burst into tears and cried profusely. Heavy sobs took over, racking her fragile body. She was soon overcome by emotion. She flung herself on the bed, sobbing into the mattress. I hesitated but held her hand quietly for a moment as if afraid of her. Scared of intruding into her grief, I let my hand fall gently and walked quietly out of the room. Jewel continued to cry and whimper like a little baby in search of her mother. Sleep eluded her. By the time the muezzin called for the early morning prayers in a nearby mosque, she was already worn out with sadness and insomnia. That was when she made a very important decision.

Now that my impotence was firmly established, I decided to live the rest of my life without a woman to hide my shame. I knew that I should be angry with my country for sending me to a war that has robbed me of my youth as well as my virility, but I refused to be bitter. My father, though a soldier, had never taught me to hate anybody or have any regrets in life. He was much more interested in serving God and his country in line with the American Legion's slogan 'For God and Country', a motto he had adopted as our family motto. That was why I took the decision that early morning in my uncle's house in Janbullo, Kano to take refuge in my military work with the promise of becoming a world class soldier and a patriotic Nigerian. Just like my gun, my country will now be my wife to whom I will shower all my love and attention.

CHAPTER ELEVEN

Another very important decision taken at the end of the high- ranking meeting in Maiduguri was the need to send some soldiers for a two-month training in Counter Insurgency (COIN) Operation in Victoria, Australia. The decision was taken when the guerrilla tactics of the Boko Haram such as ambushes, mine explosions and invasion of Army Bases were becoming rampant with disastrous results. It had become obvious that Nigerian soldier were ineffective in the war against the Boko Haram because they lacked the wherewithal to execute a non-conventional or guerrilla warfare.

Despite series of reports on the urgent need to counter the Boko Haram guerrilla tactics, it took the Maiduguri meeting to finally spur the Abuja Military High Command into action. In selecting the soldiers who would be sent for the training, emphasis was put on fitness, loyalty, educational competence as well as evidence of past performance. After a rigorous selection exercise, I was finally selected as part of the first batch of 200 soldiers to go for the training.

We arrived COIN Training Camp after a few days.

The Australian weather was horrendous. There was rain, accompanied by a sporadic, howling cold wind which increased regularly until it became permanent. Day after day, the rain poured in torrents while we were protected only by our raincoats as we toiled on the training camp. We were informed that the camp's location as well as the timing of our training were carefully arranged to give us a tough training session.

During the first week of training, we went through a strenuous physical test to ensure that we were physically fit for the strenuous demands of guerrilla warfare. Part of our training involved fifteen-kilometer run across mountainous terrain carrying a 30kg load on our backs. Firearms and weapons handling training were integrated throughout the one- month training period.

Since Boko Haram often used sympathisers in the local communities to carry out suicide missions as well as gather intelligence, we were also taught how to infiltrate their ranks. We went through mountaineering training as well as survival training which involves coping without communications and limited supplies for up to a week. Resistance to interrogation training was also part of our training. Due to the occasional need to survive during the harmattan period in the Sahara, we did sub-zero training which involved our being fully submerged in ice-cold water and carrying out physical training drills in cold weather without our tops.

Apart from a small office building, there were no other buildings for shelter on the expansive and rough training terrain where we ran, jumped, and swam sometimes drenched to our underpants and boots under the rain.

"Since you chaps are supposed to face your enemies in the open, it is important for you to undertake your training in the open," Sergeant Strongman Fisher, our physical instructor said during one of our early morning drills.

One rainy afternoon, after ten days, the physical fitness part of our training came to an end as the theory classes began. During our introductory lesson in the classroom, we learnt that before we could embark on our COIN, we must have a basic understanding of Guerrilla warfare. According to Captain Tom Warrick who took us on the introductory aspect of the subject, "Guerrilla Warfare is a form of irregular warfare in which small groups of combatants such as paramilitary personnel, armed civilians, or irregulars, use military tactics including ambushes, sabotage, raids, petty warfare, hit-and-run tactics, and mobility, to fight a larger and less-mobile traditional military."

The young-looking tall Captain also made us to understand that the major aim of Guerrilla warfare is to magnify the impact of a small, mobile force on a larger, more cumbersome one. "Successful guerrillas weaken their enemy by attrition, eventually forcing them to withdraw. Tactically, guerrillas usually avoid confrontation with large units and formations of enemy troops but seek and attack small groups of enemy personnel and resources to gradually deplete the opposing force while minimizing their own losses. The guerrilla prizes mobility, secrecy, and surprise, organizing in small units and taking advantage of terrain that is difficult for larger units to use," he lectured.

It was as if the military expert was very conversant with the Boko Haram when he said, "In addition to traditional military methods, guerrilla groups may rely also on destroying infrastructure, using improvised explosive devices, for example. Typically, they rely on logistical and political support from the local population. Foreign backers are often embedded within it (thereby using the population as a human shield), and many guerrilla groups are adept at public persuasion through propaganda and use of force. Today, many guerrilla movements also rely heavily on children as combatants, scouts, porters, spies, informants, and in other roles. Some guerrilla groups use refugees as weapons to solidify power or politically destabilize an adversary," he said before the next lecturer, Col. Fred Howler who addressed us on counterinsurgency, the core training of the course.

"A counterinsurgency (COIN) operation involves actions taken by the recognised government of a nation to contain or quell an insurgency against it. strictly speaking, the insurgents seek to destroy or erase the political authority of the defending authorities in a population they seek to control, and the counter-insurgent forces seek to protect that authority and reduce or eliminate the supplanting authority of the insurgents. Counter-insurgency operations are common during war, occupation and armed rebellions. Counter-insurgency may be armed suppression of a rebellion, coupled with tactics such as 'hearts and minds,' designed to fracture the links between the insurgency and the population in which the insurgents move. Since it may be difficult or impossible to distinguish between an insurgent, a supporter of an insurgency who is a non-combatant, and entirely uninvolved members of the population, counter-insurgency operations have often rested on a confused, relativistic, or otherwise situational distinction between insurgents and non-combatants," he taught.

Col. Howler, an experienced army officer who had taken part in many international peace keeping operations in the past, further informed us that "perhaps the most important challenge confronting a military commander in fighting guerrillas is the need to modify orthodox battlefield thinking. This was as true in ancient, medieval, and colonial times as it is today. Alexander the Great's successful campaigns resulted not only from mobile and flexible tactics but also from a shrewd political expedient of winning the loyalty of various tribes. The few Roman commanders in Spain—Tiberius Sempronius Gracchus, Marcus Porcius Cato, Scipio Africanus the Elder and the Younger, and Pompey the Great—who introduced more mobile and flexible tactics often succeeded in defeating large guerrilla forces, and their victories were then exploited by decent treatment of the vanquished in order to gain a relatively peaceful occupation." He concluded by giving the example of Alexander who recruited a guerrilla leader into his army and then married his daughter.

The moment Col. Howler said this, Hassan who sat directly behind me affectionately slapped me on the back and whispered into my ear, "Exactly what I told you to do; marry Safiya the daughter of Mohamed Maiduguri the former Boko Haram Leader so that we can win more of the Boko boys to our side."

I withheld my laughter and pretended to hear nothing. After a while, it dawned on me that I was struggling to pay attention to the lectures ever since Hassan mentioned Safiya's name. I had failed, for the umpteenth time, to consummate my love for her. Coupled with Jewel's hasty departure to Liberia, my heart has been a restless wayfarer as I thought of her all the time. I thought of her at dawn, when memories of her lovely face awakened me in my bed. I thought of her at night when the heaviness of my heart from the accumulation of her deep passion for me had made sleep a torture. I thought of her when I soaped my flaccid penis while taking my bath. My longing for her overtook all the noise of bullets and mortars and bombs of the warfront as well as the seductive smiles and gyrations of any other woman I had ever met in my life. I had the strong suspicion that Jewel must have informed Zainab about my problem because when Zainab called to inform me that Jewel had arrived safely in Monrovia, she had asked me to call her later for an urgent discussion. Coincidentally, Safiya also called me on the day we were scheduled to travel to Australia for the COIN training.

"I'm calling to wish you a safe trip," she said.

Surprised that she knew I was travelling, I asked, "How did you know that I was travelling?"

"I always know about these things," she replied and laughed before saying "I miss you a lot."

Since our previous discussions had never been romantic, I was taken aback by her statement, and I didn't know what to say. My decision to remain womanless for the rest of my life so as not to be hurt again by my sexual incapacity was still heavy on my mind. It was this fear of being a rafto that made me to physically flee from her that evening. I wanted to wipe her out of my memory and sink the ghost of her nakedness in my subconscious but the more I tried to bury her image in the sand of my emotion, the more her dark, slim, and beautiful silhouette stalk my mornings and evenings like a dancing apparition. I was shocked when I found myself saying "I also miss you."

"When are you coming to see me in Kaya?" she asked.

When I informed her that I wasn't sure of my next posting she said, "I could fix your next posting back to the IDP Camp here in Kaya so that we can see each other regularly. I yearned for us to be alone together again when we can laugh and play with each other."

I jolted to life when my colleagues started leaving for lunch. The lectures resumed after lunch. Various lecturers taught us the theoretical aspects of guerrilla warfare and consequently opened our eyes the training now opened our eyes to the things we never thought of. We soon began to understand how the Boko Haram insurgents had been able to hoodwink us despite having better trained officers and men. All the tricks used by the insurgents against us were now in our hands. We now realised the wide difference between conventional and unorthodox warfare. So impressed was Major Chike Eneh, one of our Staff Officers that accompanied us on the trip, that he did not know when he blurted out, "had we have this kind of training many years ago, this war would not have lasted this long."

The lecturers made us to realise that the wide availability of the internet has also caused changes in the tempo and mode of guerrilla operations in such areas as coordination of strikes, leveraging of financing, recruitment, and media manipulation. While the classic guidelines still applied, today's anti-guerrilla forces need to accept a more disruptive, disorderly, and ambiguous mode of operation.

"Insurgents may not be seeking to overthrow the state, may have no coherent strategy or may pursue a faith-based approach difficult to counter with traditional methods. There may be numerous competing insurgencies in one theater, meaning that the counterinsurgent must control the overall environment rather than defeat a specific enemy," Col. Howler explained. As he spoke, my mind went to the two different factions of the Boko Haram and its other allies such as ISS and ISWAP that operated in the same Northeast of Nigeria. This explained the perpetual string of the war, I reasoned within me.

After the lectures came another gruelling session, a course in the usage of weapons especially those being used by the insurgents. The first set of weapons we studied were those used for counter terrorism such as battle rifles, assault rifles, machine guns, sniper rifles, submachine guns, and handguns, explosive devices such as air force weapons, army weapons, cannons, grenades, machine gunsge" , marine corps weapons, mortars, navy weapons, rockets, light machine guns, general purpose machine guns, among others.

In view of the ferocity of the insurgents that we were fighting, we were also introduced to the modern versions of Heavy Machine Gun (HMG) for vehicles, infantry, helicopter door mounted as well as the rotary-barreled types, automatic cannon, grenade and missile launchers, surface-to-air missiles, anti-tank missiles, Shoulder-launched Multipurpose Assault Weapon (SMAW), Multi-role Anti-armor Anti-tank Weapon System (MAAWS), Mine Dispenser, Mine clearing systems, etc,. These were a real trove when compared to our outdated and sparse arsenal back home that consisted essentially of AK-47 riffles (7.62x39 mm), APMGs, APC, Anti Aircraft (13.2x96 mm), Shilka bullets, truck bullets and pistols.

We also took part in shooting exercises that mainly employed either the 25-pounder gun-howitzer for field artillery, or the 4.5-inch howitzer for medium and heavy artillery. Other weapons used for training included the heavier 9.2-inch howitzer and the 12-inch howitzer. I never knew that the Military Depot had such a massive facility with about 250 instructors and a total of 2,000 staff. According to the camp commandant, the establishment could cater for 590 officers and 700 other ranks at any given time.

Part of our training was a day and night exercise mainly in the form of simulations to protect ourselves against enemy attacks. This, we were told, was very important in view of the occasional surprise attacks from the Boko Haram insurgents on our military formations in Nigeria. We were dropped off one early morning in a far end of the training depot and asked to dig protective trenches inside which we were to stay and await the enemy. Digging was difficult because of the hard terrain. When we complained, our instructor quickly reminded us that it was the dry season back home and the grounds of the Northeast area would almost be rock hard by then. By the time we were able to dig two feet, we all had blisters in our hands, and we still had three feet more to go.

"The earlier you finished digging, the earlier you will commence the exercise," our instructor said. We commenced the simulations around midday. Twilight was setting by the time we completed the exercise. We were exhausted and almost fainting when we finally got back to our camp late in the night. We were all looking forward to a good night rest after the hectic day's work when two burly instructors who introduced themselves as Captain Knor and Captain Dawn came forward to address our class.

"My job is to address you on a very important style of combat, called 'hand-to-hand combat,'" "Sometimes, you may need to catch an enemy by surprise or even defend yourself. Therefore, it is very important for you to learn this technique of combat. I will teach you how to toss any man right on his head and break his arm on the way down if you choose to do so. I don't care if you only weigh 90 pounds, as you'll see much later during my instructions, your physical size has nothing to do with it. We were still savouring the scary bit of information when his colleague, Captain Dawn came forward with another technique that he guaranteed could shatter another person's jaw as well as several incredible "military tricks" that will take us from absolute rookie to a master fighter in just a few short hours.

"I will equally teach you how to snatch a loaded gun right out of a, insurgent's hand so fast it will literally tear his trigger finger off. You would also learn how to get away from a larger attacker who surprises you," Captain David informed.

As expected, the 'Hand Combat' training session was rigorous, but we were all fit and did very well to the satisfaction of our instructors. One of my colleagues was unimpressed with that aspect of the training. "This 'Hand Combat' thing is only useful when you can see the enemy. Most times, those Boko Haram boys are always hiding from us only to surprise us by planting mines on the roads or ambushing us," he murmured. All the same, we were happy to learn some new techniques which we could use to defend ourselves whenever possible.

One Saturday morning when we thought we would be given the weekend off, we were summoned by the fire alarm to the dining hall and were introduced to five white men dressed in full combat gear. We were told they would be going back to Nigeria with us.

"These gentlemen will work with you for the remaining weeks of your stay here as your Technical Advisers and afterwards accompany you back to Nigeria to continue the work," said our camp commandant.

"When one of us asked what the duties of the Technical Officers would be, the Commandant said, "Due to the brevity of your course here, we can't cover everything. These advisers will continue to with the training in Nigeria as well as supervise your activities back home at the war front."

It was much later that it was revealed that our 'Technical Advisers' were actually retired Australian soldiers who now plied their trade as 'Mercenaries'.

"Who is a mercenary? I have never heard of such a term before," one of my mates asked.

Luckily, Hassan who had always been ahead of many of us in his love for reading answered, "A mercenary is any person who is specially recruited locally or abroad to fight in an armed conflict. Many mercenaries are usually former soldiers and usually foreigners. They are usually well paid in US dollars," he added.

"Like how much are they paid?" another soldier asked.

"I don't know but it is usually a lot of money in US dollars," Hassan said.

Another soldier wanted to know why our commanders referred to the white soldiers as 'Technical Advisers' and not 'Mercenaries' which is their identity. Hassan informed us that the UN had declared the use of mercenaries illegal hence the need to hide their identities.

"In 1989, the General Assembly adopted the International Convention against the Recruitment, Use, Financing and Training of Mercenaries. The Legislation confirmed that mercenary activities seriously violated one or more legal rights. The motivation for a mercenary's activities always threatens fundamental rights such as the right to life, physical integrity, or freedom of individuals. Such activities also threaten peace, political stability, the legal order, and the rational exploitation of natural resources. It is for this reason that mercenary activities must be considered a crime in and of itself and be internationally prosecutable, both because it violates human rights and because it affects the self determination of peoples. In this crime, the mercenary who participates directly in the commission of the crime must be considered a perpetrator with direct criminal responsibility. It must also be borne in mind that mercenary activity is a complex crime in which criminal responsibility falls upon those who recruited, employed, trained, and financed the mercenary or mercenaries, and upon those who planned and ordered his criminal activity," Hassan quoted, obviously from a crammed document.

I also said that the suggestion about using of mercenaries came up during the Maiduguri Conference when a senior officer suggested that we should use them as was done in other several countries experiencing similar problem in insurgency and terrorism. The senior military officer gave the examples of South African and Russian mercenaries as some of the 'soldiers of fortune' with a good track record of providing quality counter-terrorism training through various private military and security companies. They have assisted several governments in overcoming insurgencies in Angola, Sierra Leone, Iraq and Afghanistan, he had said. He especially singled out the South African soldiers whom he claimed have extensive experience conducting mobile operations in hostile environments and can provide immediate access to airpower. The officer concluded by saying that mercenaries would be particularly useful in fighting Boko Haram in the Sambisa Forest, a dense area approximating 60,000 square kilometers in the northeast of the country which has become the insurgents' stronghold.

He was quickly countered by another of his colleagues who believed that the deployment of mercenaries was not a long-term solution, as they did not address the root causes of our crisis – in this case the regional appeal of Boko Haram as a credible alternative to a perceived illegitimate and disinterested government. Objecting, the earlier speaker insisted that the objective in hiring the mercenaries was to seek a quick and immediate curtailment to the violence Boko Haram has been visiting on Northeast Nigeria, and not for what he called 'any ideological correctness.'

Later in the day, we sought for clarifications about the mercenaries from one of our Staff Officers. He reiterated the point that the Nigerian Military were using Technical Advisers and Instructors and not mercenaries.

"What we have are trainers who came from security companies to help us manage and learn how to use some of the much more modern weapons because there is no time. We are in a war situation, and we need the capability to use the weapons immediately. A private military advisory and training company could assist a dysfunctional state by providing the initial professional and neutral framework to serve as a core around which new security forces can be formed and moulded. Although Nigeria has a well trained and capable military, we lack functioning structures and systems and may be plagued by the lack of mutual trust in the residue of an internal conflict. In our own case, because the Boko Haram had some religious undertones in its formation, the movement has many sympathisers in the rank and file of the military. A professional and neutral organisation can therefore be more effective in the resolution of many issues that have been allowed to hang for a long time. Such military assistance can also fill those gaps and simultaneously create an opportunity for our country's own surviving professionals to recover and begin to rebuild. A private military advisory and training company can equally assist a functioning country that is recovering from a conflict, or which faces a sudden threat and must quickly build up armed forces. Often, a country in such a position will need foreign assistance but may not be keen on committing itself to any one country and may then opt for a private company. It may also be acquiring equipment from countries antagonistic to each other, which could create real practical problems where training teams of those countries were to encounter each other on site. A neutral training team from a private company can offer real advantages in such a situation," he said.

We spent the last two weeks of our training period carrying out maneuvers and exercises with our 'Technical Advisers'. We had real weekend camps where we carried out war simulation exercises and were later attached to Artillery instructors for our Artillery trainings. It took us a long time to learn to set up the rocket launchers which when fired, shot off across the countryside with a tremendous explosion, to our great delight. On the same afternoon we were treated to a battalion assault by another set of visiting British soldiers. We watched as the paratroopers were dropped right overhead and saw them land, form up, and move into action.

With just four days to our return to Nigeria, we received the depressing news of the invasion of Baga, a fishing town on the shores of lake Chad in the remote Northeast of the country by the Boko Haram. I recalled that the town had always been a bone of contention between our forces and the insurgents. We were the first to burn down the town after driving out the insurgents who had taken over the town after attacking our garrison three years earlier. Two years later, they took us by surprise, drove us out and stayed in the town for six weeks. During that period, they killed more than 2,000 people – mostly young men, hunted down and executed as punishment for the resistance the town's vigilante had put up even as the Nigerian military fled. At that time, young women were rounded up and taken away to bush camps and forced to marry fighters on the ideological grounds that all women of marriageable age must have a husband. Again, we reorganised ourselves and drove them out but not before they set the town on fire.

News reaching us now indicated that our men had once again fled at the approach of the jihadists who rode into the town on motorbikes and captured military vehicles. We were informed that the men that drove into Baga belonged to Islamic State of West Africa Province (ISWAP), a faction of Boko Haram based in the northern fringes of Borno State and the islands in Lake Chad. Not only has the group proved a militarily potent threat, capturing a string of bases and a significant amount of equipment since mid-last year, they also represent a political challenge to the Nigerian government. Whereas it was believed that orthodox Boko Haram led by Abubaker Shekau, was an exclusivist movement that regarded everyone living outside its zone of control a legitimate target, ISWAP saw the political value in not slaughtering potential future citizens of the more inclusive state they are trying to build, based on sharia law, in the Lake Chad region.

In 2016, the split in the movement centered on Shekau's methods – his treatment of villagers, and the indiscriminate bombings and shootings that took the largest toll on civilians rather than the security forces. ISWAP's propaganda promotes the idea that Muslim civilians are safe with them. The jihadists invaded Baga and allowed those that wanted to leave to do so – the only penalty was a small "loading tax" paid to the vehicle drivers from which they took a cut. That would have been almost unimaginable under Shekau, with throat-slitting execution, the common punishment for those caught trying to escape his territory. Under ISWAP, young women were not harassed, men were not made to cut their trouser legs above the ankle as a sign of piety or to grow their beards.

Before we received orders to move to Baga immediately and recapture the town after our training in Australia, Safiya had called, "I am sorry dear, you would be going to Baga in two days time. I tried everything possible to bring you first to Kaya but because of your exclusive training in counter insurgency, the military headquarters urgently need all of you in Baga," she had said.

"Exactly, Safiya!" I had enthusiastically replied, not wanting her to see me as a weakling. "I am first and foremost a soldier and after all the expenses of this training, it is only normal for the government to benefit from its investment," I said. "By the way, what is so attractive in Baga that has necessitated the series of see-saw activities in the town?" I asked her, out of curiosity.

"Fish! Plenty of Fish," Safiya said. "It has been estimated that the money from the fish market is what the Boko Haram is using to prosecute the insurgency, as such, it is very important for them to hold the town," Safiya added.

"But if the place is so lucrative, why are young people always eager to leave the place anytime there is a change of government," I asked.

"It is out of fear. Once the military retakes Baga, the fear is that anybody found in the town would be assumed to be a jihadist sympathiser and that could mean detention in Maiduguri's notorious Giwa barracks, or worse."

"See, Bukar, with the coming of ISWAP to Baga, many people will prefer to stay on the islands controlled by them rather than in Maiduguri. All that ISWAP required was for people to pay their taxes to the oragnosation, then they can stay safely in their *daulah*, their so-called Islamic state and do their business."

"And the Nigerian government would accept that?" I asked, managing to hide my disgust.

"The Nigerian government may not recognise it, but ISWAP is very much aware it is competing to convince several young men and women that their *daulah* is a credible alternative to the Nigerian state. ISWAP levies taxes on fishermen and farmers and in return digs wells, provides security, rudimentary healthcare, price caps on basic food items and trader-friendly policies to encourage the flow of goods. Until mid-last year, life was hard on the islands, but ISWAP's success in clearing military bases along a corridor to the Niger border has boosted business," she said, fiercely.

"You are now speaking like a Boko Haram propangadist," I said.

"Not at all, Bukar. I am talking like a realist. You know that I mix a lot with people from both sides, Nigerian soldiers, Boko Haram insuregnts as well as refugees. They tell me a lot of stories, just like one Abdullahi, a trader who shuttles between the islands and Maiduguri informed me how really impressed he was about life in ISWAP's *daulah*. But he noted that friction usually developed between the local community and ISWAP commanders when sentencing under sharia was perceived too harsh, or when the jihadists did not trust locals who usually refused to join them to fight."

In my eagerness to know as much as possible about

Baga since it would be my next station, I prodded Safiya for more information about Baga and ISWAP.

"At the beginning of the year, ISWAP was going through political changes. They arrived in Baga, proclaiming they were 'Mamman Nur people' – a reference to their charismatic veteran commander, a key player in the split with Shekau. But as everybody in Baga knew, ISWAP leaders had killed Nur several months earlier. He was accused of back channel ceasefire talks with the government and alleged to have pocketed money from the ransom paid for the release of 100 school girls captured in Dapchi in March last year. It was a shameless hijacking of Nur's still popular brand by ISWAP."

"So, there were deep splits in the so-called ISWAP?" I asked.

"Well, you can always expect such things. Their attempts to cling on to Nur's legacy suggest some nervousness following his death. In the ensuing instability, the previously ISWAP-approved leader, Abu Musab al-Barnawi was replaced in March by a new so-called governor, Abu Abdallah al-Barnawi," Safiya revealed as I struggled to pinpoint where her loyalty lay.

"But I still don't understand how anybody can still be in any way ambivalent over which side offers the greatest protection and support after 10 years of a war that has killed over 35,000 people and displaced more than two million. I consider this a terrible indictment of the Nigerian government and its counter-insurgency campaign," I said.

"Exactly!" She exclaimed. "It is more reason why you people should change your style of operation. Some of those young refugees I interviewed at the IDP camp complained bitterly of lack of job in Maiduguri and would prefer to live in the Islands controlled by ISWAP if ISWAP can keep to their promises."

I disagreed with Safiya on her last statement. "On the other hand, I also know of some young people who despite all the litany of grievances of living in Nigeria – governmental neglect, corruption, the daily indignities suffered by the poor – cannot wholeheartedly trust ISWAP and still prefer the Nigerian government."

"Although your governnemt portrayed ISWAP as an externally derived problem, part of a "cluster of terrorist groups" based in the Sahel, supported by so-called Islamic State, "sneaking in to commit terrorist activities." This does not match the profile of an ISWAP commander I once met while distributing food and medicine to some Boko Haram insurgents recently. According to the Commander who joined Boko Haram in 2010 and had always operated inside Nigeria, religion is the only reason they are doing what they are doing. I was shocked when he considered himself a committed jihadist who has totally rejected any idea of compromise with the Nigerian government and instead fully expected to die for his cause. Out of the eight people from Baga that I interviewed in Maiduguri during my work, none supported jihadist violence. They all wanted this war to be over, had suffered too much in the name of religion, and enthusiastically hated Shekau. But when asked if they would support ISWAP if it was a political party that renounced violence but retained support for sharia law, there were near unanimous nods of agreement. It is the inability of successive Nigerian governments to care for its citizens fairly and justly that was regarded as the foremost problem," she said.

At the end of her long argument, I told her that whatever may be the problem with Nigeria, I still believed that the issues could be amicably resolved without recourse to war. She laughed.

"Don't worry," she said. "Once you finish your assignment in Baga, you will come over to Kaya. I have really missed you and want to see you again."

"I also miss you," I said, in my eagerness to please her.

Deep inside me, the last thing I wanted was a woman in my life. I have had enough humiliation from my sexual handicap and would not entertain further embarrassment.

Propelled by my unbearable pain of repressed libido, I had followed my colleagues to town where we had gone to unwind. While my colleagues went after the young, attractive native Australian girls that populated the small bars and hotels of the small town, I had sought out a woman with whom I thought I would be comfortable, I soon found one with flaccid breasts but affectionate smiles and whose price was well within my reach. I thought that with her experience and maturity, the middle-aged woman would be able to calm the fire in my bosom. After paying the required ten Australian dollars and despite all the efforts she put in to arouse me, I left the brothel an hour later without getting intimate with her. The prostitute's demeaning laughter continued to echo in my ears and each time I recalled it, tears would swell my eyes.

"Bukar...Bukar......are you still there?" Safiya's voice over the phone, called him back to life.

CHAPTER TWELVE

The battle to the recapture Baga town from the insurgents commenced exactly at midday one sunny Saturday. We had returned from our counterinsurgency (COIN) training in the forests of Australia two days earlier and were ready to deploy all the skills acquired in the last two months. We also had a very courageous and useful bunch of Civilian Joint Task Force (JTF) members who guided our movements as they were familiar with the terrain. Because of what we had heard about the penchant of the Boko Haram insurgents to plant mines on the way, our convoy was led by a newly acquired mine sweeper while a tank, led our attack. Our armoury was well stocked with devices such as air force weapons, army weapons, cannons, grenades, rockets, light machine guns and general purpose machine guns among others. While some of us sat behind pick-up trucks, the luckier ones were cramped inside the armoured personnel carriers.

To counter the ferocity of the enemy, we also had in our cache, an ample supply of HMGs mounted on vehicles, infantry as well as the rotary-barreled types. Also included were automatic cannon, grenade and missile launchers, surface-to-air missiles, anti-tank missiles, shoulder-launched multipurpose assault weapon, multi-role anti-armor anti-tank weapon system, mine dispenser, mine clearing systems and personal assault weapons such as AK-47 rifles.

The entire day before the D-day was spent at the briefing room of Giwa Barracks in Maiduguri where we saw indisputable and shocking video evidence of the attack on the towns of Baga and Doron Baga by Boko Haram militants during which more than 3,700 structures were damaged or destroyed.

"Of all Boko Haram assaults analysed by Amnesty International, this is the largest and most destructive yet. It represents a deliberate attack on civilians whose homes, clinics and schools are now burnt-out ruins," Major Gideon Musa, Company Commander elucidated.

In Baga, a densely populated town less than two square kilometres in size, approximately 620 structures were destroyed by fire while in Doron Baga, over 3,100 structures were destroyed in the approximately 4 square-kilometre town.

During the video presentation at the briefing, a man in his fifties was shown as he relayed what happened in Baga during the attack: "They killed so many people. I saw around 100 killed at that time in Baga. I ran into the bush. As we were running, they were shooting and killing." The man was later discovered by Boko Haram fighters and detained in Doron Baga for four days. Those who fled said they saw many corpses in the bush. "I don't know how many but there were bodies everywhere we looked," one woman told Amnesty International. Another witness described how Boko Haram were shooting indiscriminately killing even children and a woman who was in labour. "Half of the baby boy was out and she died like that," the man said.

Our confidence got a further boost when our Technical Advisers from Australia joined us with their own equipment which included some night vision apparatus and high-tech precision telescopic sniper. So confident we were of victory that as our tanks, trucks and gun carriers departed Giwa Barracks that day, we broke into a song.

We are H- A- P- P- Y,
We are H -A- P- P- Y,
We know we are,
We are sure we are
We are H- A- P- P- Y
HAPPY!

As we rumbled along the streets of Maiduguri on our way out of the city, several people lined the streets to wish us goodluck as they chanted: *Allah ya tsare! Allah ya kiyaye Anya! Asaukalafiya!*

An hour after Maiduguri, we came under attack. The attack took us unawares as we were not expecting to see the Boko Haram boys until very close to Baga. At least that was what our intelligence reports indicated.

As our leading tank responded, we quickly disembarked from our trucks and took shelter. The shelling started to thunder again. Our tanks boomed their response as we ducked under whatever shelter we could, tense, rigid and waiting. Continuous fire, defensive fire, curtain fire, mortars, tanks, machine-guns, hand-grenades – the situation continued for a long time. Suddenly, we heard a whistling noise behind us which got louder and louder before crashing with a loud roar. As we ducked, a massive wall of fire shot up about a hundred yards in front of us. Part of the sand dunes and craggy hill ahead of us were hit as a giant crater appeared in the bowel of the earth. As we watched with awe, more hissing sounds came over our heads, more shells were fired in our direction.

"Take cover!" somebody shouted. "Take cover!"

Unfortunately, the terrain was flat and there were few areas for protection. Some of us ducked behind the tanks and trucks while others flattened themselves to the ground. The late afternoon sun turned into darkness as more explosions went off around us amidst a cloud of smoke and fire.

"Mines…mines…. We have driven over mines," somebody shouted as the earth exploded all around us. Another massive hole opened in front of us where another mortar had landed while sky high columns of sand, rocks and debris came raining down on top of us. The pattern continued for a while. Heavy shelling with intermittent whistling sound followed by a confetti of sand, rocks and debris all intermingled with the cries of the wounded and dying that filled the air. The shelling was stronger than anything else and there was very little anyone could do for anybody else. A piece of shrapnel hit my helmet and bounced off. I froze.

A second hail of shellfire commenced from the direction of the insurgents. So massive was the volume that the sound of the raging earth, the echoes of the concussion as well as the twisting and burning vehicles overshadowed the roaring of guns, mortars, and shells. The air was now foggy with smoke, with the pungent smell of nitroglycerin, sawdust, and graphite swirling in the air. As we fired the mounted guns, the recoil made our truck to shake as the echo rolled out round the surrounding valleys and hills.

As the shelling from our enemies continued unabated, it became clear to us that we had underrated these boys. We started firing faster than the insurgents as our tanks and Technical Advisers took control after recovering from the unexpected attack. We were able to repel the boys as they disappeared into the surrounding bushes leaving behind a wreckage of burnt vehicles, the dead and the dying and tons of debris.

The surrounding countryside was strewn with the corpses and mutilated bodies of our wounded and the dying as their cries and whimpering floated in the bucolic air like a funeral dirge. Our medics went to work in the smoky and eerie environment, ferrying the mangled and injured away with stretchers. Like some of my other colleagues, I was lucky to get away with only red and swollen eyes, but my hands, elbows and knees were raw and bleeding in many places. All around us were scraps of burnt and twisted metals, blown-up earth and trees littered with remnants of unburnt uniforms waving in the wind like ghostly shrouds.

They were the mementos of our overconfidence, evidence of wrong intelligence reports, a heavy dose of sabotage and an encounter with a deadly force.

When all was quiet, our downcast and teary Company Commander (CC) did a roll call. He stopped at a ragged bunch of dirty and crusted one hundred and twenty faces of what was left of the two hundred happy soldiers that left Maiduguri the previous day. And instead of our buoyant and confident spirit, our thoughts were in shambles and our morale terrible low. In addition to the eighty dead soldiers, out of the ten armored personnel carriers (APC), twenty Toyota pick-up trucks, three rocket-propelled grenade launchers, two hundred machine guns, and a large quantity of ammunition that we left Maiduguri with the previous day, we only had five APC, ten trucks, one rocket propelled grenade launchers and less than a hundred machine guns left.

"We have to return to Maiduguri. We need reinforcements and we need to replenish our stock" the CC said, breathing heavily with his head bowed.

We did a final combing of the surrounding desert for our dead and dying, picked them up and stowed them in the trucks and returned to Maiduguri. The following week, we planned another assault on Baga.

"This time around, we must keep our cards to our chests," our new Company Commander (CC) Major Isyaku Biu who had appointed me as his ADC told me as I helped him to arrange his papers and files. "Our last expedition was sabotaged. Apart from the wrong intelligence reports that we were served with, all our plans were leaked. Our objective, Baga is 160 kilometers away, yet we were attacked just about 60 kilometers outside Maiduguri, a whole 100 kilometres short of our objective."

"I agree with you sir. The ambush was well planned and executed. It took place in a desolate and flat terrain with very little cover. That was why it was easy for those criminals to pick us off like rabbits. The insurgents also mined our route. That was our greatest disaster," I said.

"Yes, Bukar. The mines. But what really baffled me was why those mine sweepers did not work. I think that somebody must have tampered with the vehicle and the systems. The captain who operated the tank was a trusted hand. I can't say the same about those mechanics and technicians. Many of them are Boko Haram sympathisers," the Major said.

"I also think, sir, that we have to thank our Technical Advisers (TA) for rising to the occasion. Our casualties would have been more if not for them," I said but Major Isyaku shook his head.

"You mean those bloody mercenaries? No, I disagree with you," he fired back at me.

"Mercenaries? I thought that the government denied using mercenaries only Technical Advisers?"

My CC burst into laughter. "What's the difference? Look, Bukar, you are a small boy. I will give you a copy of yesterday's paper so you can read what I am talking about. Whether, Mercenary or Technical Adviser, they are all the same thing and they are useless… absolutely useless! I understood that it took your so called 'Technical Advisers' more than ten minutes to know what to do when you guys were ambushed. Ten minutes is a long time in an emergency. That was why the casualty was that high. Eighty soldiers on the spot and ten more in the hospital, that's unacceptable!! From the report I got, it was our tanks that saved the day and not those over-pampered and overrated mercenaries. You know how much they are paid? 500 dollars a day…500 dollars a day just as feeding allowance. Seventy percent of their professional fees which I understand is close to half a million dollars each having been paid to them before they left their home countries. Compared that to the chicken feed of 1000 dollars per month that we are being paid. It is not as if we are also not good. The problem is lack of good equipment and poor welfare package. If our salaries can be improved and half of the money being wasted on those bloody *batures* can be used to procure better equipment for us, we would also perform," Major Biu said as he chewed on his kolanut.

"But sir, they also came with some equipment which we don't have…they demonstrated some of them to us in Australia and…."

"Which equipment? The equipment they brought

was for their own personal protection, body armour they call it. That's why none of the six mercenaries that went with you sustained a single scratch. The equipment that could have helped the army as a whole were night vision equipment which makes it easy for them to work at night so that they would not be seen during daytime. If you recollect, I was one of those officers who spoke against their use at the Maiduguri Conference a few months ago. I emphatically told the Conference that hiring mercenaries is not the solution to our problem. Apart from the fact that these mercenaries do not know our terrain as much as we do, the exorbitant money they are being paid can be better used to procure better equipment for our forces and pay our soldiers a more robust salary. This apart from other challenges such as internal sabotage, corruption among our big *ogas* among other serious problems. Look, at the appropriate time, all these will be tabled before a world conference."

True to his promise, Major Isyaku handed me a copy of The Daily Mandate one of the popular newspapers available to us in our military base. On the front page was a big headline: **NIGERIAN MILITARY FINALLY HIRES MERCENARIES.** According to the paper;

Despite repeated denials by the Nigerian government that the country hired mercenaries in the war against Boko Haram, The Daily Mandate has obtained credible information, including pictures, which prove that several dozens of Australian ex-soldiers were involved in combat roles against the insurgents in the Northeast.

Credible information available to this newspaper indicates that an advance team of 12 mercenaries arrived Maiduguri yesterday after being engaged by the Nigerian government to train its troops as well as fight the insurgents.

According to information from highly placed military sources, the government's initial plan was to bring in foreign military experts to train a special squad of Nigerian soldiers for the purpose of locating the missing Chibok school girls, but it altered the plan because of deteriorating security in the Northeast. When reports surfaced of foreign fighters in Nigeria, the government strenuously denied it, claiming the foreigners seen in the Northeast were only in the country to offer training to the troops.

"What we have are trainers who came from security companies to help us manage and learn how to use some of the much more modern weapons because there is no time; we are in a war situation and we need the capability to use the weapons immediately," a Nigerian Government official said.

The government's admission of the presence of the mercenaries came last year from a government media consultant. According to the Consultant, Nigeria recruited 'Special M Forces' to help in the air while government troops took control of land operation. He said the government kept the employment of the 'technical advisers' a top secret because of the sensitivity surrounding it, even though some chose to call them mercenaries, the newspaper concluded.

After a thorough postmortem of the failed effort to reclaim Baga by the Nigerian troops from the Boko Haram insurgents, the army high command decided to adopt a different approach to the new assault. The new operation which was code named Operation Desert Tiger (ODT) had three components.

1. An amphibious assault on Baga from Lake Chad with the active support of the Chadian Army under the Multi-National Joint Task Force (MNJTF)
2. A land attack from Maiduguri but this time, after a thorough sweep of the 160 kilometres distance by a set of mine sweepers to be solely serviced and manned by our Technical Advisers
3. An air attack which would soften the ground 24 hours before the commencement of the operation.

In furtherance of our decision to avoid another sabotage, details of ODT were only known to very few top Military Officers. This in addition to the good selection of participating soldiers and good equipment contributed in no small measure to the overwhelming success of the operation. With the cooperation of Chadian Military authorities under the MNJTF, our troops that had been earlier airlifted were dropped on the Chadian shore of Lake Chad from where we commenced a successful an amphibian assault on Baga and the nearby Doron Baga. Despite our success, we lost two boats when the insurgents shot their engines. The water borne attack had taken the Boko Haram insurgents by complete surprise especially since they didn't have the equipment and the right personnel to fight that kind of battle. After our Air Force had pounded the Jihadists position for several hours, our ground forces as well as our amphibious forces from the Chad end were able to pin the insurgents down to a small radius around Doron Baga. This resulted in bloody encounter as the insurgents, having seen that they had been hemmed in on both sides, fought for their lives.

It was also obvious that the insurgents had no answer to the power of our airforce. The air hostilities commenced with two of our aircrafts sweeping down over the Baga/ Doron Baga junction where the insurgents had their camp. The result was that many of the terrorists were killed while many their vehicles and equipment were heavily damaged. But it was Baga that got the worst of our air raids. In one swoop, just before the commencement of both the land and amphibian attacks, more than twenty vehicles belonging to the Boko Haram were destroyed alongside tons of ammunition which had been stored in some warehouses near the shore of the lake that were normally used to store fishes.

After the serious 'softening of the ground' by our airforce, the Boko Haram were no match for our ground forces. Though the battle was severe for the first few hours at the Doron Baga/Baga junction, our forces soon had an upper hand and rolled over the remaining insurgents who could not escape through their usual route across Lake Chad. The insurgents suffered a large casualty including four Libyan mercenaries who had been actively coordinating their attacks. The discovery of the mercenaries had finally confirmed the rumours that had been trending for a while that most of the superior fire power usually credited to the Boko Haram boys were the handiwork of their hired mercenaries mostly from Libya and Iraq.

Our troops liberated Baga four days after our second attempt. The Battle of Baga was very expensive, the operation was worth every money spent. Apart from helping us to cut off the insurgents from the very lucrative fish market by the shores of Lake Chad through which they got money to prosecute the insurgency, the battle also confirmed the long-held belief that the insurgents having been using the services of mercenaries for a very long time. This, revelation guided our future operations.

Hours after we had liberated Baga from the Boko Haram, the insurgents deployed propaganda to deny that they lost. We also learnt from intelligence reports that the insurgents had mined the town with about 1000 mines. That was why our CC still ordered that we should shell the town as we tried to negotiate our ways round the mines when we entered the town the following morning. As we entered the small town, the remaining citizens took to their heels. Some of them particularly, the young and able- bodied ones were probably scared that they would be arrested on the suspicion of having aided the insurgents. After all the confusion and the shooting had come to an end, we saw many dead bodies of the insurgents and civilians littering the dusty streets.

Though we had fully occupied the town, we still had to go from house to house on a 'mopping up' operation just to make sure that we did not make the mistake we made the last time we routed out the insurgents without confirming that they had been totally decimated. Leading the slow and equally dangerous 'house to house' search were members of the Civilian JTF who were very familiar with the terrain and the people. I was very impressed that despite the casualties suffered during our first and second operations on the Baga, these courageous young men were still eager to help us.

In view of this, I was unhappy to later read in some newspapers that some international humanitarian agencies lambasted us for what they regarded as our high handedness in the prosecution of the Baga war. It was the belief of some of the agencies that our use of a lethal combination of amphibian, air and ground attack on a small fishing town such as Baga – a densely populated town less than two square kilometres in size, with a population of just 300,000 was unnecessary.

As the spokesperson for one of the agencies argued, "I am shocked by the violence and intensity of this attack, where several cluster bombs, about 25 per cent of which did not detonate were dropped. Apart from the huge environmental degradation that would follow many years later, the hills and valleys of this very rich agricultural region will continue to be a killing field to many farmers and their families through these undetonated bombs."

To drive home his point, the spokesperson used

the Southeast Asian country of Laos as an example. According to him, " Laos has the unenviable distinction of being, per capita, the most heavily bombed country in the world. An average of one ton per citizen was dropped between 1964 and 1973. This included some 288m cluster bombs, about 30 per cent of which did not explode on impact. Forty-five years after the bombing stopped, the hills and valleys of northern and eastern Laos are peppered with live ordnance that continues to kill and maim farmers and their families. For many years after the war, the land was so heavily mined that much of it could not be cultivated."

To add to the confusion about the fight against the insurgency, some northern elites were also of the belief that the government is not sincere with efforts to tackle Boko Haram especially with its military approach. They see this as a deliberate attempt to destroy the North and its economy given that only innocent people are being killed by our forces. What they perceive as the best solution to the crisis is the declaration of an amnesty for Boko Haram members, similar to that of the Niger Delta.

The extent of the insurgency problem was further brought to light when the President shockingly announced that 'some sponsors and sympathisers' of Boko Haram are in the executive, legislative and judiciary arm of his government. Given the increasing sophistication of the attacks of the group, many Nigerians agreed with the President. But the government failed to publicly identify and prosecute the elites in government circles who have direct or indirect connections with the insurgents. This is even though some Boko Haram members have mentioned some names within the circles of the Nigerian elite. Besides, it was equally unclear if justice would be done on a few politicians that have been arrested for their links with Boko Haram because of the corruption and hijacking of the Nigerian judiciary. The counter-terrorism effort of the government is also being challenged by humanitarian concerns from domestic and international quarters. There were mounting criticisms by human rights organisations, international organisations, and western nations over the casualties of the anti-terror activities of our Joint Task Force (JTF) in northern Nigeria. In one of its recent reports, Amnesty International raised concerns about the 'unlawful killings, dragnet arrests, arbitrary and unlawful detentions, extortion and intimidation' by JTF in Borno State in its war on terror.

Earlier, the local National Human Rights Commission has complained about extrajudicial executions in the ongoing war on terror. Consequently, reports suggested that there had been a great deal of migration of people from the conflict zones for fear of killings and arrests by JTF. A migrant told a local newspaper, "We want to leave because yesterday morning, military men came shooting in our places. A woman was hit by a stray bullet in her breast. We don't know where to go…Nobody is cautioning the JTF, they arrest anybody and have been breaking into our houses."

As a patriotic soldier who has suffered a lot in my bid to save my fatherland from terrorists, I always found it very painful anytime our well-planned military action in Baga is criticised. Human Rights Watch and the United States Government, for example, were not happy with the attack. It was reported that the United States withdrew its military assistance following the outcome of the raid. As a spokesperson of the Human Rights Watch was quoted as saying, "It is very unfortunate that the Baga military operation whereby the Nigerian Military tried to dislodge the Boko Haram insurgents claimed over 187 lives who are mostly civilians including the loss of several properties,"

I wondered where these same groups of critics were when Boko Haram was busy decimating hundreds of villages and towns in the name of Jihad. Rather than worry about the hundreds of land mines that the Boko Haram had reportedly planted in the small 2 square mile town as well as its lethal implication to the civilian population, it is worrisome that what irked these 'humanitarian agencies' was our legitimate efforts to get rid of the insurgents.

However, it was gratifying to see that out of the whole lot, Amnesty International seems to have done favourably well with well balanced reports especially on the decimation of Baga by the insurgents, "Satellite images released by Amnesty International today provide indisputable and shocking evidence of the scale of recent attacks on the towns of Baga and Doron Baga by Boko Haram militants. The detailed images showed devastation of catastrophic proportions in two towns, one of which was almost wiped off the map in the space of four days. Of all Boko Haram assaults analysed by Amnesty International, this is the largest and most destructive yet. It represents a deliberate attack on civilians whose homes, clinics and schools are now burnt-out ruins.

The organization also explained the serious refugee problem that accompanied the incident: "Thousands of people have fled the violence across the border to Chad and to other parts of Nigeria including Maiduguri, the capital of Borno State. These people are adding to the hundreds of thousands of internally displaced people and refugees, who have already stretched the capacity of host communities and government authorities. Amnesty International is calling on the governments of Nigeria and Chad to ensure these displaced people are protected and provided with adequate humanitarian assistance."

With my experience as a soldier, I had come to the sad conclusion that people really don't know about the truth about war. They knew nothing about the ordeals we go through as soldiers, the tumults in our hearts. Both sides of opinion on the Boko haram war shared a suspicion, of each other. Unfortunately, while the war was fought by the children of the poor, of farmers, mechanics, and construction workers, the elite promoted an uninformed, diversionary public debate.

The establishment that sent us to fight the Boko Haram did not send its sons and daughters. In fact, the children of the establishment, just like their fathers, had joined the class of the cynics with a very bad impression of the war as well as the soldiers who are fighting the war. Many of these pampered children see us as expendables, disposable materials or canon fodder for the comfort of the establishment and their offspring.

Whatever may be the views of analysts on the Battle of Baga, or the whole Boko Haram operation, what is clear is that I, Lance Corporal Bukar Jabbie Salisu, just like Nigeria, had now become another impotent victim of the saga. And while Nigeria had enough money and time to tackle her own political impotence, money and time were not my friends in solving my own sexual impotence. That was when I resolved that even though I would remain a patriotic Nigerian, I would be on the lookout for anything from the war that I can use to improve my lot and that of my family, most especially, to solve my current sexual handicap.

My thoughts were interrupted by the voice of the Company Commander when he ordered me to see him in his room.

"Bukar or ECOMOG or whatever you are called," he said smiling.

"You can call me ECOMOG sir," I said as I smiled back at him.

"I am very impressed with your performance. You are a real professional soldier. If you continue this way, you will go far."

"Thank you sir."

"Although we have officially come to the ned of our operations here in Baga, I have instructions from Maiduguri to keep the Company here to protect Baga. We don't want to make the same mistake we made the other time when we left town or kept just a Platoon of thirty soldiers behind only for the Boko boys to take over the town. You have done very well, and I will retain you as my ADC."

"Thank you sir." I saluted.

"Good. Now, you know that there is not much money in this our Military duty except, perhaps those who involve themselves with criminal activities such as extortion, inflation of invoices or pilfering of soldiers' allowances. All these I cannot do."

"Correct sir," I said.

"Good. Baga is known for fish. There used to be a very thriving fish market here known all over this area as well as Chad and Niger republic. In fact, the main reason why the Boko haram insurgents have been interested in Baga is because of the fish business. That is what they have been selling to fund their nefarious activity. Unfortunately, since the onset of the insurgency, normal fishing activities have not been possible except for the Boko Haram who has been stealing the fish. Now that we have routed them out, I have orders from Abuja to allow the normal fishing activities to resume, you get me?"

I nodded in agreement.

"What I want to do is to constitute a small Task Force to coordinate the activities of the local fishermen to make the fishing activities orderly and smooth. However, apart from the fish which the fishermen have promised to be providing for the soldiers' meals, they also want me to be part of the fishing business. I have been assured that the business is very lawful and lucrative, you get me?"

"Yes sir," I said, a bit uneasy.

"Good. In view of my busy schedule, you will be my link man with the fishermen, you get me?"

"Yes…Yes…sir." I stuttered.

"Good. So tonight, by ten o clock you will come back here for a meeting with the representatives of the Fishermen to discuss the details of the business, you get me?"

"Yes sir," I said as I remembered that I needed money for my surgical operation.

Chapter Thirteen

We fortified our camp in Baga with a high barbed-wire fence followed by a six feet deep perimeter ditch. Mounted at every corner of the Barracks on 20 feet high platforms were powerful searchlight which could sweep the surrounding countryside as well as the calm and sedate Lake Chad. Equally mounted but discreetly covered with camouflages and tarpaulin sheets where big mortar guns which could blast any object more than 800 metres away. Even though we had completely routed out the Boko Haram insurgents from the town, we were not taking any chances. We had been inundated with stories of how they had, on many occasions, sprung surprise attacks from various hideouts on the outlying islands on Lake Chad. Though things appeared to be very quiet in the town, our CC insisted that we familiarise ourselves with the partially empty town.

The following day, we made a quick tour of Baga and the smaller fishing town of Doron Baga by the edge of Lake Chad, in the northeastern part of Borno State, Nigeria. As we did, I noticed in the far distance, a hovering mist above the early morning sun that gave a magical appearance to a handsome but humble town with its adorable lake. Our first visit was to the Duguri and Dabar-Wanzam fishing communities and settlements, both in Baga town where we learnt that over thirty persons died as several others sustained gunshot injuries in the onslaught.

As we went round the fishing communities with their huts and corrugated roofed houses, the few remaining citizens, mostly fishermen who were still in town greeted us warmly. The morning was warm and clear, the sky blue, so also was the lake. Even at that early hour, the beach was already active with some swimmers, fishermen and fish traders.

In a stretch of the long white beach, some boys were playing soccer. Their ball strayed to where I was standing. I picked it, toss it up and kicked it back with an old instep I learnt several years ago. The ball flew into the air in the direction of the boys. I turned back to my solitude sentry duty, watching as a nearby fishing trawler as it offloaded its cargo of fishes. A young man approached me; he wanted me to buy some fish. I politely declined. Another one came, a photographer. I posed with the fishermen and some traders, my feet in the warm, salty lake smiling faintly, knowing full well that I had to hurry up.

Sitting round an abandoned old boat, some fishermen were resting while others were repairing their fishing nets in preparation for another nocturnal trip. "The fishermen prefer to work all night and bring in their catch in time for the fish market the following day," a fish trader whom we met at the beach said. From him we learnt of the insurgents' hideout: several high-density islands on Lake Chad.

"You also need to visit those Islands and secure them against the possibilities of any attack," he added. The Islands mentioned included Madari; Mari, Kaukiri, Duguri, Shuwaram, Kirta-Wulgo, Kwallaram and Dabar Masara. According to our informant, after our last attack, the insurgents fled into the islands. He wanted us to continue its pursuit to eliminate them and make the place safe and forestall the possibilities of their using those islands as launching pads for future attacks on Baga.

Our CC was prepared to match unto the island immediately, some of the Civilian JTF boys in our team advised us to inform Maiduguri before setting out because of the possibilities of running into the insurgents and suffering another bloody encounter. Another member advised us to also seek for the support of our Air Force because of the prevalence of a species of cattail reed called kachalla on the lake which might make movement difficult for boats to be used to convey our troops.

While awaiting the response for our requests for a reconnaince to the Lake Chad Islands as well as air cover, my CC proceeded with the meeting with the fishermen whose means of livelihood were disrupted by the insurgents. The fishermen's leader, Mallam Ado Abdulahi who is the Chairman of the Association of

Nigerian Fishermen, Lake Chad Basin chapter, was in his forties. He commended our troops for reclaiming Baga and other communities in northern Borno. Abdulahi who was among thousands of persons displaced by the recent conflict, said that the military demonstrated valor and professionalism to oust the insurgents, leading to the liberation of communities in northern Borno and Lake Chad region. He acknowledged that thirty of his members died during the encounter but urged the military to take the fight to various Islands in the Lake Chad, where the insurgents had fled during the encounter to clear remnants of the criminals hibernating in the area and end the insurgency.

According to the Chairman of the Fishermen, "Fishing is important to Doron Baga as well as the northeast regional economy. From the local market in Borno, fish is transported across the country and into neighbouring markets in Cameroon, Niger and Chad, whose borders converge at the lake. The prolonged insurgency has, however, led to a dramatic decline in the abundance of artisanal fishermen in the region. Fishing communities along the Lake Chad basin have suffered an exodus of fishermen and fish traders to presumably safer havens within and outside the country. Boko Haram lurks on the lake and when they do not kill us, they take 10,000 naira to allow us to fish. With the insurgency in the area, fishing is fast becoming a struggle. Our men must sail in secret, forced to evade both Boko Haram jihadists. Even, the military don't spare us as they usually accuse us of helping the insurgents to fund their criminal acts through the taxes and levies that we pay them. Since the beginning of the hostilities, more than 200 fishing towns have been razed by the jihadists.

At the peak of the insurgency between 2013 and 2014 Boko Haram reigned controlled the lake. That prompted the authorities from Niger, Chad and Nigeria to place embargo on fishing in an attempt to cut off the insurgents' economic supply lines. We are now happy that the army has regained control of most territories, forcing the jihadists to retreat further into the lake, a difficult terrain to access. But we need your cooperation in making sure that the insurgents are not allowed to return to harass us again," he noted.

The Chairman of fish traders lamented on how the insurgency had crippled an otherwise very lucrative business. "In the past, more than 200 trucks would leave Baga to supply markets all over the country, reaching as far as Lagos and Port Harcourt, Nigeria's southern megacities. By 2016, thanks to the official reopening of the Baga market and the resumption of traffic along some key highways of Borno state, it appeared that some normalcy was returning to daily life. But my members are complaining now that the army and local authorities are conniving to extort them. My members have reported cases of soldiers who seized their fish stocks transported by road. The traders also accused the authorities of harming their trade by forcing them to fix prohibitive prices on the commodity from the Lake Chad area. I am asking the government to intervene and reverse the trend so that we would not be forced to abandon the business. During the occupation of Baga by the insurgents, ISWAP did everything possible to neutralise the market by creating two major fish markets outside Nigeria, one in Kusiri in Chad, while Nigerian traders mostly from Southeastern Nigeria now access through Mubi in Adamawa state. The second fish market created by the group is in Kinchhandi in Niger Republic where traders from Hadeija in Jigawa and Kano states access for their market stocks.

In his response, our Company Commander thanked the fishermen, traders, and other citizens of Baga for their support to the Military as well as their understanding of the situation on the ground. He traced the causes of the Nigerian government's decision to close Baga-Maiduguri route in 2014 and to reopen same some years later and in the process raising once again, the hopes of stakeholders in the fish business.

On the accusation of new and excessive taxation, Major Isyaku said that the officials he spoke to confirmed that the cost is justified because of the added cost of security escorts in the volatile environment.

After the meeting, we decided to visit the Doron Baga fish market which is located about six kilometres from Baga town. We learnt that the market used to be the biggest fish market in the West African subregion. The volume of traffic from Doron Baga to Maiduguri and other parts of Nigeria was determined by the fishing seasons and market days of the settlements along the Nigerian shores of Lake Chad. On the market days, multi million nairas worth of cartons and sacks, are moved through trucks to Maiduguri and then to Lagos, Enugu, Ibadan, Onitsha, and Ilorin. Financial analysts estimated the monthly value of Borno fish industry at N1.4 billion. According to the United Nations Food and Agriculture Organization, the industry produces up to 100,000 tonnes of fish annually and was valued at as much as $220 million at its peak.

It was at the market that the CC introduced me to the Chairman of the Fishermen Association. The Chairman fixed a meeting between the two of us later that evening. "I will be in a grey Golf car in front of the Army Barracks by ten," he said.

As we departed the Fish Market, I was accosted by one of the fishermen, a middle-aged man. He had the moderate version of the Shagari cap. His oblong face created ample space for the lines of Kanuri tribal marks which melded well with his very dark complexion.

"Oga Soja,"

"Yes, what can I do for you?"

"*Don Allah*, I want to discuss something important with you," he said. "It's about my wife."

I saw the earnestness written on his face, but felt that the occasion, time and venue was not right.

"OK can we see tomorrow by that kiosk over there?" I said and gestured towards the kiosk.

"*Toh, nagode*," he said, looking less agitated.

The appointed time came. He uttered a second *nagode* and went straight to business.

"My name is Aminu Kolo. I lost my livelihood and home when Boko Haram sacked my community here in Baga and abducted my wife, whom they whisked away to their enclave in Sambisa Forest. She was later rescued in 2016 when the military launched battles against them. To my shame and embarrassment, she returned with child. It broke my heart to find out that besides the two-year-old child with her, my wife was four months pregnant for her Boko Haram husband. To further humiliate me, three weeks after she returned home, *shaytan* took over my wife's heart and she fled back to the forest to live with the man," Aminu narrated.

"My wife made me a laughingstock. While I struggled to make peace with my agony and take her back, she was dying to return to the insurgent who kept her as a sex captive and impregnated her. One day, while I was on a fishing expedition, she stole the N30,000 I saved from my petty fish trade. It was everything I had. And she absconded from home. She left a note with a neighbour's wife, promising that her Boko Haram husband would refund the money and the dowry I paid on her. She said she could no longer survive on my meagre earnings from fish," said Aminu who now begged me to help him get a civilian job in our barracks as a cleaner so he could make enough money to return to his fishing business. I was deeply moved by the poor man's story and was able to convince my CC to hire him in our camp as a cleaner.

I was surprised to learn that Aminu's story was a very common tale in Baga and indeed, the whole of the Northeast. Apart from their penchant to loot and kill, the insurgents have also specialized in the abduction of young women as sex slaves. The pitiful thing is that even after being rescued, some of these women still prefer to go back to their Boko Haram husbands whom they usually claimed pampered and treated them better than their former husbands.

When I asked why the women behaved that way even to their real husbands, I was informed that in addition to being pampered with money and gifts, some of those women are usually indoctrinated into religious bigotry.

As we awaited the permission to carry out a reconnaissance on the outlying islands on Lake Chad to checkmate the activities of the Boko Haram, there wasn't much to do in Baga. I had never been so happy and relaxed since I joined the army. For the first time in my adult life, I was able to appreciate the early morning dew, the smell of flowers, as well as the warm evening breeze by the lake side. I had two things any soldier needed to keep him happy: good food and rest. It may not be much, but at the battlefront, it meant so much to us.

Unfortunately, too much of anything, including the good things of life is bad. It is also easy to get used to anything, even, the good life. Which can be dangerous for a soldier. Before now, natural things such as the darkness and the wind were taken with utmost caution, I now took them for granted. Sounds and smells that were supposed to warn us of danger have also been forgotten. Rather than the previous state of alertness, all I now felt was the warm sea breeze as it caressed my face and soothed my lungs. Instead of mortars and guns, what I saw were images of girls, fields of flowers, and white clouds. The evenings no longer brought the terror of invisible enemies, bullets and mortars but the chirping of birds, aroma of delicious food and the perfume of beautiful women. Fearful that we would become rustic and careless, our Commander organised some activities to keep us in shape. That was how we soon fell into a routine of exercises, parades, guard duties and relaxation. The news of the return of peace and security to Baga had gone round the surrounding towns and villages including Maiduguri even up to nearby Niger, Cameroon and Chad. Before long, many of the natives and foreigners started trooping back to the fishing town, while previously locked restaurants, pubs, night clubs and brothels resumed operation.

As Planned, I had a meeting with the Chairman of the Fishermen Association, Mallam Ado Abdulahi later that night. The businessman, in his late forties was expensively dressed in a casual French suit made of an expensive looking material. In his breast pocket were pens of different colours. He wore a gold necklace with a pendant shaped like the Nigerian Coat of Arms. The same also adorned one of his fingers among other rings. Ado who claimed to have a Nigerian father and a Chadian mother also spoke French.

Ado told me he had been in the fishing business for the past twenty years and that despite the three-year-ban on fishing in the region, he was never out of business.

"Despite the ban, I was able to build an expensive house in Chad, my mother's hometown. Even here in Baga, when most people including the army could not afford fuel to operate their generating plants and vehicles, I managed to generate electricity in my house twenty-four hours a day. I also have twenty trailers apart from my personal cars which have always remained on the road no matter the security situation in this region. I have been able to get by all these years because of my good links with the Military, Customs and to some extent even the Boko Haram boys…"

"Boko Haram?" I asked

"Well… yes, actually what I mean is that since I pay whatever tax they demand from me, they leave me alone," he added before finally asking me for the Bank account number for the remittance of the Company Commander's agreed allowance which I supplied. I was taken aback when he told me not to hesitate to let him know my own personal needs, as he was willing to settle them. As if to prove his point, he handed me a box of provision for my personal use. At the top of the box was a bulky, brown envelope.

"Help me manage this," he said, "I should have taken you somewhere to for dinner, but I have to hurry up to see off my boats going out for their usual all night fishing expedition." I thanked him.

"What time would they be back?" I asked, eager to see the fishermen when they brought in their catch in the morning.

"About four in the morning." "I can send my driver to come and pick you around that time tomorrow in case you wish to have a look."

After obtaining permission from the CC, I was up by four o'clock the following morning for the trip in Alhaji Abdullahi's car to watch the fishing boats as they made their way back to shore. It is easy to fall in love with Baga and her lovely white beaches that ran along the wide blue waters of the sedate and languid Lake Chad. At that hour, in the distant glow of the moon, I saw the fishing boats spread on the sea like black butterflies on an apple yard as the fishermen returned from their nightly duties. Occasionally, the echoes of their voices and nocturnal activities came to me in my vantage position not far from the beach. Sometimes I stayed up far into the night just to watch the boats as they roamed about the lake. In the past, they would have been afraid of Boko Haram insurgents who lurked in the fringes of the lake. Today also, they were spared the occasional heavy rains and storms. To see the fishing boats out on the lake with their sails bellowed by the wind under the full glow of the midnight moon was one of the most moving experiences of my stay in Baga. I often became completely absorbed as I watched the interplay of gentle lights and translucent shadows as they danced together on the surface of the lake so much so that I sometimes forgot that I was a soldier fighting a war and not a tourist on a vacation. I was still transfixed with awe when, in the light of daybreak, the boats arrived the beach to deposit their huge harvest of fish. The haul was amazing, at least to me: catfish, tilapia, sardines, lobsters, kingfish, rockcod, red and blue snapper as well as prawns and squids. I soon made friends with the fishermen and was allowed to pose for photographs with a lovely looking catch.

The following week, we got signals for the assault on the outlying Islands of Madari; Mari, Kaukiri, Duguri, Shuwaram, Kirta-Wulgo, Kwallaram and Dabar Masara on Lake Chad where remnants of the insurgents are belived to be hiding. It was a light, grey, early morning when we lined up at the waterfront as Major Isyaku Biu addressed us.

"In a few minutes time, the aerial bombardment of some of the high-density Islands on Lake Chad will commence by our Air Force. The purpose of the operation is to clear remnants of the criminals hibernating in the area and bring this insurgency to an end. We have resorted to the aerial battle for two reasons. First, the insurgents are more familiar with the terrain more than us, as such, a purely ground battle may be to our disadvantage. Secondly, the presence of the popular reed *Kachalla* on the lake may make a purely amphibian assault very slow, therefore, there is the need for a softening of our enemies' positions through aerial bombardment. In order to reduce the number of human casualties, we have sent out undercover agents to encourage the people especially the fishermen and traders to stay off the Islands for today. To have the best possible impact on the insurgents, we shall proceed immediately by motorboats and stop midway to our destination for about 30 minutes to allow the air bombardment to commence thereafter, we shall proceed to complete our assignment."

We got on the motorboats which glided smoothly on the placid lake. Far into the horizon was a lovely and calm turquoise blue lake while overhead, a column of dainty white sea birds with golden beaks flew gracefully. It was as if they were aware of our mission and had been assigned the dignifying duty of escorting us on our perilous journey. Moments later, we chanced upon columns of fishermen who gaily waved to us from their small and fragile looking boats. It was obvious that they were praying for us, judging from their supinated palms and quietly moving lips. We also passed some tiny strips of Islands hemmed by water so clear you would think you were cruising on a river. As the journey progressed, some craggy mountains and sheltered bays with seductive looking white beaches emerged one after the other from the midday mist. We remained alert as we peered into the surrounding vast emptiness of water clinging tenaciously to our arms bathed in the rarefied sea air in the swaying boats. For a while, the horizon emptied out with nothing in sight for miles. We were like this for a while when suddenly, a thread of distant land materialized out of the mist as some of the islands came into view. That was when the Commander gave the order for us to cut the engines of the boats as we floated in the quiet vastness of water. All was quiet for a while before we heard the distant overhead rumble of engines and before long, two of our aircrafts came into view. They soon thundered over us then swooped down ahead of us to release their lethal loads. The resultant explosions quacked the surrounding serenity as columns of fire, earth and water erupted. Twice the aircrafts dived and twice the earth and sea quaked.

Mission accomplished, the two *Jirgin Sama* returned to their bases. That was when our boats cracked to life as we sped towards the ruins, us guns at the ready. The advancing boats had some snipers standing on the bows, their machine guns fitted with telescopic sights as directed by our Technical Advisers three of whom were in the boats with us. Ever so often a shot rang out from our snipers as they picked out the insurgents from that far distance. The machine-guns are rattled away, and I saw some dark figures falling into the water as shell fire erupted from another set of islands. We quickly slipped into the water, our helmets right on the back of our necks and our mouths only sufficiently above water to let us breathe. Amidst the hail of shell fire and machine guns, our boats reached the first set of islands, and we wade across the water onto dry land.

A few minutes later, we were in the heart of the

Islands. And as the midday afternoon sun filtered through the fishing huts and mud houses, we ran through the narrow streets in the hot humid weather firing our gun batteries. We ran as fast as our feet could carry us as the shells continued to fall with dull thundering noise. I was glad that I was fit as my limbs carried me on even though I was panting with a lot of effort. The situation changed as the crash of shells pounded against my ears as remnants of the jihadists now launched a counter-offensive. I quickly dived into the earth as the dull thunder-like distant explosions flew above my head. We increased our gunfire as the bullets hissed, and the shells growled over our heads. The insurgents took to their heels, but the gunfire continued in pursuit for a while then gradually died off. Numbed with exhaustion, hunger but happiness we finished mopping up the Islands and headed back to our camp in Baga.

To celebrate our victory, the Commander allowed us to go out for two hours just to let off steam. Aware of my predicament, I didn't want to follow the others, but my buddy, Hassan would not have it.

"Come on ECOMOG, you deserve some fun after today's hard work," he shouted in the presence of other soldiers. To avoid being termed antisocial, I joined them as we walked towards the middle of the town where the night clubs and drinking joints were located. We were so happy with our victory that we started drinking even before eating the rice and stew that the grateful and impressed hotelier had provided for us. Then somebody put on a popular fast paced music. As we danced, some girls, whom we were told came from Cameroon, joined us. We did not understand French, but it didn't stop us from enjoying the seductive way in which they danced. We were soon all giddy with drink and lust and before I knew it, the other soldiers had disappeared into some rooms with the girls. I was now left on the dance floor with a thin and light complexioned energetic dancer. She laughed a lot and as she danced, her short skirt was blown by the overhead fan to expose a lot of her seductive thighs. I warmed up to her as I hugged and kissed her. She held me tighter and returned my kiss. Her light skin glowed under the fluorescent lights while from her mouth came words that I couldn't understand.

Though a trained soldier who could handle and dismantle all forms of lethal weapons, who could organise a column of soldiers to liberate a town from the grips of despicable terrorists, I found this woman business a difficult one to execute. A business that does not warrant any thinking or special training nor any further training. I gave up resisting the pressure of her dainty red lips on my own, so I closed my eyes and allowed myself to be further drawn into her arms hoping that the generous dose of *burantashi* which I had taken earlier in the day would save me from the impending shame and humiliation.

Thinking that I was only being shy or naive, the Cameroonian girl continued to whisper words of encouragement into my ears alternated with seductive narratives that her many years of professional work had taught her. However, frustrated by my solitude and cold response she had shouted over the din of the music, *"Comprenez-vous Francais?"*

When I shook my head, she grabbed my hand and steered me towards one of the rooms behind the bar. And as we moved down the corridor, I caught sight of two of my friends in the half- lit rooms they had earlier entered. That was when I panicked. Like a goat being led to a slaughter slab, I tried to wring my hands away from the Cameroonian girl so I could flee before my handicap became known, before the whole Command got to know that I am a real *rafto*. Eager to make some money just as her other friends, the girl would not let me go. She must have been one of those whores who believed in their skills and abilities to stimulate and give courage to the timid or stimulate the unaroused. And despite the generous dose of *burantashi* which I had drank before coming to the club, I remained unarousable and allowed myself to sink into the unknown.

CHAPTER FOURTEEN

I met my sisters Zaynab and Rabia as promised at the lobby of the Halima Hotel, Maiduguri where I had accompanied my Commander Major Isyaku Biu to the integration ceremony of the newly repentant Boko Haram members. It was a few days after our victorious routing of the Boko Haram insurgents on the Lake Chad when my Commander intimated me about the Federal Government programme scheduled for Maiduguri the following week. "I have been invited and I want you to accompany me to the ceremony," he said and referred me to the headlines in one of the major newspapers of the day:

REPENTANT BOKO HARAM MEMBERS
ARRIVE MAIDUGURI.

My excitement grew stronger as I continued with the story which was prominently reported by other major newspapers: *"Some repentant Boko Haram members have arrived Maiduguri, the Borno State capital, after being set free by the Nigerian government. The released Boko Haram members include men, women, and children, who recently surrendered to troops in Niger Republic. The 'former terrorists' arrived Maiduguri airport in a military aircraft, in the company of soldiers led by a Major General who is the coordinator of the Federal Government programme on the rehabilitation of repentant insurgents."*

Although I had been in the front line of those who were eager to forgive repentant Boko Haram insurgents, I never imagined that the Federal Government would go as far making their reprieve such a big issue. I was further irked when the newspaper reported that huge amount of money had been expended on the former jihadists. *"The repentant terrorists were trained by the Nigerian Army wing charged with the responsibility of their reformation. They were rehabilitated by instructors from departments and agencies from the Federal Government and the National Directorate of Employment (NDE) with the aim of retraining them to become law abiding citizens. During the training, the ex-terrorists were engaged in therapy and activities including psychotherapy, psycho spiritual and counselling, adverse effects of drug addiction among several others. The coordinator of the program also added that the ex-terrorists were also empowered with vocational training such as barbing, shoe making/leather works and cosmetology which composed of the preparation of body cream, perfume, and liquid soap among others. The trainees were enthusiastic about their skill acquisition programme, and they are looking forward to practicing their trades after discharge from the camp. They are to further their training with NDE in their state of residence to enhance smooth reintegration."*

When I expressed my opinion that the training program was too expensive and that the rehabilitation exercises a bit premature since the war against the insurgents was still on, my boss disagreed with me.

"I don't see anything wrong with the idea. As someone who had previously interrogated some of the insurgents, I discovered that it was not all of them that became terrorists on their own volition. While some of them are religious extremists, others were coerced into the insurgency and yet others were financially induced to join. The information from the Army Headquarters revealed that most of the persons released were not actually Boko Haram members but were relatives of terrorists or persons found in the wrong place at the wrong time. It is therefore necessary to treat everyone on their own merit."

"But sir, how are we sure that these so-called converts have truly repented and how would the families of their victims feel when they see the same people who killed their relatives now roaming free in the society?" I questioned.

"The former insurgents have confessed their past misdeeds, denounced their memberships of the group, asked for forgiveness and taken oaths of allegiance to Nigeria. I believe they are now good citizens. I do... What the Nigerian Government has done, is a globally accepted practice. During your training in Zaria, were you not taught how countries like South Africa, Vietnam and Rwanda among other countries who went through cases of genocide and civil wars handled their post war rehabilitation issues?" He asked.

When I replied that we were not, the CC then went on to give me a lecture on the Truth Commissions set up by South Africa and Rwanda among other countries that also experienced the kind of problem Nigeria went through.

"The case of Rwanda is even very apt. After the horrendous genocide between the Tutsi and Hutu, the country in 2008 established the National Unity and Reconciliation Commission with a mission to promote unity, reconciliation, and social cohesion among Rwandans and build a country in which everyone had equal rights and contributing to good governance. At the end of the day, the Commission was able to prepare and coordinate the national programs aimed at promoting national unity and reconciliation, including mechanisms for restoring and strengthening the Unity and Reconciliation of Rwandans and of educating, sensitizing, and mobilizing the population in areas of national unity and reconciliation. These are the same things Nigeria is trying to achieve with the policy of reintegration of repentant Boko haram insurgents," he concluded.

At the opening ceremony of the two -day event at the well fortified Halima Hotel, a short distance from the Maimalari barracks, the representative of the President in welcoming guests to the ceremony, gave a background regarding the repentant insurgents,

"We have just delivered 25 persons, comprising men, women, and children. The former Boko Haram members laid down arms and surrendered to the Niger republic government, who contacted the Nigerian government to take them home. So, we have brought them home safely and brought them here as part of the government's de-radicalization programme. Out of the 254 repented Boko Haram members treated, 95 have already been handed over to their respective states while the remaining 157 reintegrated members would soon be dispatched as follows: Adamawa will receive three persons, Yobe seven and Borno 143. Three persons are from Chad Republic." I noted inconsistencies in the numbers but was too disenchanted to worry about that.

The Borno State Government also weighed in and pledged to provide the returnees with psycho-social support, food, clothe, and platform for skills acquisitions that will enable them to gain skills before they are reunited with their families."

Once I was able to confirm that I would be accompanying my CC on the trip to Maiduguri, I had quickly contacted Zaynab and Rabia who had been itching to see me to discuss my problem which they said, Jewel mentioned to them. I had a very emotional encounter with my sisters when we finally met during the lunch break on the first day. Since they knew I had a problem, I quickly intimated them with the details including my last visit to the surgeon in Kano.

"If the Surgeon who removed the bullet confirmed

that the bullet did not hit the nerve, why then are you having this problem," a teary faced Zaynab asked.

"That was what he said but after the test carried out by the Kano Surgeon, it was confirmed that the nerve was partially damaged either by the bullet or during the process of removing the bullet," I said.

"Apart from another operation, is there no other way the problem can be addressed?" Zaynab asked again, sounding desperate.

"According to the Surgeon, there is no other way except through surgery. Even Uncle Kassim also thought that there could be another way, that was why he referred me to his trusted herbalist Mallam Askira. Unfortunately, that one too could not effect any positive change." I noted.

"Jewel also confirmed that surgery is the only solution and...." Rabia said as she was interrupted by Zaynab's phone that suddenly rang out. It was my mother calling from Monrovia. Since the inception of our discussion, Zaynab had been trying to reach her. She was in tears as she said, "My son, Jabbie, is it true what Jewel and your sisters have said?"

When I replied in the affirmative, she burst into another spate of tears, "Ha, my God, how can this horrible thing happen to me? My only son? Who will now carry your family's name and heritage?" she sobbed before passing the phone to Jewel. I had expected Jewel to also launch into another sobbing episode but to my surprise, she spoke calm, loving way.

"Darling Jabbie, please don't be disturbed. God is in control. Aunty Emine has made arrangements with a visiting top American Surgeon to help you. Just relax. All will be well," she said. Those were not words; they were a balm to my soul.

"I informed a visiting Surgeon form the US who currently works at the JF Kennedy Medical Centre about your condition. He promised to help if we can afford the treatment," Fatima said when she came on the phone.

"How much will it cost?" I asked.

"I don't know the Naira equivalent, but it is 25,000 in US dollars."

Not too sure of what the Naira equivalent would be, I brought the conversation to an end with the promise to get back to my sister. As soon as I finished the converstaion, I quickly brought out my phone and punched the calculator to get a Naira equivalent of N9m at the current exchange rate. A sudden depressing wave hit me. I suddenly felt like fainting. N9m almost the equivalent of my four years salary. Then, I remembered Alhaji Abdulallahi and his promise. I felt relieved and started breathing normally again.

Unlike the first, the second day of the Maiduguri Conference unlike the placid and calm first day, began on a very riotoous note when a Bill for the establishment of a National Agency for Repentant Insurgents was mentioned by a participant. According to the delegate, since the Boko Haram insurgency was becoming increasingly marked by extreme brutality on both soldiers and civilians, it was expedient and instructive to go back to the drawing board and adopt an alternative approach complement the military option.

"There is the need for a more strategic and comprehensive approach to entice those members of the group who, after realising the futility of the course they are pursuing have decided to lay down their arms and choose the path of peace. There is no doubt that some members of the group have defected, and many others are willing to repent given a window of opportunity and this has been confirmed by many organisations including non-governmental organisations (NGOs) that have access to them." He noted.

Another delegate who supported the Bill said that "In contrast, those captured in the battlefields will be required to, in addition to the psychological therapy, participate in the criminal justice process. The Bill would provide an avenue for reconciliation and promote national security, provide an-open-door and encouragement for other members of the group who are still engaged in the insurgency to abandon the group, especially in the face of military pressure. It would also provide the government with insider-information on the workings of the group," he stressed.

Hardly had the two supporters of the Bill finished their submissions when the hall erupted into rowdiness as those against the Bill rose to voice their objection. They pointed out that whereas victims of Boko Haram attacks had remained largely neglected in the IDP camps and had become further victims of rape, hunger, malnutrition and other socio-economic vices, the Federal Government has turned its attention to providing safe havens for those whose mission was to kill and maim and cause the many sorrows we are grappling with.

"About 1.7 million people have been displaced in Borno alone. They have caused damage worth an estimated $9.6 billion in Borno alone. About 60,000 children are orphaned. Only God knows how many children are out of school, have no access to water, food and means of livelihood. The humanitarian crisis that is coming after the war may be more dangerous than the war itself. The insurgency is going into its tenth year. Some children haven't been in school in the last ten years and we know what that means," he lamented.

They expressed shock over the proposal, saying whosoever had proposed such a bill to grant amnesty for criminals who killed, maimed, raped, and destroyed innocent peoples lives and property, and threw the country into jeopardy must be thoroughly investigated and probably marked as enemies of the state.

According to them, "If government cannot cater for the direct victims of the Boko Haram or address a yearning of the soldiers that are risking their lives to contain the insurgents, and somebody is talking of how to grant them amnesty. Nigerians must be ready to interrogate the intention of the person that sponsored such a bill."

Some human rights activists cautioned the

proponents of the bill from actively conniving with armed terrorists to introduce a satanic legislation that will overlook the mind-boggling crimes of genocides committed by terrorists in the last ten years, just to appease the same terrorists even as their victims languish in IDP and refugee camps within and outside the country.

"If this bill to legalise the freeing of arrested terror suspects under any guise succeeds, then the nation should be prepared for the consequences of their unconstitutional action because the hundreds of thousands of innocent victims of the terrorists attacks in the last decade will definitely not fold their hands whilst those who killed their loved ones are pardoned through roguish means by the passage of this criminally-minded bill that is meant to legalize mass murder. Nations which had achieved stability and national security are those which have elevated law above political, religious, ethnic sentiments. The present Federal Government must be compelled to advocate national security on the basis of respect of not only individual rights but also the rule of law, but definitely not the appeasement of terrorists. Were we not told that Boko Haram had been technically defeated? From where do we still have this large number that you want commit public funds to de-radicalise? Is this not another means by which they might infiltrate into the civil society and cause more havoc? Government should discourage that kind of arrangement and stop that bill from passing," they added.

The second big problem at the conference occurred

when some of the repentant insurgents were brought into the Conference Hall neatly dressed in glinting new uniforms recently procured for them by the government and given VIP treatment on their way to Maiduguri. According to government officials, the repentant Boko Haram suspects who were about 1,400 had previously been in detention and were only recently released. The officials who justified the policy of reintegration explained that the initiative was only targeted at low-risk Boko Haram members, those who were not captured during combat.

"Those captured in combat are processed for prosecution, but the ones that have not been ideologically indoctrinated because they were conscripted, abducted or coerced, are the ones being rehabilitated. They call them low-risk combatants. Those ones do not buy into Boko Haram agenda; they were forced into it. These repentant members have been assisting the military by providing intelligence on Boko Haram's activities," they explained.

Despite this explanation, a group of Borno elders frowned at the initiative, saying the military's operation was not well thought out. They feared that releasing the purported repentant Boko Haram militants into civilian population could be counterproductive as it would enable hardened fighters to return to the terror group to commit more atrocities. They were of the view that Boko Haram members do not repent, hence the de-radicalization programme may be breeding spies and agents of recruitment for the murderous group. They urged the President to suspend the programme.

Many of the northern elite, especially those whose families, friends and associates had fallen victims of Boko Haram insurgency, were also shocked by the proposed amnesty and were quite apprehensive over government's haste to implement it. They called on Nigerians to further interrogate the ultimate agenda of integrating the Boko Haram suspects into the military.

Their position was, however, at variance with that of some officials in Borno state commended the Federal Government over the rehabilitation and reintegration policy. They said that the community leaders had already been directed to sensitize their people on the need to accept the rehabilitated insurgents and warned against infringement on their rights.

The third upsetting development happened on the second day of the Conference. It was a personal one. After what I considered to be the warm and intimate family discussion over my health with my mother, sisters, and Jewel, I called to request a meeting with the Chairman of The Fishers Association in Baga, Alhaji Abdulahi on my return to Baga the following day in the company of my CC.

"I hope the matter is not a serious one. I hope *Oga* is happy with me?" the businessman with whom I had struck a very close relationship asked.

"*Oga* is very happy with you. The matter is a personal one. I will explain when I come."

Although I had resolved to forget all about women and marriage after the discovery of my impotency, the brief discussion I had had with my family members especially, the love and support I had seen from Jewel had made me to decide to make a last attempt to resolve my problem. I had accepted to take up the offer of the surgical treatment in Liberia. While I was convinced that my CC would readily approve a two-week compassionate leave for me by the virtue of our closeness, I was not sure that he would give me the necessary financial support for the trip. Alhaji Abdulahi was my only hope.

I was in this hopeful and relaxed state of mind when I saw a shadow standing in front of me as I made my way to the restaurant during the lunch break.

"Hello, officer," the figure spoke before I could look up.

"Safiya! What are you doing here?" I asked in a mixed mood of anxiety, fear, and a mild anger

Instead of responding, she laughed in that merry way she always did, seductively squeezing her eyebrows.

"Why are you looking like that?" she asked.

"Like how?"

"You looked frightened, as if I would eat you.

"Why would I be scared of you, when I am not afraid of Boko Haram?" I bragged.

"I thought you will be happy to see me after all these days, but you behaved as if I am not wanted," she observed.

I would have loved to agree with her and tell her

to go away and not to talk to me again, but I found myself getting drawn to the slim, dark Fulani girl and her coquettish ways. To think that I had just assured Jewel that I would see her very soon in Monrovia. Plus, thoughts of money for the expensive operation that would free us from this misery and enable us to love each other the way normal couples do. But now, I am letting myself be taken for another ride when I knew that nothing would come out of it...

"Bukar!"

I did not respond.

She called me again and almost screaming, asked, "What are you thinking?"

"About us and how lucky I am to have you," was what came from my lips but not from my heart.

"Listen, Bukar," she said, half rising. "I don't have much time. I was sent to call somebody. Let's see tonight."

"Where?" I asked trembling with fear and anxiety.

"Here in this hotel. Let's see at 7pm. I am in room 66."

When she saw my startled looks, she said, "Are you not in this hotel?" I shook my head. "The Military can't afford this place. We are all staying at the barracks... but I will come tonight. She was off.

What have I done? I asked myself. Where is the passion? Where is the libido to back up this impending visit? But I have given my word. And so that night, I went as agreed and gave myself over to her. She wore a light pink silk night dress and welcomed me with an embrace that appeared to make time stand still. She was in charge, touching me with all the freedom she knew but instead of pleasure, I felt more pain and fear. I would need a miracle to arouse the the lifeless weight in my bosom. That night, I let her do everything she wanted to do with me, as she made the effort to love me while I tried not to hurt her. Finally, frustrated, her eyes took on that dull shine that you usually see in malaria patients, and she gently pushed me aside.

"I can help you," she blurted.

I told her everything. My first ambush, the gunshot, the bullet, the operation, Mallam Askari and the planned surgery in Liberia. But I did not tell her about Jewel. Neither did I tell her about my promise to her.

Moments later when I thought she had gone to sleep, she sighed and ran her fingers through my hair.

"My poor little boy," she said, "you should have told me a long time ago." She raised herself up on her elbow as her naked breasts dangled in my face. "You don't need surgery. That will only worsen things. My father has the solution. He will cure you."

CHAPTER FIFTEEN

"The result of your Nerve Conduction Velocity Test (NCV) Test which we just did now agreed with the result you brought from Nigeria," Dr Tom Williams, the American surgeon at the Save Your Soul Specialist Hospital in Monrovia said as I sat facing him that hot afternoon.

"The result confirmed a nerve injury which may be responsible for your erectile dysfunction. You will benefit from a surgical exploration of the sciatic nerve to correct the anomaly," the man added.

"How long will the operation take?" my sister, Fatima, who had accompanied me to the hospital asked.

"Difficult to predict but it should be between one to three hours. The idea is to see if we can stitch the nerve where it was torn. If the torn ends are good enough, we won't need to stay too long. However, if the torn ends are not enough to get a good bite, then we may need to use a graft, and this may take some time," the surgeon explained.

"A graft?" what is a graft?" my sister asked in a pensive tone.

"A nerve graft is a segment of unrelated nerve used to replace or bridge an injured portion of a nerve. The graft which is usually taken from the patient often serves as a track along which nerve impulses can grow down to the target area. Grafts are selected from nerves that are considered expendable, or much less important than the function being restored. We call the procedure 'nerve repair' when we remove the damaged section and reconnect the healthy nerve ends. It becomes a 'nerve grant' when we implant a piece of nerve from another part of your body. These procedures can help your nerves to regrow. Sometimes we can borrow another working nerve to make an injured nerve work. This is called 'nerve transfer'," he said.

"Hmm, I never knew that things could be this complicated," Fatima said.

"Repairing the sciatic nerve – the largest nerve in the human body presents one of the most difficult challenges in nerve surgery, particularly when a significant gap exists. One of the major limiting factors is the absence or lack of donor nerve materials. Even in cases in which a relatively small gap exists, the donor nerves of the lower leg that are harvested and used for the repair are rapidly depleted. Insufficient autologous nerves are a major obstacle in successful repair of sciatic nerve injuries with large gaps," the surgeon said.

Can't you just glue the two ends of the nerve together?

Dr. Williams laughed. "Yes. That would be a major scientific breakthrough. In fact, new research recently carried out in the US has successfully used a chemical called polyethylene glycol

(PEG) to effectively glue two ends of a severed nerve together in rats. We are looking forward to the day when the same feat can be carried out in humans. For now, we still have to rely on the traditional method of repairing nerves."

"I read somewhere that the nerves are very small. How would you be able to see the nerve ends to be stitched together?" my sister asked.

"The surgery will be done under high microscopy and high illumination," the elderly doctor said. "Even then, as I said earlier, the sciatic nerve is a very big nerve which should not be too difficult to repair."

Still unsure of what the future had for me, I said, "What are the chances that I would retain my potency after the surgery?"

"Nerves being what they are, often take a while to heal. The best results are usually obtained when the nerve stumps are sutured together as quickly as possible after the damage. Even at that, the success rate is about sixty percent for partially torn nerves and thirty for completely severed nerves, or even three months after surgery. From your records, your injury is more than three months old. Fortunately, the result of your NCV test showed that your injury is a partial one which explains why other parts of your lower limb supplied by the nerve are still functioning well. It also means that you have a very good chance of recovery."

After agreeing with my mother, sisters, and Jewel to have the surgery done in Liberia, I had approached Alhaji Abdullahi with the request for a loan of N9 million. Since I did not want to broadcast my problem to other people, I told him that the money was for my mother's urgent treatment abroad and that I would pay back the loan from what my CC had promised to give me out of his own commission from the fish business. I was pleasantly surprised that the Chairman gave me the money as a gift and not a loan.

"I know how important it is to take care of one's mother. Remember I told you that I just completed a house in Chad, my mother's country. Actually, I built the house for her. I will therefore do everything to assist you to take care of your mother," he said.

When I expressed my surprise at his gesture he said, "I am also aware of how very poor your salary as a Lance Corporal is. You are a good and contented young man. You have never asked me for anything before neither have you tried to do any deal behind your boss. Not everybody is like that. So many of the young men in your shoes, would have tried to outwit their bosses."

With the money secured, I had gone to see my CC for a three-week compassionate leave. Again, knowing how difficult it was for soldiers to keep secrets especially in the sub-human conditions of the war, I also told him that the leave was to take care of my mother's urgent health problems in Liberia.

"I never knew your mum was a Liberian" he said when I informed him of my proposed destination.

"My dad married my mum during his service period with the ECOMOG forces in Liberia," I said.

"Ha… I now understand why your colleagues call you ECOMOG. I thought it was because of your bravery and professionalism," he said, as he approved my leave request.

When Safiya called me on phone I told her about my proposed trip for the surgery. She was not impressed, calling it a waste of money.

"All the money you made from the fishing business will just be wasted for nothing," she said.

"How did you know that I am involved in the fish business?" I asked, shocked.

"Hahaha! Everybody knows that any senior Nigerian army officer or someone close to a senior officer posted to Baga will sell fish, those in Madagali will sell cows while those in Damaturu will sell petrol," she said and burst into laughter.

"So, what would any female senior aid worker in the IDP camp do? Sell ammunitions and Nigerian Army uniforms to Boko Haram?" I countered, sarcastically. Rather than take offence at my broadside, Safiya replied; "No, we do more than that. We also pass information to both the Boko Haram and Nigerian Army then feed and sex handsome Nigerian soldiers like you." And as we later laughed over the matter, Safiya again reiterated her father's promise to help me solve my impotence problem.

"He has a very powerful Mallam who can assist you. The man is very good. He is the one that prepares charms that has made the Boko Haram boys so powerful. He has stuff that can make them to be bullet-and bomb-proof as well as invisible to the enemy."

When she noticed that I was quiet, she said, "Actually, that was not the reason for my call because I know you don't believe in such things. My main concern is about your libido because I want a strong husband. I just want you to try my father's

Mallam who, I am sure, will easily cure you without cost." She spoke vehemently against the surgery.

"Apart from being a waste of money, if something goes wrong with the operation, it can damage other things in your body. At least, you still have a good control of your legs for now. From what I learnt in First Aid, the same nerve that controls your libido is the same one that controls your legs, therefore, any mistake during the surgery could be disastrous. It would be very sad if at the end of the day you become crippled. That would be the end of your highly promising military career. I also don't want a cripple for a husband."

When I later expressed anxiety about the possibility of complications from the surgery to Fatima, she asked me to commit everything to God whom she knew would see us through. Thereafter, she suggested that I should accompany her family to church for special prayers. Although as a kid, I had gone to church on a number of occasions with my mother, I had not attended church for a long time since my adult life. It was Jewel who came to my rescue, as I struggled with the decision whether to go, she promised to accompany me, so I accepted.

And so with my mum, sister, and her family, I found myself attending the Ecumenical Church of God on Broad Street in Monrovia for the Sunday morning service. It was the day before my operation. As I entered the beautiful and well-filled church, I was struck by an architectural design which to me seemed to be a cross between the French Gothic and Western style. Apart from the several stained glass from where the early morning sun filtered in, there was a central aisle flanked by two narrower aisles dividing the church into neat sections. To provide stability for the daring architecture, the cavernous beauty was held in place by pale yellow pillars with an array of paintings of the saints and other religious icons. The building's spiritual intensity was heightened by the opalescent interior with its dazzling array of well-positioned soft lightening, well-decorated ceiling as well as soft and homely furniture.

As I quietly followed my family members to a corner of the auditorium, the resident choir broke into sonorous spiritual songs much to the applause of the congregation many of whom joined. It was amid the soul-inspiring songs that the presiding Pastor moved to the lectern to deliver his sermon entitled "Moving Forward to Fulfilment." Very much aware of my predicament and the surgical operation the following day, I listened with rapt attention as the pastor used the example of Esther the woman of courage in the Bible to convey his message. He ended with Psalm 138 verse 8: "The Lord shall perfect that which concerns you."

"Amen" I shouted on the prompting of Jewel who had quickly held my hand and dragged me to my feet. Four times did the pastor repeat his prayer and four times did I shout, "Amen" much to the satisfaction of Jewel, my mother, sister, and her family.

I joined the congregation in singing that evergreen and soul-inspiring hymn, 'Amazing Grace.' I dabbed away the tears that slowly welled in my eyes.

The day after. My surgery in Monrovia went well and I was discharged to Fatima's house a week later. Dr. Williams was very confident of the outcome of the surgery.

"Let us keep our fingers crossed, but I am quite sure we shall have a very good outcome," he said. When I asked him when I could confirm the surgery's outcome, he said, "The standard time is three months, but then you are a very fine and tough bloke. I think the military has toughened you up and so you could be okay before then. All the same, I won't want you to push your luck…". Jewel was wonderful all through my recuperating period in Monrovia as she stayed with me both in the hospital and at Fatima's house. I was very impressed when she told me that she had taken her annual leave just to be with me.

Sometimes she passed the night with me in my room in Fatima's house. And even though we were not yet married, I was already having fantasies about our life as husband and wife as I watched her sleep, evening after evening, her tangled hair on my pillow. In the half glow of the evening lamp, I admired her girlish beauty, her aquiline nose which she said was a gift from her grandfather, a mulatto of Scottish extraction. In the half-darkness of the room, I watched her smooth and steady breathing, the regular heaving of her chest. I had thought that after that night in Kano when she realised my handicap, she would have forgotten about me. But here she was, still taking care of me. As I continued admiring Jewel in the gathering twilight, I realized that the time would soon come when I would have to go back to my job. My military training and religion have taught me to always learn to live one day at a time because I have no control over what the future would bring. Tension, war, death and the strange solitude of the war front had been my lot all these past few years. For now, all I wanted to do was savour the love and peace of a devoted woman. I felt a strong irresistible pull towards Jewel. I switched off the lamp and stretched cautiously under the bedsheets to lie beside her, in what I knew was a foretaste of our future together, forever. Yes, yes, that would happen very soon, insha' Allah.

I returned to Nigeria only to be informed that my Company had been pulled out of Baga and returned to Maiduguri in what the army authorities described as 'routine posting'. The decision, I learnt, was caused by the rivalry for the control of the lucrative fish business in the lakeside town, among some of our bosses at the Maiduguri Command office, a fact that was corroborated by Alhaji Abdullahi when I went to pay him a courtesy visit upon my return to Nigeria.

"Soon after your departure for your leave, I was invited to Maiduguri where some of your bosses expressed their anger towards me for having left them out of the monthly welfare package from the fish business. They even went as far as accusing some of your bosses at the warfront of deliberately prolonging the war to continue to benefit from the fish business."

"How would they do that?" I asked, furious.

"The military command in Maiduguri believes that some of the occasional incidents of ambushes and attacks by Boko Haram were carefully planned by some Nigerian officers to give the wrong impression that the insurgency is still active when in truth, the Boko Haram had been severely decimated," he said. He assured me that even though my immediate boss had also been posted back to Maiduguri, he would still be looking after our interest.

Although I did everything possible to avoid contacting Safiya after my surgical operation and return to Nigeria, I incidentally ran into her one day at the Maiduguri airport where I had gone to receive my CC who was returning from an official trip to Lagos.

"Hello stranger" her voice startled me at the airport's newspaper stand where I was busy perusing the day's headlines.

"What are you doing here?" I asked, trying to smile to hide my annoyance at her rude intrusion.

"The same thing you are doing here" she answered.

"How did you know what I am doing here?" I asked.

How often should I tell you not to be asking me that kind of question again." When she noticed my puzzled look, she said, "By the way, I hope you are enjoying your new posting?"

"Yes...but...but..." I stammered

"But what? Don't you want to rest especially after your operation?" she asked.

"You mean, you also know about my new posting?" She nodded.

"You remember I once asked you to inform me any time you needed to be posted away from the warfront that I could fix it?"

I nodded.

"See, Bukar, some soldiers both junior and senior officers have never for one day served in the warfront since this Boko Haram business started, yet you had the same training. Some of these soldiers have influenced their postings to juicy postings away from any form of danger while you go about facing bullets and bombs daily basis. Are you the only soldier in Nigeria? Don't you think that you deserve a good rest after your very expensive and delicate surgery?"

Then in a subdued voice she said, "Instead of thanking me for giving you a juicy and safe posting, you are glaring at me as if I have committed a sin."

I saw through her disgust and felt remorse. I apologised for my cold attitude and promised to see her later that day at the IDP camp.

The IDP camp was located at the Shetima Ali Monguno Teachers Village on the outskirts of Maiduguri. Trust Safiya, she had also worked her own transfer to the place. Later that day on my way to see her there, I ran into hundreds of the IDPs who were allegedly protesting poor treatment at the Camp. The protester barricaded the major Maiduguri-Kano highway and held up traffic for about fifteen minutes. I was alarmed when I saw several of the protesters – mostly women, young men and children – destroying public signposts, especially campaign billboards of various political parties despite the presence of security men around the area.

As I tried to maneuver my way out of the melee, I overheard some of the IDPs complaining that since their arrival at the camp, the government had not been kind to them, as they were left to sleep in the open without any form of accommodation.

"It is not our fault that we are chased out of our homes by Boko Haram," one woman complained. "We were dumped here and left to live and sleep in places not fit for animals. Look at women, nursing mothers and those that have just delivered living in the open as if they are not human beings."

When I finally located Safiya where she was attending a meeting with some of her colleagues in one of the offices in the camp, she excused herself and took me to an empty shed where we sat.

"Actually, the IDPs have two different complaints" she said when I brought up the issue. "Prior to this time, the distribution of food and relief material to the IDPs has been through their village heads. However, the people complained about the lack of sincerity on behalf of these leaders. They now want us to distribute the food and relief material directly to them. The second issue has to do with inadequate and delayed supply of food by the humanitarian organisations. Both complaints are being investigated and things will soon be sorted out," she added.

"I hope so, because I feel so bad seeing people who are actually refugees suffering like this," I said.

"I know. It's unfortunate," Safiya responded. "There is no way we can ever have enough for the IDPs. We are talking about hundreds of thousands, if not millions of people who are in need and you cannot continue assisting these populations in a humanitarian form forever," she added before we directed the discussion to our personal matter.

I am not blaming you for going for the operation. What I find difficult to understand is for you to have to wait for about three months to know if an operation that cost millions of Naira can work when there is a better one that will work in just two days at almost no cost," she decried, after I had updated her on my surgical operation in Liberia.

With still two months to go to know the outcome of

my operation, I suddenly found Safiya's proposal enticing. "Supposing this your father's Mallam's treatment doesn't work?" I asked.

"Well, you have nothing to lose even though I am sure that it will work. There is no harm in trying," she said.

That was how, two weeks later, Safiya escorted me to Numbe, a small village on the Maiduguri-Kano Road, to see her father's mallam, Mallam Yisa.

In view of my previous disastrous experience with my Uncle Kasim's Mallam Askari, I wasn't expecting any positive outcome from the encounter.

Just like Mallam Askari did, Mallam Yisa also stripped me to my underpants and applied some scarification on my inner thighs while chanting some incantations. After that, he rubbed some jelly-like substance which he said was made from Zuma into the fresh wounds while chanting some 'prayers' in Arabic. Unlike Mallam Askari, he did not give me any black powdery stuff, rather, he brought out some ingredients. "This is the dried skin of ayaba," he said as he brought out dried banana skin out of a pouch. He then proceeded to grind the crispy brownish stuff in a small mortar. Next, he brought out another handful of what looked like dried ground nuts. "This is Gyada,' 'he said as he again ground the stuff in another mortar. He poured the two ground material together in a small gourd into which he poured a cup of *ruwan zamin*. "Now, our medicine is ready," he said as he handed over the concoction. "Drink it" he said. "In two days' time, you will be ready for action"

Forty-eight hours after my visit to Mallam Yisa, I was

waiting for Safiya in a small hotel room not far from the University of Maiduguri gate. As I waited for her, all the tension and anxiety of the past two days since I drank Mallam Yisa's *ruwan zamin* came to the fore. I was sweating despite the air-conditioned room. Even though, I was not sure that I would be able to do anything, I still came to the hotel just to prove Safiya wrong once and for all. That way, I would be able to finally dismiss her from my life and concentrate on Jewel and the result of my N9 million operation in Liberia. Instead of the excitement and joy that usually permeates the heart of a lover at the sight of his loved one, Safiya's arrival in the hotel did not excite me. I remained unmoved as she undressed.

I was still in fright as to what to do when she stretched out her hand. For a while, in the absolute darkness of the hotel room, I could not move but gave myself to her and before long found myself delightfully aware that I was doing something that for a very long time I had wanted to do but had imagined could never be done. Now as I floated about in delightful happiness, I could no longer resist the urgent rumblings in my bosom and the bewildered anxiety to flee and at the same time to stay forever in that celestial space where all doubts about my virility grew wings and flew away.

Safiya, still in my arms, waited until my racing heart had calmed down and the tears that had been flowing for a while ceased. Then in that sonorous voice of hers, she said, "Now, I have kept my promise. It is your turn to keep yours."

"Yes, what is your request?" I asked as I smiled, happy, relieved of my burden and convinced that her request will be a simple one that I would be able to attend to.

My heart almost came to a stop when she told me.

"I can't do that. I just can't do that," I shouted even after my recent emotional triumph.

"Shh... shh... You don't have to raise your voice," she said.

"I'm sorry, but you are asking me to commit two heinous crimes – treason and murder. No, I can't. Those are offences for which I can be executed."

"Not treason and not murder. Nobody will be killed. It is a purely humanitarian operation. We need to get food to hundreds of starving insurgents in a very remote area of Borno State. All we want to do is to ambush the food going to the military garrison in Biu and pass the food to the starving Boko Haram boys in that region. The military can always get another supply of food, but the Boko Haram have no access to food. Like I said earlier, you are not the only person involved in the operation. Yours is just to give us the details of the movement of the convoy as well as the strength of the accompanying security that will follow the convoy. Some members of the security team are with us. Once the ambush takes place, the security men will vanish, and the boys will swoop on the convoy and take away the food. That's all," Safiya said but I was not impressed.

"Look Safiya, I am not a small boy in military work, and I have undergone courses in humanitarian relief activities. I know the protocols for sending food to your so-called 'non-state-actors'. All you need is to apply to the Military High Command and your request, if genuine will be duly processed and approved. Please, don't use our love to get me into trouble," I said as the tension between us heightened.

"Yes, Bukar. That is my area of specialisation. I am aware of the protocols and due process. The problem is that they take too much time and by the time approval is given, the harm would have been done. Aid agencies are restricted from operating outside of government-controlled areas based on the Nigerian Terrorism Prevention Amendment Act, which criminalises engagement with groups the government listed as terrorists without exempting humanitarian operations. Obtaining military clearance is also a prerequisite for humanitarian cargo and staff movement in the Northeast region, while clearance from the EFCC is a prerequisite for moving cash for staff salaries and vendors or to finance essential services in remote locations. See, Bukar, getting clearance takes about two weeks, with organisations required to submit notifications.

Suddenly, the peace of the room was broken by Safiya's loud sobbing. I was alarmed.

"Safiya, what's the matter? Why are you taking an official matter so personal?"

"My father and eldest brother are in that group of starving insurgents who need urgent help. They have not eaten for the past three days," she said.

"Your father? I thought he already renounced the Boko Haram people and is now part of the recently pardoned and reintegrated insurgents?"

"Yes, he was until four days ago when he went back."

"Really? I thought he was one of our trusted newly rehabilitated former insurgents?" Safiya shook her head.

"Many of those so-called repentant insurgents find it difficult to actually stay repentant for long due to the previous indoctrination they had gone through. My father tried his best to remain repentant but the pressure from his former lieutenants including his first son was too much for him, so he had to go back to them," she said.

"Even if I wanted, I don't have access to that kind of information," I told Safiya.

"You can always get it from the CC's top-secret file. You are his ADC so you can always snoop on the file."

I was quiet for some time as I wondered how the lady knew so much about the ways of the military. Much as I wanted to help Safiya, I still found the idea of sabotaging my colleagues highly reprehensible.

Safiya knelt to plead with me.

"Bukar, you have to help me. My father means a lot to me. He risked his life to get me a good education. I can't watch him starve to death. Please, don't forget what I also did for you."

I was grateful for Safiya's assistance with my impotence, I didn't like the idea of her using it to blackmail me.

"No Safiya" I said. "You can't compare the two. You can't say that because you helped me with an ordinary issue of impotence you will now ask me to commit treason and..."

"Haba, Bukar. You call your virility ordinary? Don't become too slavish to a country that turned you into a *rafto* in the first instance. You want to equate your love for your country with your ability to have children and be happy? Don't forget that Mallam Yisa can reverse what he has done for you if you don't cooperate."

"I don't care. You can take back my libido if you like. I am an honourable soldier. Military work and honour run in my family. My father and grandfather left good records and I will not spoil their legacies." I spoke.

Safiya quietly got up and started dressing.

"Bukar, I thought you really loved me. It was the love I have for you that made me to stick out my neck for you and go all the way to make you a man. Now, it is your turn to help my father, but you don't want to do that. I never knew that you are that selfish. No problem. This is how far I can go with you. I will ask Mallam Yisa to take back your manhood. Good night, goodbye," she said as she left the hotel room.

A few minutes after Safiya left the room, I was seized by a very profound feeling of terror at the thought of losing my virility. After months of living with the monster of impotence, the recent release was gratifying, and I was looking forward to the time when I would also be able to call myself a father. Safiya's new stance, and her strange request frightened me. The more I thought about what she said, the more it began to make sense to me. 'Don't become too slavish to a country that turned you into a *rafto* in the first instance' she had said. Maybe she was right. I had heeded the call of my motherland and served her with all my diligence. Then the ambush happened, then the gunshot and then my loss of libido. If I had died, would the state have missed me? Yet, this feeling of abandonment did not make me less of a patriot because I loved my country just as much as the state did. That was why I had always defended my country with all my might. I broke into a cold sweat as the thought of remaining a *rafto* for life seized me. Moments later, I called her and arranged to give her the information she needed the following day.

Two days after the deed was done, I was assisting my CC in his office to search for a file which he urgently needed for a meeting when his phone rang. Seconds after picking the call, he let out an ear-splitting scream.

"What? I can't believe this. The whole company wiped out? This is horrific. About the worst ambush we ever had. Hey!" He slumped into a chair.

Much later, as I heard details of the ambush on our boys at Biu, I knew that I was culpable. It was either Safiya had been misinformed or she had tricked me. Whatever it was, the information I gave her had contributed to the loss of about 120 of my colleagues, including my beloved Hassan. As the whole barrack and nation descended into deep mourning, I hurried along the corridors without greeting anybody. I entered my bunk and shut the door.

ACKNOWLEDGEMENTS

MADAGALI is a work of fiction but it benefited from many people who were generous with their time and resources. I cannot name them all. They include my staff, fellow writers, friends, family, some reformed members of the Boko Haram sect as well as retired and serving members of the Nigerian security services. I am immensely grateful to them all.

I am indebted to Onyeka Nwelue, my Publisher, Abibiman Publishing for working tirelessly to produce this UK and European edition of the book to the glory of God and mankind.